CROWN HILL

Christine M. Abt

a novel

CROWN HILL

aBc Publishing and Writing
Eden, New York

This book is a work of fiction. Although certain historical figures, events and locales are portrayed, they are used fictitiously to give the story a proper historical context. All other characters and events, however, are the product of the author's imagination, and any resemblance to persons living or dead is purely coincidental.

ISBN: 978-0-9905518-0-5

The trademark aBc Publishing and Writing is registered in the U.S Patent and Trademark Office and elsewhere.

Manufactured in the United States of America

August 2014

1 2 3 4 5 6 7 8 9 10

Also by Christina M. Abt:

CHICKEN WING WISDOM
*Stories of Family, Life and Food
Shared Around the Table*

Western New York Wares Inc. (2005)
www.chickenwingwisdom.com

To Alice Christina and Agnes Marie~

To Bennett Christopher and Ella Rose~

The hearts and souls of my past and of my future.

PROLOGUE

ONE HUNDRED AND FIFTY YEARS...
evolving from a one-room shed into a groundskeeper's residence, a treasured summer retreat, a holistic commune, a cherished family dwelling,

ONE HUNDRED AND FIFTY YEARS...
hosting family celebrations, holiday gatherings, births, deaths, wakes, weddings, salons and séances.

ONE HUNDRED AND FIFTY YEARS...
of time when no matter who sought my shelter, no matter the changes they wrought, a part of my being was always extraordinary.

Stop for a minute. Stay quiet, and still. Feel the tranquility and calm, the sense of welcome within my walls.

It is that quietude that has long drawn departed spirits into me as a haven, a trusted refuge.

For the most part, the souls who have lingered within me have been kind, harboring no desire to harm. Rather, they have been in search of the needed strength to journey from this world to the next.

Yet there was once a spirit...a tortured soul...whom even my healing powers could not aid. This spirit was the essence of a gentle woman who once lived within me, a woman who created a loving atmosphere unlike any I had ever known. Accordingly, we became closely entwined in ways that can only be shared between a homemaker and her home.

Sadly, and to my enduring sorrow, fate delivered a wretchedly violent end to this caring woman's life. It was a death that inextricably wounded her soul, leaving her unable to find peace, even within my shelter. Thus, this woman's tortured spirit remained within me for years, haunted and haunting, searching for release from the earthly ties that kept her connected to her agonizing demise.

The situation was painful for us both and, over time, became unbearable. That is, until the power and wisdom of the universe interceded in the form of a heartfelt woman who helped us both to once again become whole.

It is our story that I share with you in the here and now.

BOOK ONE

MARY

CHAPTER ONE

June 3, 1884

Mary Southwick carefully navigated the narrow rungs of the wooden ladder, pausing as she became level with the upper pantry cupboards. In one balanced motion, the determined woman grabbed hold of the nearest cupboard handle and gave it a strong tug--once, twice, three times. Suddenly the glass door sprung open with unexpected ease, causing Mary's hand to ricochet squarely onto her nose.

The sharp blow caused an immediate welling in the farmwoman's eyes. Truth be told, she'd been on the verge of tears all morning. Sadness was a pattern in Mary's life that had long ago wearied her, and one she desperately wanted to end. Yet, for the last 18 years Mary possessed little power over her tears---or anything else in her life---ever since taking the vows of marriage with Owen Southwick.

The thought of her husband caused Mary to reach up and tenderly touch her cheek. She could still feel the trace of Owen's oversized palm, a vestige of his early-morning fury.

Mary's day had started peacefully enough. She rose from the iron-frame bed she shared with Owen and dressed in the cloak of morning darkness. Silently she slipped downstairs into the parlor to steal a few moments in this, her favored room. Snuggled into her grandmother's heirloom rocker, alongside the piano that she loved to play, the gentle farm wife allowed herself the indulgence of reading in the quiet comfort of her Crown Hill home.

Mary held a strong passion for books. Over the years, they provided a blessed escape from the isolation of her life with Owen. On this morning, in the pattern of her passion, the gentle woman became quickly lost in the wonder of a book written by the Englishman, William Robinson. His expertise on cottage gardens entranced the devoted gardener and time passed without her realization.

So it was that Owen's appearance above her seated body felt like a bolt of lightning, sending shocks throughout her being. In a blinding flash, the incensed husband ripped the book from Mary's hands and began an assault of demands for his breakfast. Owen's rage quickly morphed to the physical as he snatched his wife from the rocking chair. The lithe woman felt the twist of every bone in her body within the force of the angry man's grasp.

Propelling her into the kitchen, Owen whipped Mary around and forcibly drew their bodies together. With his dank breath suffocating her own, Owen pronounced that he would return shortly for his breakfast and it had best be on the table when he did. To reinforce his demand, Owen added a stinging slap across his wife's cheek before shoving her toward the stove and storming away.

Turning to the task at hand, Mary spoke a soft plea of desperation: "Dear House, help me. Please help me find the strength to endure, to withstand this life."

It was a habit the solitary farm wife had developed over the years, sharing her sorrows with the home she loved so much. Shortly after becoming husband and wife, Owen's nature turned dark and foreboding. It was a change his mother connected to other men in his family who had exhibited the same abusive tendencies as they aged.

No matter the cause, Owen began mistreating Mary out of his own anger and against her kind heart. Many a morning, she was left bereft as Owen departed for the fields, threatening to burn her treasured books if his various household demands were not met upon his return. His spiteful threats almost always accompanied by a shove or a well-placed strike.

With no recourse, Mary learned to transform the pain of Owen's abuse into heartfelt devotion to her home, giving all of herself to filling it with loving touches and comforts inside and out. As if to personify her love, Mary christened her home "Crown Hill," a name she felt reflected the wonder of this special place, set atop one of the area's highest rises. Each time Owen became abusive to her mind or her body, Mary turned to her home for the sense of comfort and care found nowhere else in her life.

Drawing on that bond, Mary tucked away her fear and all feelings of loathing, both of Owen and of herself, and focused on her husband's breakfast. Unsure of how quickly he would reappear, she kept the morning meal simple: a sliced steak and fried potatoes from the previous day's roast ham dinner. Scrambled eggs from the bounty she had collected in the hen house the morning before. As for bread, she knew the wisest choice would be to serve toast. It was the only way Mary could imagine avoiding Owen's wrath by not having freshly baked bread prepared.

Owen had always been a demanding man, especially when it came to his meals. Breakfast was to be on the table at 6 a.m., dinner exactly at noon, and supper at 5 p.m., sharp. No variations, no excuses. Additionally, no matter the food Mary cooked, Owen had long ago decreed that bread was to be baked fresh, every day.

Plating Owen's breakfast, Mary silently admitted that after almost two decades of marriage, she had grown weary of her husband's regimented meal demands. Just once, she thought, it would be nice to eat a bowl of soup at noontime rather than a heavy meal of meat and potatoes, a simple sandwich at night, instead of a three-course supper.

Of course the harried farm wife knew there was no sense in broaching such menu variations with her husband. Unless she was willing to be punished with days of silence, or worse yet a cuff across the face, Mary needed to continue her practiced pattern of meal-making, exactly as Owen fancied.

To her relief, when Owen returned for breakfast that morning, he took no issue with the toasted form of his bread. However, as Mary sat silently at the table amidst the tenuous calm, she knew her reprieve would be short-lived. It would be but a few hours before Owen would return for his noon meal with the full expectation of fresh-from-the-oven bread. It was that reality which led Mary to her post-breakfast struggle with the pantry cupboard door.

Putting aside the sting of her burning nose, the petite woman began rummaging through the pantry cupboard, pushing aside crocks of flour and sugar; shuffling containers of baking soda and salt. With extended effort, Mary reached into the back recesses of the deep cabinet. There she located a glass canning jar filled with carefully wrapped packets of herbs and spices, all of which she had lovingly grown and dried.

From her earliest memories Mary had loved gardening; as a young child squeezing clumps of earth through her chubby fingers, as a youth discovering the magic of bringing seeds to life, as an adult, becoming expert at propagating herbs into unusual combinations for her hearty stews and tempting desserts. Yet, at the moment, Mary was not the least concerned about her precious herbs. Rather, she was on a frantic hunt for baking powder.

She began the search in her oversized country kitchen, scavenging through cupboard after cupboard without success. In frustration the steadfast housewife turned to her pantry, holding out feint hope that she might have misplaced some of the leavening agent within her herb jar. Sifting through its contents, Mary softly inventoried, "Peppermint-sage, lemon-thyme, chive-parsley…sweet mother of pearl, no baking powder."

Exasperated, Mary returned the circular glass lid to the canning jar and forced the wire keeper into the notched ridge. Shoving the container back among the canisters and crocks, she soundly slammed shut the cupboard door.

Climbing down the ladder, the distressed farm wife felt a familiar sick panic spread through her every sense. How was she ever going to prepare the fresh bread that Owen expected upon his return from the fields? Hitching horse to wagon and driving to Caskey's General Store, in the nearby Town of Eden, would require time that she did not have. Panicked, Mary could imagine no other option, than to prepare for Owen's looming wrath.

Suddenly, in the midst of her dread came blessed inspiration. She could walk to the Sandrock's House, a half mile down the road. No doubt her neighbor, Elizabeth Sandrock, would have extra baking powder to borrow.

Mary grabbed her bonnet from the hall tree and whisked out the back screen door. Passing beneath the rose-covered arch that defined Crown Hill's entry, Mary paused for a deep breath and a view of her surrounding gardens. The floral scents and sights soothed the troubled woman's mind.

The Southwicks had moved to the farm upon marrying in December of 1866. Owen gifted the 50-acre property to his bride in a gesture noted by Mary, and many around them, as devoted and loving.

However, the truth of the matter was that Owen was financially unstable. He hadn't the money to afford even the down payment for the rambling farmhouse with its outbuildings and acreage.

As Mary later learned during one of her husband's brooding rants, it was Owen's father, Richard, who actually purchased the property. He entered into the transaction based on his son's promise to repay the debt. Yet, Owen's word meant little to him, as evidenced by the fact that in eighteen years' time, he had reimbursed his father less than $1,000 of the original $5,000 purchase price.

For her part, Mary was devoted to her father-in-law and grateful that he never made mention of the monies owed him, at least not to her. Mary was sure that Richard recognized the dark side of his son's nature, and surmised the indignities she suffered as Owen's wife. Mary believed that her deep love of Crown Hill soothed any guilt Richard Southwick suffered over his son's part in their clearly troubled marriage.

So it was on this sunny June morning that Mary once again took strength from the beauty of her home, her gardens and her favorite rose-covered archway. With a sense of renewal, she tied her bonnet in place and set off down the road.

Within minutes, Mary was winding her way along the driveway to the main house of the Sandrock Estate. The Georgian-style residence appeared as a grand white mansion, more gracious than any nearby homes.

Frederick Sandrock owned the property. He was a widower who generously shared the house with his brother William, William's wife Elizabeth and their three children. From the day that the Sandrocks and the Southwicks officially became neighbors, Mary and Elizabeth bonded over their mutual love of gardening. Mary was reminded of their shared passion as she approached the Sandrock's backyard. Walking beneath the wisteria-laden arbor gate, Mary paused for a moment to enjoy Elizabeth's beautifully landscaped brick terrace, to luxuriate in the scents of the perfectly groomed perennials embellishing the house's entryway. The setting was a gardener's dream.

It was mere seconds, however, before Mary's peaceful reverie was shattered by boisterous laughter spilling from the house. Mary immediately identified the ruckus as the Sandrock children.

Mary envied Elizabeth's motherhood. It had been her life's dream to produce a brood of children to nurture and love. However, she and Owen had never conceived.

Mary still winced whenever she recalled the memory of Doc Shaw scribbling the word "barren" across her medical chart. She remained incensed that Doc had denounced *her* body as their barrier to conceiving a child. She was equally frustrated that the small town physician had shared that decree with Owen. Within her own heart and soul Mary was sure that it was Owen, not she, who had been unable to create life within her womb.

Never mind, Mary steeled herself against the ever-lurking melancholy. *None of that matters right now. Concentrate on the task at hand.*

Mary approached and knocked on the Sandrock's door several times. No response. Stepping inside, to the back hall off the kitchen, Mary called out, "Hello." Again no response.

Just as she was about to give up and retreat, Mary felt the thunder of the Sandrock children flying down the backstairs. The voice of their nanny, Bridget, followed close behind pleading, "Now all of you just simmer down!"

Mary braced herself for the onslaught as the children raced through the kitchen, barreled over her body and slammed out the back door. Seconds later Bridget appeared, flustered and winded. Upon seeing Mary, the overwhelmed nanny politely nodded and began apologizing.

"Oh, Missus Southwick, I'm so sorry, mum. I really had no idea you were standing there. I was just trying to chase the children outside to blow some of the stink off them."

With no time to waste, Mary proceeded directly. "Bridget, I'm sorry to ask, but it seems that I have run out of baking powder and I have to get bread in the oven right away. Might you have some I could borrow until I can make the trip to Caskey's tomorrow?"

With a nod and an, "Of course, Missus." Bridget lumbered off to the pantry.

Moments later the helpful servant returned with a small container of the leavening agent and a respectful, "Here ya be, Mum."

Mary expressed her thanks and asked Bridget to deliver kind regards to Mrs. Sandrock. The ruddy-faced nanny offered to summon her mistress, but Mary politely declined, explaining that she really needed to attend to her baking. Though before departing, Mary paused.

"Bridget, please do tell Mrs. Sandrock that with this extra baking powder I'll make one of my special cinnamon nutmeg coffee cakes. If she likes, I could bring it over tomorrow and we could begin planning our new perennial gardens."

In the weeks that followed, Bridget endlessly repeated that snippet of conversation to all who would listen. As on the very next day, rather than sharing cake and planning gardens, Mary Southwick was found hanging from a rafter in the woodshed behind her beloved home. Yeast encrusting her stiffened hands, flour dusting a ghostly pallor across her bruised and twisted face.

Of all who ever lived within me, Mary Southwick was the most kind and loving. She cared for me in specially comforting ways, keeping me spotlessly clean and beautifully decorated, adding heirlooms, mementos and thoughtful touches to my rooms and hallways, making it so that anyone who crossed my threshold felt welcome and at home.

In return for Mary's loving care, I became her devoted guardian, her vigilant protector.

When Owen became abusive, I enticed sweet scents from Mary's gardens to permeate my being and caress her. When Mary's heart unleashed bitter tears for her unborn children, I wrapped my comforting spirit around her. Through every moment we shared, we became connected and entwined as homemaker and home.

So it was that Mary's death came upon me as an unbearable tragedy, softened only by the fact that she expired outside of my shelter.

Sadly, the violent nature of Mary's passing immediately arrested her soul. While her spirit sought release from the earthly ties that bound her, the trauma of her death ultimately rendered her powerless to pass from this world.

Frightened and unsure, Mary's spirit came to me with an intense need that spread throughout my being, invading every level, each corner of my space.

"Dearest Crown Hill, for so long you have lovingly cared for me. Now when my spirit is wounded….destroyed…I find myself once again seeking your protective embrace. Gentle friend, can you find the power within your being to soothe my pain and restore my soul? Can you somehow lift me from this torturous place, where it seems that I am so hopelessly trapped?"

Mary's anguished pleas enfolded me like a shroud of the blackest fog. By nature, and without forethought, I reacted to her pleas.

"My sweet Mary, you must know how it pleases me to again have you within my shelter. As always, I promise to embrace you with my deepest love, protect you with my strength, do all that I can to help you. Trust that it will be as it has always been."

With that solemn promise came a re-uniting of our souls. Mary and I beginning our newly shared journey…this time as spirit and protector.

BOOK TWO

EDWARD

CHAPTER ONE

July 6, 1922

Edward Randall strode down the mahogany-paneled hallway connecting his law firm's boardroom with his office. A powerful man, both in stature and demeanor, Edward had just completed a marathon series of business meetings with officials from the American Super Power Corporation, The Super Power Syndicate, the Niagara Terminals Building, the Cataract Development Corporation, the South Buffalo Gas Corporation, the Eureka Smelting Company, and Prest Air Corporation. It had been an exhausting, but necessary process.

Now, with his immediate business concerns concluded and his law docket clear of pending cases, Edward could confidently take leave of his Buffalo office to join his family at Crown Hill.

Thoughts of his family's summer home generated comforting images in Edward's mind. He loved their hilltop sanctuary set outside of Eden's rural township. He savored the peace and tranquility that he, his wife and his children enjoyed there. The only real challenge in retreating to Crown Hill was carving out the time away from his busy law practice.

Edward Randall was recognized throughout Buffalo and the State of New York as an astute businessman and a successful attorney. It was a professional reputation he had earned over a number of years and which he highly valued. Yet, in the late 1890's Edward earned repute within a vastly different realm, one directly connected to a woman named Emily French.

Miss French resided in the nearby city of Rochester, New York, some 90 miles beyond Buffalo's eastern boundary. On the occasion of Edward and Emily's first meeting, the slight-built woman was in her sixty-second year, partially deaf, and struggling with a weakened heart. Yet despite her physical failings, Emily possessed a strong inner ability for which she had become famous. She was a direct-voice medium who most regularly channeled the voice of the Seneca Indian Chief, Red Jacket.

Edward's association with Mrs. French began when he was hired by a group of Buffalo citizens to prove the medium and her powers fraudulent. Ultimately the skillful attorney was forced to withdraw from the case, as he was unable to accomplish the task. Moreover in what many in Buffalo described as a bizarre twist of fate, Edward became a devoted disciple of spiritualism and Emily French's greatest supporter.

Together Emily and Edward became experts in the realm of spiritualism, which led to their national renown. Over time, that same renown disassociated Edward from many in Buffalo's business and legal communities. It was a divide that widened as Edward re-directed much of his career to validating Emily's medium abilities. Their partnership flourished and continued for fifteen years, until the occasion of Emily's death in June of 1912.

Following her passing, Edward continued to research and write on the topic of spiritualism, although without the gifted medium's presence his spiritual zeal began to pale.

Gradually, the once-esteemed businessman returned to the world of commerce and finance and re-invigorated his law practice. Yet never did Edward Randall completely lose interest in the spirit world that he and Emily had so fully shared.

Through the varied professional peaks and valleys in this time of his life, Edward consistently relied upon the comfort of his devoted family—his wife, Maria and daughters, Virginia and Marion. The Randall Family resided in an expansively gracious home on Tudor Place in the heart of one of Buffalo's most fashionable neighborhoods. As a couple, Edward and Maria swirled through Buffalo society as in-demand salon guests and valued patrons of the community's arts and political societies.

In a matter of months the Randalls would be officially presenting Virginia and Marion at a lavish gala ball which Maria had been planning for over a year. No doubt, it would be *the* event of Buffalo's 1922 social season, and certainly the focus of many family planning conversations during their Crown Hill summer.

Thoughts of such frivolous moments ran through Edward's mind as he passed through his office's paneled hallway and entered the outer reception area. There his secretary Alice slowed his purposeful pace.

"Mr. Randall, Sir Conan Doyle telephoned. It seems he's in New York City and would like to talk to you today, if possible. Also, Mrs. Randall just phoned. She asked that you call her right away."

Edward's stomach twisted upon hearing of his wife's message. Maria was a sensible woman. She was also very independent and rarely, if ever, telephoned him. The fact that she had contacted him was troubling. The fact that she was calling long distance from Crown Hill made her message worrisome. Edward was a solid hour away from Crown Hill by train, longer by horse and buggy. If something was wrong with his family, there was little he could immediately do to help.

Heading to his office, Edward requested that Alice phone his wife at Crown Hill. When the intercom buzzed, Edward swooped to the receiver.

"Maria. Is everything all right? I was just about to leave."

Even with the usual delay in long distance telephone transmissions, Edward could sense the turmoil in his wife's voice.

"Edward I only have a moment, but I need to tell you about an incident here at Crown Hill that has upset the girls, and caused me great concern as well."

Edward's mind reeled with the possibilities of "incident," while his solicitor's practiced logic demanded clarification. Without deliberation, the barrister slipped into his well-practiced courtroom demeanor.

"Maria, could you explain exactly what it is you mean by incident?"

Ignoring her husband's condescending tone, Maria closed her eyes and reimagined the startling sequence of events as they had occurred.

"It all began with an early morning knock at the back door. Virginia went to answer and discovered a lovely young girl, whom she decided to invite into the kitchen where Marion and I were baking your favorite elderberry pie."

The thought of Maria's flaky-crust dessert momentarily distracted Edward until the sound of his wife's voice refocused his attention.

"The young lady introduced herself as Margaret Rose Jennings, but she asked us to call her by her preferred name of Rose. She explained that her mother was recently hired as a nanny for the Spaulding Family up the road and that they lived there, on the property. Rose continued that she had been on a walk and, in passing by our home, was so enchanted by the beauty of Crown Hill that she wanted to stop and meet those who lived here. She was a bit younger than our girls and quite charming, easily engaging all of us in social pleasantries. As time passed, I was about to ask if her mother knew of her whereabouts when, without any warning what so ever, it happened."

Growing increasingly impatient with his detail-oriented wife, Edward spouted, "*What* happened, Maria? What exactly do you mean by *it*?"

"That's what I'm trying to explain, Edward. In the midst of conversing with Rose, the air in the kitchen suddenly became cold. Not as if a breeze were coming through a window, but more as if a chilling winter's day had invaded the house. The change, of course, startled the girls and put me on edge as well. Yet Rose's reaction was quite different. She pointedly turned away from all of us and became riveted, staring out the kitchen window toward the old woodshed in the yard. As she stared, her body began trembling as if she were weakening, about to lose consciousness or convulse."

Maria paused, both to control her voice and to carefully collect her thoughts. Taking a calming breath, she began anew.

"Obviously I was concerned for the young girl's well-being, so I approached her. But as I reached out, she spun and pushed past me, purposefully moving from the window to the pantry door. There she stood, rooted, continuing to tremble, sobs now streaming from her being. It was all so disturbing, Edward. Truly unlike anything I ever witnessed, even in the few séances I observed with you and Emily."

Hesitant as how best to continue, Maria decided to forge ahead with the remainder of her story, hoping the details would not cause Edward to consider her foolish or worse yet, irrational.

"In the midst of all of this confusion, the kitchen door to the pantry suddenly sprang open, as if someone were trying to force their way into our home. Yet Edward, as God is my witness, there was not a living soul on the other side of that door. What there was, at least what I believe I saw, was a pale blue light, rather in the shape of an orb. And I know this may sound unimaginable, but the light appeared to move toward Rose and, well there's really no other way to describe it, hover above her, almost as if caressing her. At the same time, the young girl began to speak, repeating the same words over and over. 'It's alright. Yes, I'm here now; I'm here.' And Edward, as soon as those words left the girl's lips, an undeniable scent of sweet roses filled the room."

Feeling unexpectedly dizzy and weak, Maria pulled a chair from the kitchen table to where she was standing by the wall telephone. As her knees folded beneath her, the determined woman righted her body against the sturdy, press-back oak chair and resumed. She had to finish telling Edward the story so she could get back to her daughters, who were keeping watch over the young girl.

"Then just as it had all occurred, the orb vanished; literally disappeared into nothingness. The kitchen became all at once warm, freed from the frigid state that had kept both the girls and I immobilized. And then, from deep within Rose came a hauntingly, long and soulful wail, followed by her collapse onto the kitchen floor.

Maria's last words were distorted by disruptive static on the phone--advance notice to Edward that their connection was about to be lost.

Long distance telephone service between Buffalo and Eden, 25 miles apart, was inconsistent at best. To make matters worse, Edward knew that once the line went down, it might be hours before a connection could be re-established.

As he hung up the phone Edward felt uneasy about the safety of his wife and daughters. He was also more than curious about the young girl of his wife's description. Yet without a phone connection, there was nothing the commanding attorney could do but finish gathering his papers and quickly journey to the train station. With any luck Edward would catch the noon train and arrive at Crown Hill within two hours.

While his mind whirled with the possibilities of all that could happen in that time, his thoughts instinctively turned to a collection of memories; recollections that centered upon his friend and spiritual guide, Emily French.

The time following Mary's death was intensely painful for us both.

For my part, Owen remained living within my shelter, and as he had been cruel to his wife, he was equally unkind to me. He continued in his selfish ways, allowing me to fall into filth and disrepair until my spirit became overburdened with the darkness of his being. For that reason, neighbors and friends who had been a constant during Mary's life no longer cared to enter into or enjoy my welcome.

Adding to the turmoil, Doc Shaw officially decreed Mary's death a suicide, in complete opposition to what most of Eden believed: that Owen had murdered his loving wife.

Consequently, on full moon nights long after Mary's passing, neighboring children would gather outside my walls and derisively tempt her spirit to appear. And, although they never witnessed her, Mary's spirit was indeed present and deeply tortured by their mocking taunts.

"Dear House, I cannot tolerate the cruelty of these gatherings," Mary would lament above the children's jeers. "If I were to appear just once, I am sure they would all go away."

Mary's heart-wrenching pain impacted me as if infused directly into my being. To soften our shared anguish, I offered caring consolation.

"Sweet friend, stay within me, silent, if you can. In return, I will bring you echoes from our past: comforting piano music that you once created within me. Hear your soothing melodies. Allow the music to wash over your spirit and bring you peace."

Sadly, no matter the enduring love and support that I offered, it was never enough to completely ease Mary's pain. Eventually, in unrelenting agony, she became hardened--angry and bitter--lashing out and haunting those around and within me.

She began first with Owen, literally haunting him to death. It was a vindictive act, far removed from the true heart of my Mary. But I understood it as an uncontrollable response to the many years of cruel words and hurtful actions against her.

Mary next haunted Owen's father Richard, who took possession of my deed following his son's passing. Although devoted to her father-in-law in life, Mary's vengeful spirit tortured Richard without regard. As a result, he sold me into a progressive chain of deed holders that numbered 15 in 20 years. And despite my best efforts to calm her fury and restrain her resentment, Mary terrified every one of them.

In time, Mary's deep desire to pass became overshadowed by the pain of trying. It was a terrible plight; one that wounded me as well. No matter who claimed me as their home, no matter how I tried to create for them a place of calm and caring, I could never reassure them to the point that they could accept Mary's spirit or abide her tortures.

As the town of Eden and her people became aware of Mary's hauntings, they soon branded me as a place of unhappiness and suspicion. That repute eventually made it impossible for any living being to willingly reside within my walls. To my great despair, for years no one believed I had anything to offer other than horror.

And so I languished, empty and alone...except for the tormented spirit of my beloved Mary.

CHAPTER TWO

Maria replaced the phone receiver onto the hook. *Of all times for the phone line to go dead,* she agonized. *Why now?*

A long wail interrupted Maria's thoughts. "Mother, pleeeaasssee! Come quickly."

Maria hurriedly pushed through the swinging kitchen door into the oversized dining room, then moved beyond the matching pocket doors into the parlor.

After Rose collapsed on the kitchen floor, Maria had commanded her daughters to individually take hold of the young girl's limp and lifeless legs. While the caring mother supporting her head and upper body, the three moved the pallid child onto the midnight blue, mohair sofa in the parlor.

Re-entering the room, Maria was shocked to see Rose sitting up, appearing completely awake and alert.

"Could I have some chocolate, please ma'am?" came the girl's polite request.

Unsure of the unusual circumstance, Maria decided to send Virginia to fetch the candy jar tucked away on the top pantry shelf. Edward was passionate about chocolate and could not complete a day without savoring at least one milky morsel. Maria always kept a not-particularly-well-hidden stash in her pantry to satisfy her husband's late night cravings.

While waiting for her daughter to return, Maria decided caution would be her best ally.

"Rose, do you have recall any of what happened to you in the kitchen a few moments ago?"

"Sort of, ma'am. It's what my mother and I call my awake-dreams. I've had them all my life, but none in quite some time---not since before we came to the Spaulding's."

Maria considered the intense actions she had just witnessed in her kitchen to be a far cry from any "dreams" she had ever known. Yet as Virginia returned with the candy and placed a silver wrapped chocolate in Rose's delicate hand, the normalcy of the moment enticed the wary woman to almost believe nothing unusual had really transpired.

Nearly, but not quite.

In Maria's eyes, Rose's self-described, "dream" appeared much like the direct-voice experiences she had, on occasion, witnessed in the presence of Emily French. It was a realization that made Maria none too happy.

While her husband had become deeply involved with Emily and the proving of her direct voice medium abilities, Maria remained quite separate from their spiritual endeavors. There was something about the séances that frightened the devoted wife and mother. Accordingly, when Edward broached the subject of adding a séance room to their fashionable Buffalo home, Maria expressed her strong disapproval. However, her husband was determined. To save peace, Maria agreed to allow the spiritual retreat as long as it offered a separate entrance. It was her hope that the alternative entry would isolate all otherworldly activities and participants from the Randall's everyday lives.

Maria further extracted a promise from Edward that spiritual activities of any kind would never occur at Crown Hill. Yet now here she was, with her daughters, immersed in the very kind of spiritual circumstance that she had dreaded, with neither Edward nor Emily involved in any way.

Regardless of the circumstance, Maria had no desire to become further immersed in whatever was going on in young Rose's life. She also was not going to allow what had just occurred to further invade Crown Hill or disturb her family's summer. Maria decided that the best course of action was to help Rose gather her strength and return the young woman to her home, without delay.

"Mother, whatever are we to do with her," whispered Virginia as she drew close.

Looking into her daughter's deeply brown, questioning eyes, Maria could see the true innocence of Virginia's heart. There was no doubt that her concern for Rose was genuine.

Discreetly moving her caring child away from the parlor, Maria cradled her daughter's hands as she explained. "Once Rose feels strong enough, we are going to accompany her home."

"But Mother, are you going to ignore all those things that just happened in the kitchen? The way the girl trembled and cried and the way she started talking as if someone was there? Aren't you going to tell her mother? Don't you think someone should make sure that she sees a doctor?"

Maria knew that her reply would either pacify or further disturb her tender-hearted daughter. Accordingly, she chose her next words with care.

"Virginia, there are people in this world whose minds cause them to act in unusual ways, just as Rose did here today."

"Oh mother, do you mean like father's friend, Mrs. French?"

Again, Maria instinctively knew that her answer required thoughtful perfection.

"Virginia, Mrs. French was a very unique woman, but I am not concerned with her right now. I am talking about Rose, who clearly has some sort of problem of which her mother is aware. We cannot change that, and it is not our place to interfere. So I am asking you to help me gather her up and, with your sister, we will make sure that she gets safely down the road to the Spaulding's house."

Virginia considered her mother's words for several moments before reluctantly agreeing. Truthfully, Maria was relieved that her daughter seemed more concerned with the welfare of the girl than with the strange occurrence they had just witnessed.

Returning to the parlor, Maria found Rose and Marion snuggled together on the couch, absorbed in conspiratorial giggles. Though the scene appeared playful and quite natural, the thought of friendship between the two girls raised every hair on the back of Maria's neck. No doubt there was something unusual about this child and Maria was sure that the less her daughters knew of Margaret Rose Jennings, the better.

"Well young lady I see that the chocolate must have had magical powers, as you seem fully recovered from your spell."

Maria immediately regretted her choice of words. Ordinarily she would not be bothered by innocent terms of enchantment. However, considering the events within her home over the last hour, she found suggestions of anything magical or out-of-the-ordinary quite disturbing.

Maria became even more concerned when she noticed outward signs that the odd girl seemed to be transgressing into yet another "awake-dream." But as quickly as Rose's eyes widened and glazed they refocused as she meekly replied, "Oh yes, thank-you so much ma'am for the scrumptious chocolate."

Drained of her energies, Maria announced the time was right to escort the young girl back to the Spaulding's. She was determined that once they took that short walk down the road, Rose would be completely removed from her family's life.

Awash in the warmth of the summer sun, the foursome strolled along the winding country road to the Spaulding's driveway. From there they advanced to the door of a small cabin behind the main residence, the place Rose identified as "home" for both she and her mother. With a respectful farewell, Rose left the Randall women, entering the cabin on her own.

In ordinary circumstances Maria would have insisted on speaking to Rose's mother about the morning's odd events. But truth be told, at this point, she was relieved to have the child gone from her presence.

When the Randall women returned safely to Crown Hill, Virginia and Marion headed to the nearby vineyards for a game of hide and seek while Maria moved to the porch, onto her favored wicker sofa. Taking a deep breath, the weary woman tried to regain some sense of composure. Her attention was drawn to the horizon and the scenic beauty of Lake Erie in the far off distance. The day was crystal clear, allowing her view to extend to the sandy edge of the Canadian shoreline and the landmark lighthouse at Point Abino.

The tranquil scene encouraged positive, peaceful thoughts within Maria's troubled mind. It had taken ten years for her family's world to return to some sense of normalcy following Emily French's death. Ten years for Edward's law practice to become rejuvenated. Ten years for their rightful place in Buffalo's society to be re-established. Maria was not about to allow Rose and her "condition" to destroy all they had recouped in that decade.

As her overwrought mind and body began to release the morning's tensions, Maria assured herself that Rose's departure would allow all to be once again safe in her world. However, as she settled into the comfort of the summer's day, the mindful woman became quickly disturbed by a strong breeze traversing the expansive Great Lake and ruffling through Eden's rural landscape.

Suddenly a cool edge sliced away at the warmth Maria had enjoyed only moments before, and within that unsettling change came a series of unnerving shivers that traveled up and down Maria's spine, chilling the very fibre of her soul.

As Mary's spirit burst from my being into the kitchen, I begged her to return to me, to retreat from approaching young Rose.

At the same time, I understood completely why Mary was drawn to the child. Her pure and engaging innocence radiated through me from the moment she crossed my threshold. There was no doubt that this gentle girl held a saving grace of the kind that could help Mary's spirit. It was that glorious promise that ultimately overwhelmed Mary and compelled her to appear.

Regrettably in materializing, Mary unsettled both Maria and the girls. Their reactions made me fearful that, like so many before them, the Randalls might decide to abandon us.

In the years since Edward and Maria first chose me as their summer retreat, in those initial moments when Edward Randall made his way through me room by room, I was infused by his caring manner and by the sensitivity with which he considered my being. Both Edward's initial actions and his aura inspired me to believe that he possessed extraordinary abilities.

The fact that the Randalls lived most of each year in Buffalo, far removed from the tragedy of Mary's death and my ill-repute, allowed them to be unaware of Mary's haunting presence. Further, whenever anyone in Eden engaged Edward or Maria with suggestions of my troubled reputation, they quickly dismissed such caveats as idle gossip.

It was Edward and Maria's fearless attitudes that ultimately caused me to beg Mary not to appear to any of the Randalls until I could fully ensure their comfort in my care. It was an entreaty that she first refused, but eventually and grudgingly agreed to uphold.

Now, as Mary and I anxiously awaited Edward's arrival and his reaction to what had occurred, I agonized that my worst fears of losing the Randall family might quickly become real.

At the same time, I could sense young Rose's goodness, and how her purity combined with Edward's spiritual strength might provide the healing powers Mary so desperately needed.

Was there a way for me to ensure Edward would remain? That Rose would return? That their powers could connect and help Mary's spirit escape the pain of being trapped in this world?

Most importantly…could I keep Mary safely guarded within my protective care until all such things came to pass?

CHAPTER THREE

Though the Randalls were only in residence at Crown Hill during the summer months, they still required a year-round employee to maintain and care for their property. Being a bachelor with no ties to anyone but his mother, Arthur Smith, was only too happy to add Crown Hill to his ongoing caretaking duties at the Spaulding's estate just next door.

On this particular summer day, the all-purpose handyman's immediate Crown Hill chore was to sit at the Eden train station and await Edward Randall's arrival from Buffalo. As usual, Mrs. Randall and the girls had journeyed to Eden earlier in the week, departing Buffalo as soon as the school year ended. As Arthur understood it, Mr. Randall required additional time to put his business affairs in order, always arriving a week or so later.

While most Eden residents still traveled by horse and buggy, Edward Randall was intrigued by the new driving machines produced by entrepreneurs such as Ransome Eli Olds and Henry Ford. So it was not surprising that he became one of the first in the rural community to own a Model-T automobile. Part of Arthur's job was to learn how to drive and maintain the new vehicle; challenges that he enjoyed and easily handled.

As the train steamed into the Eden station, Arthur gave the car one last wipe down in hopes that his extra effort might earn a generous tip. However when Edward Randall alighted from the train his attention clearly was neither focused on the condition of his automobile, nor on the man driving it. In fact, the usually gregarious barrister literally passed Arthur by as he exited the train station.

"Afternoon, Mr. Randall, sir."

Hearing his name caused Edward to pause. "Oh, Arthur. Hello. Sorry, I was lost in my thoughts."

Arthur collected his employer's bags and secured them to the wooden luggage rack attached to the back of the touring car. Meanwhile, Edward climbed into the front seat of the vehicle. Unlike most that employed chauffeurs, Edward preferred to sit up front where he could feel more directly involved with the driving process.

Masterfully cranking the engine to a quick start, Arthur slid behind the steering wheel. Once underway he turned to Edward and tried to engage him, "Hope your trip was pleasant, sir."

Edward, still distracted, absently replied, "Yes, fine, thank you."

The trip from the train station to Crown Hill was two miles in distance and took less than six minutes. The biggest challenge in the journey was the steep hill at the beginning of Sandrock Road. The sharp grade caused the Model-T engine to groan and sputter, but as long as the gravity forced fuel tank was full, there was no doubt the car would make the climb.

As the two men rounded the curve in the road, passing the Spaulding's estate and approaching the hillside vista of the Randall's summer home, Edward continued to exhibit noticeable tension. Traditionally, the trip through the Eden countryside was a cathartic break, bringing out the best in the hard-working attorney. Today, however, he was rattled and displeased, not at all himself.

Arthur made a left turn into the entrance to Crown Hill and handily navigated the circular drive. As he slowed the car at the home's terraced entranceway, Edward alighted from the auto before it came to a full stop, failing to acknowledge Arthur in any way.

At that moment, Edward's thoughts were far from Arthur or any civilities. Passing under the rose covered arbor at Crown Hill's entrance, Edward was solely focused on the well-being of his wife and daughters and the strange events they had endured with the neighboring girl.

"Maria? Girls? Where is everyone?"

Edward's calls of concern echoed through the house without reply.

He proceeded purposefully from the back porch, through the kitchen, and into the formal dining room. There, through an adjoining doorway, he caught sight of his wife outside on the wrap around porch. From where Edward stood, it appeared that Maria was resting on the white wicker sofa that she had so perfectly matched with complimentary chairs and tables.

"Humpf," Edward fussed in exasperation. Quiet repose was the last thing he expected of his wife following the distressing phone call they had shared earlier.

Edward gently clicked the brass-levered handle to open the porch door. Stepping out onto the covered veranda he could clearly see that his wife was not simply resting. She was soundly asleep under the cover of a brightly striped Hudson's Bay wool blanket.

Loudly clearing his throat, Edward attempted to make his presence known. Failing, he bent close to his wife and employed a more direct manner. "Maria, my dear, wake up."

In a far-away fog, Maria heeded her husband's call and began to respond. Gradually, she awoke to the intensity of Edward's steel gray eyes willing herself to consciousness.

"Oh my," she responded with a startle. "Edward, when did you arrive? I just sat down for a minute. A chill came off the lake and I wrapped myself in this blanket for warmth. I must have dozed off."

Concerned and slightly confused, Edward launched into a lawyerly interrogation. "Maria, where are the girls? Is everything all right? What happened to the young neighbor child? What occurred after we spoke?"

"Heavenly days, Edward. Let me get my wits about me." Maria sat up and pulled several deep breaths of warm summer air into her lungs. As her mind connected with her memory, she began to explain.

"Let's see. After I spoke with you, the young girl…oh yes, Rose…she recovered quite quickly from her fainting spell and actually seemed fine. So the girls and I walked her home and that's all. Nothing else happened."

Even from within her sleepy haze, Maria knew that she did not want to further disturb her husband by mentioning that the girl had almost slipped into another trance before leaving. No. She was not going to give Edward any further reason to become involved. At this point, Maria was dedicated to re-establishing her family's tranquil summer at Crown Hill and she was quite sure that meant dismissing Rose and everything connected to her from their lives.

"Father, Father, you're finally here!" Edward heard their voices well before the girls scrambled up the adjoining porch steps. Unlike their mother, Marion and Virginia desperately wanted to recount the details of their unusual morning to their father. After quick embraces, they proceeded to describe each moment in detail.

As Maria watched her children animatedly describe the frightening experience, she silently made a firm vow. Young Margaret Rose Jennings would never again be welcomed to Crown Hill. Further, Edward would never again be allowed to so much as raise the topic of spiritualism in their summer home. Case closed. No discussion, no lawyerly debates.

And if for any reason Edward did not agree, Maria was fully prepared to gather the girls and return to Buffalo for the remainder of the summer.

Or forever, if need be.

I was concerned about Maria. I had come to care for her deeply and did not want either her or her daughters, who took every cue from their mother, to anguish over their lives within me.

To that end, while Maria settled on the porch, I summoned peaceful powers to soothe her and allow her rest. Yet the respite from the day's events was far short of what Maria truly needed.

From their conversations within my shelter, I was aware that Maria had remained detached from Edward's professional relationship with Emily French. I had witnessed their conversations, during which the devoted wife voiced to Edward her deep fear that the spirits who spoke during Emily's direct medium experiences might one day remain with them.

Edward assured his wife that those to whom Emily gave voice were peaceful and kind spirits, presenting no harm to their family. As time passed without incident, Maria came to accept her husband's assertions as truth.

However, when it came to summers within my shelter, Maria demanded, and secured a promise from Edward, that I would remain a respected retreat, free from séances and spiritual activities of any kind.

Now with the arrival of Rose, and Mary's shocking appearance in response, Maria was suddenly unsure of her family's safety within my walls. She was frightened and I understood her fear. I also knew the traumatic hauntings that Mary could undertake.

I was caught between my desire to comfort Maria and my promise to help Mary. Both women were strong and determined. Both women were in search of peace and comfort. Ultimately, both women wanted and needed Edward.

The question was, if forced…which of these two women would Edward choose?

CHAPTER FOUR

The telephone's high-pitched ring echoed through the cavernous Waldorf Astoria penthouse. As the hotel butler moved to answer the phone, the suite's occupant, Sir Arthur Conan Doyle, drew his leather wing chair closer to the oversized marble fireplace set against the far living room wall. Settling down to read, the esteemed novelist kicked off his comfy leather slippers in a resolute attempt to warm his always-cold feet.

Sir Arthur made the trip to New York from his home in Sussex England as part of a North American speaking tour on spiritualism. While in Manhattan he also planned to attend the Society of American Magician's annual banquet with his fellow colleague, Harry Houdini.

The *Sherlock Holmes* author had become fascinated with the subject of spirits and fairies in the late 1890's and ultimately penned a number of magazine articles on the topics. With his elegant stature, his heartfelt good nature and his passionate belief in the spirit world, Sir Conan Doyle soon evolved into an in-demand speaker on the topic, traveling around the world to share his considered perspective.

This current speaking tour fully evidenced the accomplished author's popularity as his original three-day lecture schedule at Carnegie Hall had quickly expanded to seven appearances to accommodate the many clamoring to attend.

In between his lectures, Sir Arthur luxuriated in the world class amenities of his hotel suite, working his way through a collection of recently published books on spiritualism whose titles intrigued him.

At the moment, Sir Arthur was deeply immersed in a tome written by an American acquaintance, Edward Randall. The book was titled *The Dead Have Never Died*. While the two men had not met in person, they corresponded regularly on the topic of spiritualism, connected through their mutual friendship with Houdini. It was Sir Arthur's intent to meet Edward during his ongoing speaking tour, which included an appearance at The Hotel Lafayette, in Randall's hometown of Buffalo. Reading the man's book before meeting him was essential to Sir Conan Doyle.

"Excuse me, sir, a Mr. Edward Randall is on the phone asking to speak to you," the butler formally announced. "He said that he is returning your call."

"Thank-you, Robert. I'll speak to Mr. Randall in my room." The Waldorf Astoria's penthouse provided guests with telephones in the main living area as well as in the bedrooms. It was a standard of luxury known in few hotels around the world.

Closing the bedroom door behind him, Sir Arthur lowered himself into the overstuffed chair positioned next to the antique nightstand beside the bed. He lifted the receiver from the ornate French phone and offered a hearty greeting.

"Edward old chap! Jolly good to finally speak in person."

Edward responded in kind, and apologized for allowing a day to lapse before returning the noted author's phone call. From that point, the two easily worked their way through the required social pleasantries until Sir Arthur redirected the conversation.

"I say, Edward, when I complete my lectures here in New York, I am engaged to speak at The Hotel Lafayette, which is right in your bailiwick. I was wondering perhaps if we might meet and enjoy some conversation over a spot of tea, or a fine malt?"

Edward was relieved to hear the renowned author's invitation and replied without hesitation. "Sir Arthur, it's so good of you to ask and actually I was wondering the same thing. Only I was hoping that your schedule might permit you a few days at Crown Hill, our family's summer home. We are not terribly far from Buffalo, and my wife and daughters would be thrilled to meet the famous creator of Sherlock Holmes. Additionally, the extended time might allow us to engage in discussions of a spiritual nature."

"A quite right idea, Edward," Conan Doyle responded enthusiastically. "Actually, after my Buffalo lecture appearance, I have time set aside to travel to the spiritualist assembly at Lily Dale, which I understand is located not too far outside the city. No doubt I can accommodate a visit to Crown Hill in that time as well. It would seem, old chap, that our great minds think alike!"

"Agreed, Sir Arthur! Our summer home is located in a quaint rural town named, Eden. Conveniently, it is located on a direct path between Buffalo and Lilydale. So make your plans accordingly, and know that you are welcome to stay with us at Crown Hill as long as you please."

"Excellent, Edward! Many thanks for your most gracious invitation. I will make my plans and be in touch."

Exchanging proper good byes, the two men completed their conversation with the promise to soon re-connect.

Pleased with the results of his telephone call, Edward headed to the dining room where Maria and the girls were engaged in their ritual post-dinner card game. Upon sharing the news of Sir Arthur's impending visit, Maria and the girls instantly began planning a summer party to honor the famous author.

"Wait! Wait! Ladies, wait just a moment!" Edward raised his hands in attention-grabbing exclamation. "I'm not even sure when Sir Arthur will arrive at Crown Hill. So before you start inviting people and preparing food, let's wait to hear his plans."

It was always that way in the Randall household. Maria loved to hostess for any and all reasons, and her daughters were definitely following in their mother's footsteps.

"Well, it doesn't hurt to plan, Edward," Maria responded in playful retort. "It takes more than just a day to put together a party for someone as important as Sir Arthur Conan Doyle, my dear."

After almost 25 years of marriage Edward was intimately familiar with his wife's tone. He also knew that when she made up her mind, the best litigator in the world could not change it. In acknowledgement, he kissed her softly on the cheek and replied, "Yes dearest." Then, with oil lantern in hand, Edward retreated to the study off his bedroom on the second floor, leaving his girls to plan away to their heart's content.

Truthfully, Maria and the girls fussing over menus and decorations was exactly what Edward had hoped to accomplish by inviting Sir Arthur to Crown Hill. Their excitement was the perfect distraction from the still-disturbing, Rose "incident" the day before.

Edward and Maria had discussed the occurrence at length after breakfast that morning while the girls were outside picking berries. His wife was concise and clear about her feelings. She did not want Rose to return to their home, ever again. She did not want to discuss what happened, ever again. Maria then strongly stated that if either of those things should happen, she and the girls would pack up and return to Buffalo, or perhaps even travel to their family camp in Bear Lake, Canada.

Edward was fully aware of his wife's strong spirit, yet he highly doubted that she possessed the courage to spend the summer with the girls on her own. Just the same, he had no desire to test her resolve.

The good news was that since his arrival, everything at Crown Hill had returned to its peaceful and normal nature. Now with his plan to invite Sir Arthur perfectly in order, Edward was hopeful that his family could move past the unsettling "Rose" experience, as if it had never happened. He did however intend to fully discuss the incident with Sir Arthur during his time at his family's summer home. . He was sure that their shared expertise would allow for a resolution as to what had actually happened at Crown Hill, and why.

Sitting at his desk, Edward felt smugly satisfied. He reached for his pince-nez glasses and placed them firmly onto the bridge of his nose. The disciplined barrister then took pen in hand and began writing a review of the events that had occurred with the young girl as he recalled Maria's story. He would need details for Sir Arthur to consider.

It was only minutes before Edward's self-satisfaction was shattered by a wailing scream that pierced every inch of the house.

In immediate response, Edward jumped up, knocking over the desk's inkwell in his haste. Sprinting out of his office and down the back stairs two treads at a time, he could hear Maria and the girls repeatedly shrieking his name. Darting through the kitchen, Edward raced into the dining room where he slammed to a halt.

There before Edward stood his family, seemingly paralyzed, their eyes locked onto the dining room sideboard. As he turned his gaze to the oversized oak hutch, Edward saw something dramatically different inside the mirror, something that had never before appeared. It was the tortured face of a woman staring into Edward Randall's eyes---seemingly speaking to him directly. Speaking words that he could neither hear, nor imagine.

I was devastated by Mary's actions in appearing to Rose. After the many years I had cared for her, tried to keep her from complete despair, she was now destroying everything with her impatience.

When she withdrew into me after materializing, I strongly admonished that if she did not remain quiet and away from the Randalls, I would no longer provide her shelter.

It was the first time Mary and I had ever shared unkind words and sharp responses.

"No longer shelter me, house?" Mary lashed back. "You may believe that you can banish me, but in truth, you can only make me feel unwelcome. And I will tell you that the pain of your disapproval is not enough to stop me from doing whatever I need to pass. Not now. Not any longer."

Mary's rough-edged anger was hurtful, an emotion so unknown to me and that I had only witnessed as she lashed out at others. In response, I retreated deeply into myself, closing all access and leaving Mary isolated and alone.

As that agonizing night passed into a new day, I decided to try and approach Mary with the kindness and love that had long connected us. Yet before I could reach out to her, I felt Mary summoning all of her strength and power from within me. Suddenly, a force like a tidal wave of energy surged through my being. I had no idea what to think or expect. I had never experienced such intensity in my existence.

It was then that my worst imaginings became real, as I heard the screams and witnessed the fear of Maria and the girls as Mary revealed herself to them, appearing in the mirror in an image of the woman she once was.

From that moment, there was no turning back. Mary had removed her spirit from my care and was now lost to me...completely out of my control.

CHAPTER FIVE

Although Edward had participated in over 700 séances and spiritual gatherings during his 20 years with Emily French, he had never witnessed anything quite like the vision before him in the mirror. Further sensationalizing the phenomena were the terrified pleas from his wife and daughters.

Oddly, Edward was divided in his reaction. His heart demanded that he comfort his family and protect them from what appeared to be an invasive spirit. Yet his lawyer's intellect challenged him to further investigate the apparition before him.

The decision was ultimately made for Edward as, in a split second, the woman's image vanished from the mirror.

An eerie silence fell across the house, as if all life had been completely withdrawn. The unnatural quiet was followed by a cold air that frosted the dining room and forced all of the Randalls to take deep, sharp breaths.

Maria was the first to speak. "Edward. What is happening?" she begged in a desperately whispered voice.

Edward's brain felt somewhat frozen, his words forming like icy leaden drops. "I'm not sure. I don't know," was all he could manage in response.

It was Maria who finally took charge of the unsettling situation. "Girls, I want you to go upstairs to your rooms *now,*" she ordered while protectively wrapping her arms around each daughter. Before the two could protest, she handed each child a candled lantern and pushed them toward the front hall stairway.

"Light the globes in the upstairs hallway and in your rooms. By the time you have done those things, I will be there with you."

Without protest both girls obeyed their mother, fear preceding their every step as candlelit shadows taunted them along the stairway and into the long, dark, second floor hallway.

Once the children were out of earshot, Maria turned to her husband. Edward was practically unaware of all going on around him, standing still-entranced by the sideboard mirror. Maria's words sliced through the space between them.

"Edward, I cannot stay in this house, nor will I place my daughters in jeopardy by spending the summer here. While I don't blame you for what is happening, there is clearly something, or perhaps I should say someone, who has invaded our home and become determined to be known or acknowledged. While I am sure that the idea of such an occurrence is quite intriguing to you, it is completely unacceptable to me. So, in the morning, I am going to take the girls and return to Buffalo."

While Edward was aware that Maria was speaking, he was unable to grasp the impact of her words. His brain instead raged with the image of the woman's tortured face that had only moments ago demanded center stage in their dining room.

Who was the woman? How was she was appearing from the inside the mirror? And why? Why here? Why now?

Again, from his work with Emily, Edward was accustomed to voices of spirits emanating from all corners of a room. As well, he had often seen photographs from spiritualist believers who claimed murky black and white images to be ghostly apparitions. Yet never had Edward actually seen a spirit, if, in fact, that was what he and his family had just witnessed.

"Edward!" Maria spit his name out of her mouth. "Are you listening? Do you even hear me?"

Edward had no idea what his wife had been saying over the last few minutes. It wasn't that he didn't care; it was more that he was finding it impossible to get his brain focused on anything other than the haunting face in the mirror.

"For the last time, Edward, do you hear me and do you understand that the girls and I are leaving?"

The anger in Maria's usually loving voice jolted Edward to reality. This time he definitely heard and comprehended his wife's words and realized that if he wished to avoid a long summer apart from his family, he needed to think and act quickly.

"Maria, dearest, can we talk about this? Let's at least try to find some common ground, some solution other than you and the girls leaving."

"Common ground? Solution?" Maria's words felt like tacks riveting across his body. "I'll tell you what the only solution would be. We need to sell Crown Hill. Walk away from whatever it is that has transformed our lovely summer home into this house of terror. Otherwise, there is no solution. No matter what happens, I will never again be able to walk into this house, sit in this dining room, or rest in my bedroom without concern of something unnatural or frightening about to occur."

Edward did not doubt his wife's words. Nor could he misinterpret her body language, misconstrue the look in her eyes. If he indeed wanted his family to continue their treasured summer holidays, it would seem such escapes could only happen in another place, far away from Crown Hill.

"My darling," Edward approached with outstretched arms and embraced his delicate wife. As he protectively caressed her, Edward set about detailing a meticulous defense of all that had happened in the past 24 hours.

"I completely understand how you feel and I don't blame you for wanting to leave Crown Hill, never again to return. But my dearest, can you truly allow the minor incidents of the last two days to override the enjoyment and special memories we have experienced in our many summers here?"

Edward could feel his words working their magic. His strokes across his wife's back were further soothing her fears, causing them to ebb and flow away. Edward was sure that if he could find just the right combination of words, Maria would be open to possibilities other than departure.

What Edward did not anticipate was the strength of his daughters' emotional counter defense.

"Mother, please," Virginia called out from the stairway landing. "Marion can't stop crying and we are both scared. We lit all the globes, but the shadows look like that awful face in the mirror and it's terribly frightening. Please, please come upstairs now."

The girl's words returned the icy chill into Maria's veins. Her back stiffened as she pushed herself away from Edward's warming embrace.

"I'm sorry Edward. I know how much you love Crown Hill and I too have loved every summer we have spent here as a family. But whatever it is now happening here, it is just too much."

And with that, Maria went to her daughters, leaving Edward alone in the darkened dining room. Leaving him to wonder how his life had changed so abruptly.

And why?

I was stunned by Mary's power; by what seemed to be her complete betrayal of our friendship--- all that we had shared over the years and everything that we had planned and to which we had agreed following the Randalls' arrival.

Mary's appearance in the mirror was beyond any haunting she had ever undertaken. Not only did it damage Maria and the girls, it depleted all of the spiritual strength that Mary possessed.

It was full fury that allowed Mary's spirit to materialize; a culmination of years of anger over Owen's abuse combined with frustration at being trapped on this earth with no means of deliverance to eternal peace.

Yet it was the irrational passion of Mary's fury that most astounded me. Even now, I struggle to describe the emotions that filled my being after her cruel haunting of the Randalls.

Intense fear emanated from Maria and the girls.

Focused curiosity and shock poured from Edward.

It was so unnatural for this loving family to experience such distress within my care.

Further compounding Mary's disastrous haunting was the angry exchange between Edward and Maria following her disappearance from the mirror. Their discordant words slashed painful gaps in the core of my being. In a matter of minutes, not only had I lost Mary, I was losing the family who had so lovingly restored me in so many ways...and all I could do was helplessly observe.

CHAPTER SIX

A cloud of white steam infused the air as the train chugged its way into the station. While the engineer slowed the string of rail cars to a stop, a porter alighted from the first passenger car, a riser of portable stairs in his hand. In one neat motion, the uniformed rail man adeptly positioned the steps on the ground.

As if on cue, a tall distinguished-looking gentleman emerged from the train and briskly navigated the stairs. He was dressed in an elegant three-piece suit complete with a striped tie and straw boater hat. His face was highlighted by a well-tended moustache.

As the man paused to scan the surrounding rail yard, Arthur had no doubt that this was his passenger. Accordingly, he approached and introduced himself.

"Good afternoon. Sir Conan Doyle, I presume. My name is Arthur Smith." Pointing toward the nearby Model T, Arthur continued. "I am the chauffeur for the Edward Randall Family. Mr. Randall sent me to transport you to Crown Hill where he awaits your arrival. Welcome to Eden, sir."

"Quite right. Eden. A perfect name for the countryside I have enjoyed during my train trip from Buffalo. And you are spot-on, Arthur. I *am* Sir Conan Doyle, my pleasure to make your acquaintance. Now, if you would be so good as to gather my bags, I will make my way to the car and we can be off." With a flourish Sir Conan Doyle moved toward the car, leaving Arthur in search of the famed author's luggage.

Upon locating the three, fine-leather valises, Arthur firmly secured them to the Model T's baggage rack. Moving to the front of the car, he cranked the engine to a fine hum, whereupon he slid across the driver's seat, shifted the car into gear and began the short journey to Crown Hill.

In minutes, Arthur was navigating the Model T around Crown Hill's circular drive. The sound of crunching gravel beneath the tires coupled with the loud exhaust from the car's four-cylinder engine, clearly heralded their arrival throughout the property.

Anxious to greet his guest, Edward quickly made his way downstairs from his second floor office. Passing through the kitchen, he exited to the back porch precisely as Sir Conan Doyle alighted from the car. The two men met midpoint along the brick walkway to the house, beneath the rose-covered trellis.

"Edward. Jolly good to finally meet, face to face."

"Likewise, Sir Arthur. Welcome to Crown Hill."

Upon sharing a dignified handshake, Edward guided the Scotsman into the house and through a brief tour of the main floor, ending on the gracious wraparound porch.

"I say old chap, the view from here is quite spectacular." The eminent writer strolled and inspected the covered veranda, end-to-end, "I can see exactly why you and your family are devoted to spending your summers here. And by the by, when might I enjoy the privilege of meeting your lovely wife and daughters?"

Sir Arthur's question caused Edward's mind to reflect on the final moments before Maria and the girls had departed, days earlier. He recalled valiantly pleading with his wife to stay, using the same entreaties he had offered throughout their sleepless night.

"My darling, please reconsider. Please don't allow these few isolated incidents to separate us."

Edward knew that the intensity of his steel gray eyes were having their impact on Maria's soul, as they had from the moment the two first met. He could sense his wife's heart softening, compelling her to follow his lead. However, the appearance of their daughters quickly hardened Maria's mindset.

"Mother, we're ready."

Virginia and Marion stood before their parents, pale and exhausted. The disturbing incident involving the sideboard mirror had thoroughly frightened the sisters, frightened them to the point that they were having difficulty sleeping in their feather-down brass beds. Moreover, since the haunting appearance, the girls had become fearful of venturing at all from their mother's side, day or night.

Witnessing his children's distress, Edward was forced to admit that Maria was doing what was best---removing them from the terror that now seemingly defined Crown Hill.

As the family filed out the back door and passed beneath the trellis to the waiting car, the Randalls appeared to be in collective mourning. Virginia and Marion softly kissed their father good-bye. Edward embraced each one in a wholehearted hug. Husband and wife next united in a touching embrace that lasted but a moment. Then, with a final wave, the three were off for the train station, leaving Edward with a heavy heart of lingering thoughts and fears.

"I say, old man, everything quite alright?"

Sir Arthur's query restored Edward's mindfulness.

"Yes, I'm sorry Sir Arthur. My mind wandered there for a moment. You asked about meeting Maria and the girls. To be honest, they have taken unexpected leave of Crown Hill. They departed last week for Buffalo and since have traveled on to our family compound on Black Lake in Canada."

"Departed, you say? I hope it's nothing in the nature of an emergency or an illness."

"Fortunately, no. Although if you were to ask my wife and daughters, I have no doubt they would say that there had been an emergency. You see, recently, a most unusual spiritual occurrence took place here at Crown Hill."

"Spiritual occurrence? How fascinating. Are we talking voices, or apparitions, objects flying through the air? Have you performed temperature tests or conducted séances?"

The intensity of Sir Arthur's questions tweaked Edward's sense of reason. To this point he had focused only on the ways that his family had been affected by the woman in the mirror. Listening to his guest's queries, Edward felt a bit foolish that he had not considered the matter from a more scientific perspective.

"Actually no. That was one of my reasons for inviting you here. I wanted to share details of the occurrence and draw upon your expertise, discuss your thoughts."

The respected spiritualist was intrigued. "Well then do tell, my friend, and we shall see what we can see."

Settling into adjoining, oversized wicker chairs, Edward began. "Last week while in my office reviewing correspondence, I suddenly heard my wife and daughters shouting my name. Rushing downstairs I found them all in the dining room, frozen in fear by an apparition of a woman's ghostly face in the sideboard mirror. The image was haunting and remained visible for several seconds. Equally unsettling, it seemed to be speaking directly to me, but not in sounds that could actually be heard. Then just as oddly as it materialized, the image disappeared."

"I say, old chap, this is all most intriguing." The celebrated mystery writer extracted a leather pouch from his weskit pocket. Out of the pouch he pulled a pipe, which he tapped sharply several times along the edge of his handmade leather boot. "Tell me my good man, have you undertaken follow-up to attempt to apprise who it was that appeared? Has the apparition returned since?"

Again, Edward felt quite sheepish as he replied. "Truthfully, Maria decided that with everything happening she and the girls were no longer safe here. In fact, initially, she demanded that we sell Crown Hill and never return. So I did nothing while they were still present. As for further appearances, no. Nothing more of a spiritual nature has happened since that night. My hope however is that, between us, we will be able to discover who it was that appeared in the mirror and why this woman suddenly began haunting. Perhaps then I can put an end to this odd spiritual activity, which I am hoping will encourage Maria and the girls to return."

Pausing to better collect his thoughts Edward continued. "So, Sir Arthur, now that you are here and have heard my story, might you have a willingness to help?"

The distinguished author filled his pipe with fragrant tobacco from the leather pouch. Holding match to bowl, he inhaled deeply and with the sweetness of his custom-blend infusing the humid summer air, he replied.

"Most certainily. I would be delighted to aide you, Edward. I am pleased that you have invited me to Crown Hill to witness whatever we may discover. I will say that my first and instinctive response is that your woman in the mirror is a spirit who, due to unknown circumstances, has not yet passed.

"Agreed," Edward responded. "I believe that to be the truth as well. As you know, Emily French and I discovered a number of spirits still on earth, long after their physical beings had passed. Many of them were in search of a way to cross over and so I am familiar with this type of encounter. What I cannot understand is why this woman has appeared *now*. We've summered at Crown Hill in peaceful tranquility for years. Suddenly, with no apparent reason, this woman materializes. It's odd."

The men continued in conversation for several hours, until the setting sun reminded Edward of his hosting duties.

"Sir Arthur, I apologize. I have completely forgotten my manners. You must be hungry and most likely tired from your trip. The house keeper left us a cold plate dinner and, if you would like, we can dine here on the porch."

"Sounds absolutely capital!" the Englishman responded. "And a healthy tumbler of scotch would make it all the better, old chap."

Edward and Sir Arthur enjoyed a dinner highlighted by conversation on a wide range of topics. They reviewed the controversial reactions to Doyle's book, *The Coming of the Fairies*. They discussed their mutual acquaintance, Harry Houdini. They delved deeply into the current storm over the infamous *Blue Book*, a publication providing tricks of the trade employed by fraudulent mediums.

After several lost hours, Sir Arthur pointedly brought the conversation back to their ultimate purpose.

"Edward, let us pour ourselves another finger of scotch and go into the dining room. I would like to inspect this sideboard of yours and its mysterious mirror."

The prospect of beginning both enticed and unsettled Edward. His natural curiosity and deep belief in spirits encouraged him to jump to the task. Yet the recall of his strong physical reaction to the woman in the mirror was not easily dismissed. He disliked identifying it as such, but Edward believed he was actually fearful of what might lie ahead.

Sir Arthur, on the other hand, appeared exhilarated by all aspects of the happening. In fact, he had already poured himself another drink and was making his way from the porch into the dining room. Edward could do little else but follow.

Once into the room, Edward lit the gas sconces lining the walls. At the same time Sir Arthur headed directly to the sideboard, like metal to a magnet. The spiritualist stood before the solid oak furniture in reverential silence. He ran his hands over and around the smooth wood-grained top, reaching out and carefully exploring the attached setback mirror.

Edward was intimidated by what he observed. It appeared as if his guest was executing some sort of solemn ritual. Uneasily, he stepped back and allowed space for whatever rite was underway.

Finally Sir Arthur spoke.

"I say old man, this is a fine piece of furniture. Solid and well made. I cannot imagine it being anything more, but I do not doubt that your story is true. At this point, what I would like to do is head off to a good night's rest. Then in the morrow, refreshed and energized, we can begin again the task of trying to solve your mystery."

To Edward's relief, Sir Arthur's presence before the sideboard had not incited spiritual activity. Drawing closer to both the man and mirror, the calmed host responded.

"Certainly, Sir Arthur. That would be fine. And I apologize if I have rudely kept you up too late discussing my personal concerns."

"Not at all, my dear man. I've thoroughly enjoyed our evening together. And please, call me Doyle. It is the moniker used by those who know me best".

"Alright then, Doyle. Let me close up the house and I will show you to your room." Edward collected the dinner dishes from the porch and deposited them in the kitchen sink. Before taking her leave, Maria had arranged for the chauffeur's sister, Agnes, to begin working at Crown Hill as a housekeeper and cook. Edward reasoned that she could take care of the dishes upon her arrival in the morning.

Returning to the dining room, Edward lit the candled lamp on the sideboard and extinguished the wall sconces one by one. Together, the two men climbed the treads of the formal front stairway and passed along the hallway to the guest suite, set privately in the back of the house.

Edward toured Sir Arthur through a sitting room with a small divan and an ornately carved oak and leather rocking chair. He then progressed to the bedroom highlighted by an oversized cast iron bed and a connected dressing room complete with plush towels and quilted hangers. Edward was always pleased by the special touches Maria put in place for family and friends who joined them at Crown Hill.

Lighting Sir Arthur's guest room lamp, Edward pointed out the nearby lavatory and the back stairs, which led to the kitchen. With the layout of the house defined, the two bid each other good night and good dreams.

Settling into a sound night's sleep the men slumbered peacefully. As they dreamed, both were completely unaware of a light glowing in the dining room, radiating intensely from the sideboard mirror. Both were unconsciously insulated from the sounds of sorrowful weeping permeating the house.

As Maria and the girls prepared to take their leave, I desperately wanted to change their plans, to soothe them in ways that would entice them to remain with me. Yet truth be told, I was as distraught as all of them by Mary's appearance in the mirror. That distress, in turn, diminished my abilities to provide their much-needed comforts.

For the first time since Mary's passing I was exhausted by the emotional turmoil that her spirit had created in my being. As a result, the welcoming scents and peaceful auras in which I always surrounded those in my care were now absent, completely drained from me. Worse, I was wholly unaware of Mary's spirit and the next frightening actions she might undertake.

I had not felt Mary within me since her haunting appearance in the mirror. After so many years together, it was oddly disturbing to be without her spirit.

Initially I was somewhat concerned, wondering where she had gone. Yet at the same time, I was relieved to be free of Mary's pain; her tortured yearnings. For the first time in longer than I could recall, I felt at peace.

So it was that Mary's return that night felt like a slowly churning storm; her sorrowful words filtering through her heartbreaking sobs.

"I have returned, my beloved Crown Hill; returned with a contrite heart and a wish for your forgiveness. I know that I went against our agreement in appearing to the Randall Family. All I can tell you is that I was helpless to prevent my deep emotions from overtaking me. Truly, the intensity of my feelings compelled me to do something, anything, that might deliver me from this painful death on earth."

Unsure of my heart, I remained silent. Within the space of my quietude, Mary continued her act of contrition.

"That is why I went away from you. I had to gather my strength and compose my soul. Dear friend, if you can find it in your heart to forgive my actions, I will follow whatever lead you set. Even should you ask me to take leave of your shelter, I will do so."

Mary's repentant aura warmed the chill that her haunting had draped upon me. I could feel my wooden beams and boards gently expanding and relaxing. Once again, my being opened in welcome to my friend.

"Sweet Mary, we have been of one heart for too long to allow anything but tenderness between us. I do feel a joy in your return and assure you that I will never deny you my shelter. At the same time, I believe I have the news that we have long awaited. Circumstances may be transpiring that could generate the strength and power to free your soul."

As I wove together the stories of the girls and Maria's departure and Sir Conan Doyle's arrival, Mary once again settled into me…as it had been and was always meant to be.

CHAPTER SEVEN

The sound of a crash echoing through the house jolted Edward from his sleep. Scarcely awake and completely unaware, the barrister could not quite conjure the source of the early morning commotion.

In the light of day, Edward's concern over the woman in the mirror had faded. However, the spiritualist's instinctive reaction to the loud crash was the vision of an overturned dining room buffet.

With heart pounding, Edward peeled himself from the comfort of his down-filled bed and donned his dressing gown. Knotting the velvet belt in place, Edward slid into his comfortably worn, leather slippers set just inside the closet. Properly garbed, he made his way through the front hall and down the stairs, hesitating two treads short of the main floor.

Cautiously, Edward peered around the stairway wall, into the dining room.

From his perch, Edward could clearly see that the buffet and the mirror, perfectly upright and in place. *Silly fool*, he chided himself.

"I say! Was there an accident of some sort?" Sir Arthur's words reverberated down the stairs in a timbre that literally dropped Edward to the floor.

"Sorry old man," Sir Arthur offered as he descended the open stairway. "I had no intent to startle you."

"Not a problem, Doyle I'm fine," Edward offered with a twinge of aggravation in his voice. "Just not quite awake."

As the two men began strategically inspecting the dining room, they discovered the source of their early morning alarm among shards of a broken vase upon the floor. At the same moment Agnes pushed through the swinging door from the kitchen, broom and dustpan in hand. Seeing her employer and his guest in nightclothes caused the flustered servant to stop short of the debris.

"Oh dear, I'm so sorry if I disturbed you gentlemen. And I will gladly pay for the broken pottery, Mr. Randall, sir."

Edward was so relieved to discover that a simple accident was the source of the crash, he immediately reassured the middle-aged woman.

"Not to worry, Agnes. Just clean up the mess and then please serve us breakfast on the porch. Repayment will not be necessary."

The two men made their way to the wraparound veranda, where they luxuriated in the summer warmth and exchanged early morning pleasantries. In short order Agnes presented a sumptuous breakfast of fresh blueberry pancakes topped with her famous blackberry syrup, accompanied by a platter of steaming pork sausages. For good measure, the skillful cook also served up two fluffy cheese omelets made from eggs delivered fresh that morning by a neighboring farmer.

"I give you this, old man," Sir Arthur remarked in exchanging his emptied plate for his pipe. "There's never been a better breakfast served than that which we've enjoyed here this morning!"

Edward had to agree. While his wife prepared wonderful meals, Agnes was an artist in the kitchen. Edward always looked forward to those occasional summer days when Agnes would take over Crown Hill's kitchen duties and spoil the family with her flavor-filled menus.

With their stomachs overly full and their minds restfully numb, Edward and Sir Arthur turned their gaze to Lake Erie's horizon. Together they languished in the rising sun that cloaked the porch, sharing the sweet scent of Sir Arthur's pipe tobacco. As the moments passed, the two men relished the silence between them, completely comfortable in Crown Hill's embrace.

Eventually, Sir Arthur interrupted the quiet.

"So my friend, I have been thinking. Is there anything in particular that seems to have set off this apparition in the mirror? What I mean is, do you think that something of a specific nature has encouraged this spirit to appear?"

The same thought had crossed Edward's mind. It seemed strange that this woman, whoever she was, had just appeared without rhyme or reason.

"Not really." Edward replied.

Even as he spoke, instinct tugged at his awareness *What*, he thought? *What am I missing?*

"You are absolutely sure then that there has never been any sort of spiritual activity here at Crown Hill?" Sir Arthur continued. "No séances, or levitations, or readings of any kind?"

"Absolutely. At least for as long as we have been here," Edward replied. "Maria made me swear a solemn oath when I built the séance room at our home in Buffalo, that I would only conduct spiritual activities there. She was adamant about it and I have been respectful of her wishes."

Sir Arthur took several long puffs on his meerschaum pipe before again engaging, "Well, I must say old boy that were it not for your extensive spiritual experiences with Mrs. French, I would almost be inclined to think that what you saw in that mirror was a reflection of light or shadow in some form. But you are too experienced to misunderstand or misjudge such things. So I am compelled to believe that, as I explained last evening, what has happened here is the apparition of a soul unable to pass. Yet why this spirit has come along at this point in time, I cannot quite imagine."

Edward felt uncomfortable with Doyle's assessment. In all his years with Emily she had been the one to directly connect with all spirits. Clearly, whatever was now going on at Crown Hill, Edward was at the center of the experience and it made him uneasy. Sir Arthur's next comment served to tighten Edward's stomach further.

"Well dear chap, if there is nothing to consider---no obvious spiritual activity other than the one appearance in the sideboard mirror---we have two ways in which to proceed. We simply wait to see if anything happens again, or we conduct a séance to see if there actually is a spirit present and if we can make a connection."

Edward knew that Sir Arthur's séance suggestion was the obvious next step. Still, undertaking such spiritual activity without Emily felt inappropriate. As if reading his mind, the intuitive Scotsman spoke again.

"I would venture to guess, my good man, that you are wishing Emily French could be here at this moment. As I understand from people who were in her presence when she channeled, she was a quite right, astonishing medium. In fact, I have been told that it seemed as if spirits were literally in wait for her to open her soul to them."

Sir Arthur's words struck a deep chord in Edward. As a key turns a lock, Edward felt his mind once again opening to his strong spiritual connection with Emily. The moment was both stunning and euphoric. It was also illuminating in that Edward suddenly realized what was missing from the mystery of the woman in the mirror. It was so incredibly obvious--- the young girl from the Spaulding's. She was the missing link.

Upon our reuniting, Mary and I shared a restful night. The next morning, as the sun awakened and warmed my roof and walls, I felt renewed hope rise within me. Edward and Sir Arthur would help Mary. I had no doubt. What I never imagined was that they would be aided by another.

Edward's conclusion that Rose was key to Mary's hauntings led the two men to the decision to meet her, get to know and assess the young girl.

My initial reaction to their plan was one of concern.

I was already fully aware that Rose's innocent presence could entice Mary to appear. I also understood that whenever the child was closeby to Mary, I had no control, no ability to reason or ensure that Mary's actions would not terrify people and drive them away.

I began searching for Mary within me. I needed to advise her, make sure that she knew exactly what was happening, and where the two men's actions and interactions with young Rose might lead.

I could not find Mary within my shelter. Thus I turned outside, looking for her among the out-buildings and vineyards. At last, I discovered my tender-hearted friend in a place I never expected, lingering inside the woodshed where she took the final breath of her earthly life.

Within the aged building I became awash in the sweetness of Mary's rose-scented fragrance. It was a delicate perfume that she loved and always wore; one that permeated my being during the many years of our life together. For a brief moment, it was as if Mary were again alive.

"Mary? Mary, please talk to me. I know you are here. I can feel you and recognize your lovely rose scent. I have much to tell you and it's all good, positive. It hurts to know that you are here in this place where your life came to an end. Please....please..."

From the recesses of the ramshackle shed came the voice I longed to hear.

"Dearest Crown Hill, I remember my last moments in this woodshed. I was at first afraid, then peaceful, then shrouded in a darkness that burdens me still. Yet in those moments, between the peace and the darkness, my thoughts were of you, dear friend. The times we shared in the gardens, tending my precious herbs, the many days cooking and baking in the kitchen for those we loved, summer evenings on the porch savoring the brilliant sunsets over the lake. My

final life moments were filled with memories of the great happiness you brought me and the constant protection you offered me.

The combination of Mary's heartfelt words and the dusty atmosphere of the woodshed generated a strong aura of her final life moments. Overwhelmed by the sensation, I could do nothing but listen as Mary continued.

"Crown Hill, know also that when my spirit passed from my body, my first thought was to return to you. I knew somehow you would help me, if you could. And if you could not, then you would love me and that would be enough."

While Mary spoke in hushed tones, the intensity of her words flowed directly into my core. There was no escaping the importance of Edward and Sir Arthur connecting with Rose. There was no escaping this place in time. There was no escaping the sense that the universe was drawing all together… all of it within me, for a purpose.

CHAPTER EIGHT

It took only moments for Edward and Sir Arthur to groom, dress, and set off for the Spauldings. Since the distance from Crown Hill was just a half-mile, the men decided to work off their generous breakfast by walking.

As they journeyed, Edward became lost in thought. How could he have been so obtuse? Why had it taken him days to realize the significance of all that had occurred at Crown Hill and connect it to this neighboring child? In recalling his wife's story, Edward now had no doubt that the girl was central to the mystery of the woman in the mirror.

Each step Edward took toward the Spaulding house delivered increased adrenaline through his body. As he reached the apron of the neighboring driveway, he realized that his intensity had caused him to leave Sir Arthur behind. Mortified, Edward stopped in wait for his colleague, harnessing his nervous energy by trying to recall the name of the child he and Doyle were about to meet.

Edward recalled that Maria had made mention of her identity, but for the life of him he could not think of the girl's name. What did come to mind was that the child was the daughter of the Spaulding's new governess. Edward instinctively realized that he needed to approach both the girl and her mother with thoughtful care, not overwhelm them in any way. If Edward were right, that this child was the link to the spirit now haunting his home, she was central to restoring peace at Crown Hill and within his family.

"I say old chap. You set quite a pace when you walk!" The words wheezed from Sir Arthur as he reached Edward's side. "I can see that I am going to have to cut down a bit on my meerschaum in order to keep up with you."

The physical strain evidenced in Sir Arthur brought Edward's attention front and center.

"I apologize for my rude behavior Doyle. My mind is racing and it has set my body to a similar pace. Let us proceed along the driveway in a more reasonable manner."

Walking together the men approached the entry to the stately home. Raising the weighty, brass door knocker, Edward soundly rapped upon the Spaulding's front door. It was only moments until Helen Spaulding appeared.

"Oh Edward, how wonderful to see you. Our summers are always made special when you and Maria and the girls arrive." Glancing over Edward's shoulder at Sir Arthur Helen queried, "Are they with you?"

Edward hesitated before responding. Over the years, Helen had become a valued neighbor and a good friend. Yet she was widely acknowledged in Eden as a community information source, or "gossip" as Edward more bluntly defined her in conversation with Maria. He had no intention of providing Helen with idle chatter to spread throughout the town.

"Maria and the girls are all in good health and spirits, thank you, Helen. And may I introduce you to a friend of mine who has come for a visit, Sir Arthur Conan Doyle."

Hearing the author's name caused Helen to literally jump out the doorway toward the two men. The life-long Eden resident was an avid reader, particularly of mysteries. Her love of the Sherlock Holmes series was well known among her family and friends. In fact several years earlier, during a particularly blustery winter season, Helen attempted to write her own mystery novel in the style of the revered author.

"How do you do my dear lady," Sir Arthur offered in his most cultured brogue.

Hearing Sir Arthur's voice affected Helen to the point that she was momentarily unable to speak. Ultimately, a deep smile spread across her face as she reverted to reality.

"Oh Sir Arthur, I am so thrilled to meet you. I am a true Sherlock Holmes devotee. Please come into my home. Let me get you some tea along with some of my fresh-made blueberry muffins. Do tell him, Edward, about my delicious baked goods."

Before either man could protest, Helen whisked them up the steps, through the front door and into her comfortably elegant parlor. Sailing out of the room with an, "I'll be right back," Helen left her guests to ponder how they might best proceed. After several moments of contemplation, Edward gave voice to their primary concern.

"Any suggestions on the best way to handle this situation so we don't spook these women?" Edward squirmed in his seat as he realized the double entendre of his words.

Sir Arthur was about to share his thoughts as their hostess reappeared in breathless euphoria.

"Here we are, fresh muffins and hot tea," Helen veritably waltzed into the room balancing a sterling silver tray with antique teapot, fine china cups and matching plates. Complementing the tea service was a picture-perfect basket of muffins. Edward was about to decline Helen's offering with the excuse of their already-consumed breakfast when Sir Arthur interrupted with a request.

"Dearest Helen, would there be any butter and jam for these delectable baked goods?"

"Why certainly, Sir Arthur." Again, their hostess took leave without pause. Edward looked to his friend in amazement. The mystery writer returned the glance with a sly smile.

"No, my good man, I am not hungry in the least. But I have an idea of a way to promote our purpose here. Perhaps we could explain that we are undertaking research for a book that I am writing and we have need of someone to transcribe our notes. That someone should be of an age and stature that a small amount of money, along with the experience of working in our company, would suffice as compensation."

Edward understood the mystery writer's plan, but wondered about its wisdom.

"Doyle, what about that job description makes you believe Helen will offer the services of her nanny's daughter?"

"Elementary, my dear Randall," the accomplished author answered with a wry grin, "my charm!"

When I finally persuaded Mary to depart from the woodshed and return to my shelter, her spirit was broken, her heart stripped of all its strength. She was fully resigned to the idea of enduring thiw afterlife to which she had been condemned. It was almost as if in revisiting the woodshed, she had died a second death

Understanding this, I tucked Mary's spirit into the core of my being and wrapped her in the loving joys of all that we had shared during her earthly life. Within those comforts I renewed my promise to help her find the necessary peace to move on to a world of light and grace.

"Dearest Crown Hill, it matters not any longer. I have accepted that after these many years, I am destined to remain trapped in this earthly hell, doomed because of a death that I could not control. I no longer have a will to rail against this destiny. Rather I ask only that you allow me to remain within you, trusting my solemn word that I will never again haunt, rather simply endure."

Words cannot describe the devastating sorrow that connected our spirits at that moment. I felt Mary's complete despair as if it were my own. Still the thought of Mary forever within me as a spirit of desolation was impossible to accept.

"Mary I have loved you too long to abide by your request. You were a kind and loving woman throughout your life, and deserve to experience the rewards of your nobility.

With that said, of course my answer to you is yes. Yes you may always remain within me, as long as I exist. But at the same time, I will not be a part of your enduring anguish. Rather, I will remain true to my promise to help you find that which will set your spirit free from the insufferable demise your body endured."

As I waited in patience for a reply, sounds of silence resounded within my walls...broken only by moments of Mary's softly anguished weeping.

CHAPTER NINE

The slight young girl passed quietly into the Spaulding's parlor. She looked neither at Edward nor at Sir Arthur, but instead moved immediately to her mother Elizabeth's side. Helen had summoned Elizabeth and her daughter upon hearing Sir Arthur's need for transcription help.

"Rose, I would like you to meet our neighbor, Mr. Randall. I believe you met his wife and daughters the other day. They live in the big white house on the hill next door".

The delicate fourteen-year-old cast a glance toward the two men seated across the room. They found her gaze mesmerizing, with her deeply blue eyes framed by lush lashes, her face highlighted by a waterfall of auburn curls. Edward offered his best fatherly smile while extending a gentle greeting.

"Hello Rose. I am pleased to make your acquaintance. My daughters told me all about your visit to Crown Hill. It's nice to have this chance to meet in person. This is my friend, Sir Arthur Conan Doyle. He is an author who has come here to do some research for a new book that he's writing."

Again, the girl looked shyly at the two men, offering a delicate smile in place of words. Edward pressed on.

"We were wondering if you might be interested in working for us at Crown Hill during the next week? It would be just several hours a day, re-writing and organizing some of Sir Arthur's notes."

At the suggestion of returning to Crown Hill, Rose became transformed. Smiling brightly she responded, "Oh yes, sir, I'd like very much to do so." She then turned to her mother with an animated request, "Oh please mother, may I?"

Looking first for an affirming nod from Helen, Elizabeth agreed that her daughter could work a few afternoons for the gentlemen, as long as the child's household chores were completed and only after she had eaten her lunch. Speaking directly, the protective mother added that she needed her daughter to return to the Spauldings by 3:30 each afternoon to care for the barn animals and help feed and bathe the Spaulding children.

With the details agreed upon, Elizabeth delivered one final condition. "I have heard that Agnes Jones is temporarily in your employ. I must insist that Agnes always be present whenever Rose is at your house. No respectable young woman would ever be found alone in a home with two men, famous or otherwise."

Elizabeth's stipulation caused both Edward and Sir Arthur to flush in embarrassment. Not only were both men fathers to daughters about Rose's age, each was very much in love with their wife. The thought of any type of wrong doing with this innocent young girl had never crossed their minds. Rather, they were completely absorbed by the mission of reaching the spirit they believe was connected with the young woman.

"Of course, all of those conditions are fine," Edward responded. "And we'll pay 5 cents a page, if that is acceptable?"

While it was not an overly generous amount, to Rose it was more money than she had ever earned working for her mother. The girl could barely contain her excitement as she blurted out a reply.

"Oh yes sir. That would be wonderful. When would you like me to start?"

It was at this point that Sir Arthur joined in the conversation.

"Let's say tomorrow afternoon, around 1:30? That way Mr. Randall and I have the early part of the day to prepare."

"Very well sir. I shall see you tomorrow at Crown Hill at 1:30 p.m. promptly."

"Alright Rose," Elizabeth commanded. "Time to go about our business."

With that, mother and daughter departed.

Emitting a high-pitched giggle, Helen flirtatiously asked, "Now Sir Arthur, if you don't mind my asking, what is this new book of yours about?"

"Well, Madame, I never give away the plot of a book in progress," Doyle answered in his most charming demeanor. "Suffice it to say that I am writing about spiritualism and the ways in which those who have passed communicate with the living."

"Oh my. Oh my! The very thought of such a thing makes chills run along my spine." Helen nervously fluffed her perfectly coiffed hair. "Are you sure that a young girl such as Rose is the appropriate person to help with this project? I mean it is quite an unsettling topic and she is so impressionable. I wouldn't want anything untoward to result. You know, nightmares or things of that sort."

With another burst of off-key laughter, Helen revealed her true intent.

"Perhaps you could use someone a bit more *mature* to work with you, Sir Arthur. Actually, now that I think of it, I might be able to clear my busy schedule and make myself available. I am an avid mystery reader and I do have some background in writing the genre."

Taking pity on his cohort, Edward quickly diverted the conversation. "My, what a generous offer, Helen. But we could never impose on a woman of your talents for menial transcription work. I'm sure that Rose is more than capable of managing the tasks involved in copying over Sir Arthur's manuscript. And now, I'm afraid that we must be on our way. Much to do, you know."

Determined to continue her interaction with the illustrious author, Helen immediately responded, "Well, alright then, I'll accept your abrupt departure, but only if you promise to return for dinner on Friday."

Edward graciously sidestepped the request with a "possibly" reply and deftly exited the house, Sir Arthur close behind. Making their way down the driveway, the ever-optimistic Scotsman gave a hearty chuckle. "Well, I thought that was jolly good."

"I thought it was a nightmare," Edward responded. "I felt as if we were lying to all three of them. And what happens now if the woman in the mirror does re-appear to Rose and we haven't told her mother the whole truth? What will we do then?"

"See here, my good man. We did not lie. We simply created a job as a means of returning the child to the scene of the crime, so to speak. And who knows what will happen when she comes to Crown Hill tomorrow? Perhaps this spirit of yours will not even appear. Perhaps whatever happened, or what you and your family witnessed, is over and done with as quickly and oddly as it started. Point of proof, consider the fact that nothing has occurred since my arrival. I say you are making a mountain out of the proverbial mole hill."

The men walked the remainder of the distance between the two houses in silence. As they approached the Crown Hill drive, Edward stopped, turned and looked directly into Sir Arthur's eyes.

"Let me just make one thing perfectly clear. I do not want anything to happen to this young girl while she is here."

"And you think that I would?" Sir Arthur countered. "Edward, you are acting as if I brought this spirit into your home and that I am responsible for its involvement with Rose. I have no ties to this whole experience, other than serving as your friend and wanting to help solve your mystery. So, let us agree that we are in this project together, as partners, and we will not go forward on any action unless we are both quite right with the process."

The truth of Sir Arthur's words impacted Edward like a sharp blow across the face. He immediately regretted his words and offered an apology, which the Scotsman good-naturedly waved away.

With peace restored between them, the two men strode along Crown Hill's winding driveway, entering the house to exit onto the porch. Once comfortably settled, Agnes served them a late lunch of rare roast beef on her specialty kimmelweck rolls, topped with salt and caraway seeds. She complimented the sandwiches with German potato salad. While they ate, the cohorts laid out a plan for the following day.

As the intense afternoon sun ebbed into a magnificent amber horizon, the two men welcomed the evening over generous tumblers of scotch and fine Cuban cigars, gifted to Sir Arthur by Harry Houdini. There they remained without interruption, discussing the meaning of life and death into the night's starry moonrise.

I listened intently as Edward and Sir Arthur laid out their plan for meeting with Rose. As they plotted, I tried to balance the possibility of all they envisioned with the disappointing realities Mary and I had experienced so many times since her passing. At the end of the night, I could not help but believe that this time, with these two men and with this young girl, it could be different.

That was the message of hope I took to Mary in the midst of the night. Yet unlike my mindset, her sense of optimism was tempered.

"Dearest Crown Hill, what is it that makes you believe so in Sir Arthur? We have known Edward long enough to trust in his nature and abilities. But what of this man who has befriended him?"

"Sweet Mary, I would say that in all ways, his good natured heart appears to lead him, which makes him a balance to Edward's logical nature. As for his spiritual abilities, it would seem that he is genuine and unafraid, which re-enforces Edward's same demeanor. I believe that together these two men possess the strength and courage to understand and deal with the tragedies your spirit has endured."

Mary dropped deeply into my being, staying silent and still. I could only imagine what she was feeling, the long and exhausting time that she had been forced to remain on the earth with no ties, no foundation, no ability to go forward or back.

After so many years of agony, to even begin to consider that the torture might soon be over had to be overwhelming. Further, somewhere in all of her imaginings lurked the reality that if and when she were able to finally move on she would be leaving me.

"Crown Hill?"

"Yes my Mary."

"What about the girl?"

"What about her?"

"What is her purpose? Why has she come into our world?"

"I believe it is due to her purity of heart and soul, dearest. While Edward and Sir Conan Doyle have the strength to free you from that which keeps you earthbound, Rose's innocence can illuminate your path to the spirit world. Without her goodness, your release from all earthly ties will be impossible."

Her silence again walled Mary away from me.

As the night sky faded into the dawn's sepia hue, I felt a deep fear welling up within me, from a source I knew only too well.

"Crown Hill?
"Yes, sweet friend, I am here."
"Please, do not leave me. I cannot face this alone."
"I understand and I am here for you...always."

CHAPTER TEN

Rose could hardly sleep. The prospect of earning money by copying words onto paper filled her mind with imaginings of chocolate candies and satin hair ribbons that she would soon be able to buy. At the same time, she was troubled by the awake-dream she had experienced at Crown Hill.

Rose was a sheltered child, aware of little outside the protected world in which her widowed mother, Elizabeth, had raised her. As a result, the young girl was completely content with her life and surroundings. It was a perfect existence, marred only by the onset of the disturbing, awake-dreams.

The visualizations first began when Rose became a "woman," as her mother explained the rivulet of blood dribbling between her legs. Whenever it became Rose's "time of the month," she would inevitably experience a spell where one minute she would be talking and laughing like any young girl, and the next her eyes would glaze over and she would pale, trembling convulsively in place. After a few moments the episode would end as abruptly as it began, with Rose dropping into a faint. When she awoke the disoriented girl would be weakened, with little if any recall of what had transpired.

As Rose matured, her spells became stronger and more clearly connected to what Elizabeth feared was an evolving spiritual sensitivity. What the concerned mother found most alarming was in the midst of these trances, her daughter would often engage in conversation as if communicating with someone clearly not visible. The resultant sense of fear within Elizabeth made her determined to do everything possible to keep Rose's condition a secret, kept between parent and child.

However Elizabeth's determination to safeguard her daughter's condition eventually weakened, following one particularly distressing awake-dream. The intensity of Rose's response to whatever engaged her spirit that day triggered wild imaginings within Elizabeth over the evils that could threaten her child. Desperate for help, she turned to her own mother and cautiously explained all that she had witnessed.

In response, Elizabeth's mother revealed a family history of women who had acted much the same as Rose. She termed them "seers," and said they possessed the ability to talk with those who had passed.

Learning of her family's lore did little to comfort Elizabeth. She immediately dismissed it as Irish poppycock and made her mother promise never to reveal Rose's condition. Yet the seer story remained with the frightened woman. She found herself fearing for her daughter's soul and offering daily prayers for the young girl's salvation.

Whether due to Elizabeth's holy invocations or not, Rose's awake-dreams began to play out in a more consistent fashion and, mercifully, always when the young girl was at home. In fact, no one outside of Elizabeth had ever witnessed her daughter's odd spells. As a result, the anxious mother chose to identify them as more of a medical condition than any sort of spiritual occurrence, which helped lessen her angst.

For Rose's part, she followed her mother's lead, accepting the intense dreams as part of an ongoing medical disorder. While she could neither predict their frequency nor recall their evolution, Rose learned to manage the physical demands of the spells with doses of chocolate, which she tried to keep always nearby to help revive her body. Overall, it seemed as if the odd happenings were becoming quite manageable. That is until the day that Rose made her way to Crown Hill and her awake-dreams became known.

When the young girl found herself resting in the Randall's parlor and realized what had happened, she was unsure how to proceed. Although Mrs. Randall and her daughters seemed most kind, her mother had continually warned her that no one should ever be told about her condition.

True to her mother's warning, Rose had not elaborated on her medical disorder to the Randalls and obviously had no control over entering into an awake-dream in their presence. All the same, Rose knew inherently that she needed to prevent her mother from ever finding out what had happened that morning at Crown Hill.

So it was in walking up the driveway to the Sandrock's house with the Randalls alongside, Rose quickly made the decision to go directly to the cottage where she and her mother lived. With any luck, her mother would still be at the main house and would never see the procession of neighbors escorting her home.

When Maria suggested that they wait for Rose's mother to come to the door, Rose assured the concerned woman that Elizabeth would be busy in the main house with midday duties. With that explanation and an assuring smile, Rose turned and entered into the cottage, escaping any further inquisition.

Now lying in her loft bed, reviewing the day's surprising visit from Mr. Randall and Sir Conan Doyle, Rose found herself consumed with excited thoughts about returning to Crown Hill. And fearful wonder if more uncontrollable awake-dreams might await.

In truth, I was concerned for the child.

From the moment she crossed my threshold I could sense the purity of Rose's spirit. After witnessing her connection with Mary, I had no doubt that her appearance at my door was in accordance with some greater plan.

Yet, the manner in which Edward and Sir Arthur were deceiving both the child and her mother raised my concerns.

What if Rose was unable to endure all that was required to set Mary's spirit free?

What if something went amiss during the séances planned by the two men?

I reviewed the troubling possibilities over and over, becoming obsessed with a multitude of frightening outcomes. While I was dedicated to freeing Mary's spirit from the earthly hell in which she was trapped, I did not want another traumatic incident, or something worse, to happen within my shelter.

I could only imagine avoiding such tragedy by communicating with Edward. I needed a way to connect with him that would encourage his most careful consideration of Rose and her spiritual gift.

I began with Mary.

"Mary, please come near so we can talk."

"I am here, dear friend."

"I hold great concern about young Rose. While there is no doubt she is essential to you, I need to be sure she is protected. It is my hope that you understand the same and will do whatever is required to ensure her well-being. Dearest Mary, I believe we need to reach out to Edward. Bring him thoughts that will help him safeguard the child."

Mary's response was immediate.

"What is it you think could happen? What concerns you so?"

"I am not sure. It's really not a specific idea or fear, more a feeling that something could go terribly wrong. And this child does not deserve to suffer while engaged in helping us."

"Kind heart, I understand your care for Rose. She is a beautiful child with a radiant soul. That is exactly why I was drawn to her when she first came to us. Yet without a specific reason for your protective feelings, I'm not sure what it is you want Edward to think or do. Dear Crown Hill, while I love you, I have endured many years of spiritual pain and sorrow within your shelter. Now when it seems that finally I

may be freed from my earthly bonds, what is it that you would have me do?"

Listening to Mary's voice I could sense her long-endured pain, feel her depleted spirit. Hearing her words, I realized that Mary could play no part in reaching out to Edward.

Thus I was caught in a triangle of worry. While I passionately desired Mary's release from this earth, I was concerned for Rose's safety and needed to protect my own being as well.

I did not want to become overwhelmed once more by a painful human tragedy as happened with Mary's death. Such sorrow had almost destroyed my being once. I would not, could not, allow it to happen again.

In considering all things, reaching out to Edward would have to become my purpose…mine alone.

CHAPTER ELEVEN

Edward tossed and turned throughout the night. In the dawn of the new morning, he found himself searching for guidance and struggling for inspiration as to what should be done.

In a matter of a few hours Rose would appear at his door, ready to undertake her role as Sir Arthur's official transcriber. Edward felt terribly guilty. The job was but a thinly veiled excuse to try and attract the spirit that had appeared during the girl's initial visit to Crown Hill. Yet in discussing the subterfuge with Doyle, the spiritualist proffered a valid point.

"I say old chap, 'tis quite possible that the spirit may not even appear again. The woman in the mirror might very well be gone from Crown Hill, as oddly as she arrived."

Edward wanted to believe in such a possibility, but his instinct was that it was only a matter of time before Rose and the spirit were again connected.

Right now, Edward's primary concern was protecting the innocent child from being overwhelmed and frightened by any spiritual happenings that might occur. If only he and Sir Arthur had been truthful with Rose and her mother, this circumstance would be much easier to manage. On the other hand, Edward's lawyerly logic forced him to acknowledge that if they had explained their quandary to Elizabeth, she might never have allowed her daughter to return to Crown Hill.

The more Edward considered the problem the more disturbed he became. Finally the barrister decided to rise and go to his desk. At least there he could write to Maria and express how much he missed both she and the girls. Perhaps, he thought, communicating with his wife would help clear his thoughts.

Edward had not heard from Maria since her departure. Between the distractions of Sir Arthur's arrival and connecting with Rose, there had been no time to really consider his family's absence. With his conscience now hammering away at his righteousness, Edward found himself drawn to thoughts of his devoted wife and his sweetly impressionable daughters. Unfortunately, those thoughts also increased his compunction over deceiving Rose. No matter which way his mind turned, Edward was mired in self-reproach.

Two quick raps on his bedroom door startled Edward halfway off of his chair. .

"Had no intent to intrude old chap. Rather I was heading down for an early morning spot of tea and noticed your light. Everything tip top?"

Edward really didn't know how to answer his friend's query. Nothing was overtly wrong, but nothing felt quite right either. His wife and daughters were miles away, his family spending their summer season apart. His favored vacation residence felt foreign and unfriendly. And at the base of all of his concerns, Edward felt almost evil about the manner in which they were involving young Rose in their spiritual quest.

"To tell you the truth Doyle, I'm just feeling a little unsettled about everything going on right now, both at Crown Hill and in my life Try as I may to analyze and condense it into a matter of right and wrong, it's not that easy. So I guess I'm out of sorts about everything. If I have layered my concerns on you, I apologize."

"Not at all, my dear fellow. I can certainly understand your mindset. What do you say we both get a cup of tea and begin our morning on that wonderful porch of yours? Undoubtedly a breath of fresh air, along with the early morning sunrise, will serve us both well."

Once relocated to the porch, the men savored their tea along with generous slices of Alice's egg, ham and cheese pie. They topped off their hearty breakfast with the housekeeper's delectable scones topped with her concord grape preserves, made with freshly picked fruits from the adjoining vineyards. While savoring each morsel, Edward and Sir Arthur judiciously reviewed their plans for the day.

"I believe that when the young girl arrives we should unquestionably bring her into the dining room and have her begin to transcribe notes at the table," Sir Arthur began. "I also think it will be quite important to seat her facing the sideboard and mirror."

"I suppose," Edward reluctantly responded. He immediately added, "I want to be sure that we don't leave her alone in the dining room, or in any room for that matter, in case the spirit does appear again. We need to always be in close proximity so that we can witness Rose's reaction should any spiritual activity occur." As a contrite afterthought, Edward added, "And of course to make sure that she is protected from all harm. Not to be bothersome on this point of protection, but I'm realizing a sense of failure in not protecting my own young girls as well as my wife from the impact of this spirit. It is vital that I do not fail again with Rose."

"Absolutely, my dear chap and I completely understand and respect your viewpoint," Sir Arthur agreed. "Now, the only other thing we need to discuss is the séance."

The mention of the word caused Edward to shudder. When Emily was alive, the two had partnered in many spiritual engagements. However, since her passing Edward rarely ventured into the spiritual realm. Such undertakings were no longer as comfortable as they had been with Emily. To think of delving into the world of spirits without the guidance of his trusted friend, or worse yet by relying on an innocent and unaware youngster, it was unsettling.

"Come now, old man," Sir Arthur spoke, recognizing his friend's discomfort. "You and I have been independently involved in many séances over the years. I have no doubt that we will be able to handle whatever comes our way. Chin up. There really is no reason to worry."

Edward smiled weakly and nodded. He wished he could be as sure-minded as Sir Arthur. Taking a deep breath, the troubled lawyer was about to broach their possible need for a darkly quiet séance room when Agnes materialized at the porch door.

"Excuse me sirs, but there's a young girl here to see you. It's Rose Jennings from the Spaulding house up the road. She says that she's supposed to start working here today, something about copying a book. What would you like me to do with her?"

An uncomfortable tingle crept along Edward's spine like a multi-legged spider. Why had the child come to Crown Hill so early? He clearly recalled Sir Arthur stating 1:30 in the afternoon as their appointed starting time. Nervously, Edward wondered if somehow the child's mother had discovered their devious plan and commanded her daughter to withdraw from the project. In a state of distress he offered a softly pleaded invocation. "Emily, I can only hope that you are here to guide us."

"I beg your pardon sir, but is Emily the name of your wife?" The question came from Rose, now standing beside Agnes in the porch doorway.

Caught off guard, Edward deflected the girl's question by issuing a sharp command, "Agnes, take the young lady into the dining room."

As the housekeeper led Rose to a seat at the dining table, Edward and Arthur followed closely and settled into chairs opposite the child. Lacking direction or protocol, Edward began by asking a question.

"My dear Rose, whatever are you doing here so early in the morning? You aren't shirking your duties at the Spauldings are you?"

"Oh no, sir, not at all," she earnestly replied. "Actually, I got up early and finished all my work. Then I packed my lunch and brought it with me, promising my mother that I would be sure to eat. You see, I have been known to get wrapped up in whatever I'm doing and forget to take nourishment. Then I can become faint. It always embarrasses my mother so, and she doesn't want anything like that to happen while I'm working with you here at Crown Hill."

The young girl's pure intent and sincerity of response added to Edward's discomfort over the less-than-honest situation. Again he felt his conscience reproach him.

What Edward could not possibly fathom was that the roles he and Sir Arthur were playing in this drama were no longer of their own plan or accord. Rather, the universe was now in control of all that was about to happen within Crown Hill, including the imminent interaction between the living and the dead.

I felt Rose's presence from the moment she appeared at my door.
I felt Mary rising up within me as the child crossed my threshold.

The strength of their converging spirits felt uncontrollable, much like a powerful tidal wave rising to envelop all in its path. As I struggled to remain steadfast, I wondered how I would manage Mary and support Rose at the same time? How would I balance their individual beings in concert with their strong connection?

My concerns quickly became irrelevant as Rose proceeded fearlessly from the porch into the dining room. Immediately I felt Mary move as well, but to where I was unsure. I decided that rather than try and prevent or control Mary's actions, I would wrap my protective powers around the child. Yet as I drew near, a force prevented me.

"Stop. Stay away. Do not interfere."

It was a message delivered into my being, without context or connection. Whose words were they and why?

Mystified, I searched within for Mary.

"Mary, where have you gone? Answer me. What is happening?"

Not a word. Not a motion. No sense of her spirit, anywhere.

Disoriented, I turned my attention to the dining room. Agnes had withdrawn to resume her kitchen duties. Edward, Sir Arthur and Rose were seated at the table beside the buffet in which Mary had appeared. All seemed in peaceful order. At the same time tension streamed through me, filling my every room.

If I should continue to radiate such apprehension, Edward and Sir Arthur would undoubtedly struggle to create the tranquility needed to connect Rose and Mary.

Drawing on the quietude of my being, I focused on how best to aid them in their circumstance.

Instinctively, I wanted to extend myself to Rose. I felt compelled to move her away from the oak sideboard, away from the mirror where I could still imagine Mary's tortured face. Once more I moved cautiously toward the innocent young girl.

"Stay away from the child. Leave her."

The voice carried a force that halted me. I was now fully aware that something, or someone, with momentous power was within me. It was clear that I no longer held control of my own being...or anything that was about to occur within my walls.

CHAPTER TWELVE

Rose was completely unaware that arriving early for her work with Sir Arthur and Mr. Randall would cause them consternation. Yet truthfully, it would not have mattered even if she had known. The girl simply could not wait beyond mid-morning to make her way to Crown Hill.

Rose was unsure why she found the rambling old farmhouse so intriguing.

No doubt, she had enjoyed meeting Mrs. Randall and the girls during her first visit. However, Agnes has already informed the young girl that the Randall women had departed from Crown Hill unexpectedly, with no apparent plans to return. Obviously, their presence was not at the root of her inexplicable attraction.

Further, while Rose valued the money she was going to earn from Sir Arthur, there was something more than dollars and cents compelling her to the neighboring hilltop. So it was on that late summer morning, as the sensitive child entered Crown Hill and settled into a chair at the dining room table, something odd stirred within her.

A wave of nausea? A need for food perhaps?

Dreading the onset of an awake-dream, the wary child asked her hosts for permission to eat a piece of fruit from her lunch.

Without waiting for a reply, Rose pulled a red, ripe apple from her brown bag and took a delicate bite. Her simple action kindled an image within Edward's mind of the Garden of Eden's devilish asp and its sinfully tempting fruit. The wicked impression triggered further consternation within Edward about their deviant plans for this innocent girl.

Stop! Edward silently commanded his unwavering brain. The sensible lawyer knew that he needed to halt his anxious imagination or his present circumstance would worsen.

Perhaps, action would alleviate my relentless fears.

"Sir Arthur, shall we put young Rose to work?"

"Most certainly, Edward," came the famed writer's reply. Rising from the table he directed, "Young lady, you finish your apple. I shall retrieve my writings and a journal into which you can transcribe and will return directly." With that, Sir Arthur left Rose and Edward to each other's company.

Between bites of her fruit, Rose smiled sweetly at Edward. In striking up a conversation, Edward realized that her genuine nature reminded him of his own daughters.

"So Rose, Virginia and Marion were pleased to meet you when you last visited."

"Oh I'm so glad, Mr. Randall, sir. I enjoyed meeting the girls and Mrs. Randall as well. They were all so kind to me. I am sorry that they are no longer here. I was hoping to see them again."

"I agree with you, my dear, I am saddened that they are not here as well," Edward replied. While speaking, he moved purposefully around the table and onto the chair next to Rose, remaining constantly vigilant of the sideboard mirror.

"Perhaps next summer you and my daughters will enjoy some time together, hiking through the vineyards and playing in the fields." Edward's suggestion turned his thoughts to his family reuniting at Crown Hill. The images distracted him until Rose's softly spoken question refocused his attention.

"Please sir, is there some place that I can put this?"

Rose's long, graceful hand held out the brownish core of the once red fruit. Edward pointed her to a small wicker basket at the table's end where she deposited the seed-filled remains. Sliding back onto her chair, Rose tucked away her brown lunch bag just as Sir Arthur returned.

"Here we are my dear: My writings, a journal for transcribing, several pens, nubs and ink. Edward, might you have a blotter on which young Rose could work?"

Edward retrieved a green blotter edged in dark brown leather from his office and placed it on the table in front of Rose. Stepping back, he made a visual sweep of the dining room, ending at the sideboard mirror. Nothing out of the ordinary, nothing unsettling.

Sir Arthur returned to his chair and began detailing Rose's work while Edward was left with nothing to do but observe. Watching in silence, the unnerved barrister realized the moment as nothing more than ordinary. Without conscious awareness, a long, deep breath seeped from Edward's lungs. His body relaxed. His mind refocused.

Was it possible that Sir Arthur was right? Had the spirit, which had so terribly frightened his family, disappeared as curiously as it had materialized? Was all of his worry about Rose for naught?

Edward relocated to a seat in the corner of the dining room where he could command a view of the young girl at work, as well as the possible comings and goings of all, human or spirit alike. As Sir Arthur and Rose consulted on the transcription, a quiet rhythm of life permeated the room.

All proceeded peacefully for several hours until the blast of Eden's noon whistle heralded Agnes' arrival. She appeared carrying luncheon plates of roast pork sandwiches topped with thickly rich gravy. The accomplished cook served side platters of buttered carrots and her specialty, potato pancakes laden with orchard fresh applesauce and sour cream. The melded smells encouraged the trio to immediately put aside all else to enjoy the delicious repast.

"Thank you so much for lunch," the brightly smiling girl spoke directly to Edward. "It is so much better than the jelly and butter sandwich that I packed this morning."

Jelly and butter sandwiches had been Edward's favorite as a young boy. It had been years since he enjoyed the sweet, creamy taste treat. "Well, I tell you what young lady. You can just leave that sandwich here with me and I will eat it tonight as my bedtime snack. That way your mother won't be concerned that you are not eating well enough while you are here."

The thought of the grown man before her enjoying a jelly and butter sandwich made Rose giggle, which quickly rolled into full out laughter that became contagious to the two men beside her. Within minutes the three were laughing heartily, tears welling in their eyes.

The sounds of their merriment compelled Agnes into the dining room to investigate whatever was happening. Upon seeing the trio collectively dissolved in laughter, the dour woman shook her head and retreated back to her household duties.

When at last the three gained their breath and regained their composure, a true sense of joy permeated the house. Gone were the feelings of dread and foreboding that had existed only moments earlier.

"Well, my dear Rose, I believe that we have accomplished quite enough for one day," Sir Arthur spoke in his inherently kind demeanor. "Let us plan on your return tomorrow, but a bit later in the afternoon, as agreed upon with your mother. We should be able to complete the transfer of my notes by week's end and I will pay you your wages then."

While Rose had no desire to leave, she was respectful of Sir Arthur's wishes. Obediently she collected her writing materials and set them on the sideboard, where they would be out of the way. Her placement caused Edward to inwardly cringe, but no matter his sense of dread, there was not a sign of a spirit in the sideboard mirror, in the dining room or anywhere within his extended view.

Rose bade the men good day and slipped out the kitchen door and with her safe departure Edward and Sir Arthur exhaled a shared sigh of relief. The young girl's presence at Crown Hill had gone without incident or mishap.

"I say, well done old chap," Sir Arthur offered with a hearty slap on Edward's back. "You see, just as I predicted. All is well. Now let us again set off for that charming porch of yours and enjoy some afternoon sherry, shall we?"

Edward had to agree, the morning had been uneventful, quite pleasurable actually. Rose was a charming young girl and whatever had happened during her initial visit at Crown Hill seemed to be but a thing of the past. Sir Arthur was right. Celebratory sherry was appropriate and, indeed, needed.

The two men basked in the warmth of the summer season and toasted to their health and continued good fortune. While enjoying the heat of the sun and the singe of the sherry, both were blissfully unaware of the uninvited force that had invaded Crown Hill that morning. And of the war of wills that was about to begin.

From the intensity of Mary's reaction to Rose's presence, I fully expected her to reach out, to appear, to do something to try and unite with the child's spirit. Yet once the disturbing voice warned me to stay away from Rose, there was no reaction from my Mary. When I was warned a second time, again with no reaction, I realized that her spirit was no longer within me.

I opened myself to every corner, to every floor in search of my sweet friend.

Nothing.

Finally, I stilled my worry, and waited.

"Dearest Crown Hill, please help me."

It was faint.

"Mary?"

"Dearest, I am outside of your shelter, but know that I have not purposefully retreated from you. Rather I have been forced away by the intensity of that which has invaded your being. Please hear me and know that I am still near, still in need of your loving support, now more than ever."

The idea that there was a power strong enough to drive Mary from my care was inconceivable. Further, that this power possessed the strength to invade my being and force actions over which I had no control...again, unthinkable. Who, or what, possessed such power?

"Mary?" I called again

Silence.

"Mary? Can you hear me? Can you feel me reaching out to you?"

Silence still.

A core of fear rose up within me like an uncontrollable bile. Cold air seeped into my being with an intensity that I could not arrest.

Never had I experienced such sensations within my walls.

Never had I been overpowered in every sense of the word, by any earthly force.

Confused and anxious to comprehend what was happening, I looked to the sideboard mirror. There I witnessed a blackness that deflected all images. As I stared into the nothingness, I called out, "Who are you? What are you?"

The response to my questions came with an intense blast of icy air that swept through me, "It matters not who I am. Know only that I am here to ensure that the spirit of Mary remains."

The reply transformed my fears to anger. "What do you mean? What purpose of yours is served by continuing Mary's suffering?"

A freezing cold again accompanied the response. "Mary will remain here always and nothing you undertake will change that. That is all both of you need to know and understand."

This time my reply came without thought. "And who are you to invade my being and try to control what goes on within my shelter? What makes you believe you have that right?"

Frigid air spread through me as if every bit of warmth on the earth had been depleted. A vase from high upon the sideboard came crashing to the floor splintering into glass shards, as if someone had angrily thrown it to the ground.

"Mary is to remain here on earth and I have the right and power to make it so. I warn you, stay away from the child and all others attempting to free Mary's spirit, as she is mine to control."

An eerie silence followed, accompanied by a stream of warming air. The loud crash from moments earlier drew Agnes into the dining room. As I watched her inspect the glass shards on the floor, I wondered if she would imagine something more than a random accident causing the vase to fall and break. Would she sense that something with a vengeful power had entered my space and taken control?

Could anyone feel it? Or somehow control it?

For the sake of all concerned, I hoped so...as it was clearly evident that I could not.

CHAPTER THIRTEEN

The day dawned with a sweltering air, draping across Crown Hill like a thick woolen blanket.

In the early morning light Agnes was busy cooking, perspiration freely streaming down her face, arms, and legs. The accomplished housekeeper was determined to produce the entire day's meals before the stifling humidity intensified and made her kitchen tasks completely unbearable.

As she put the finishing touches on a batch of sweetened biscuits she hoped would suffice as a dessert base for both lunch and dinner, Agnes became aware of stirrings overhead.

Sir Arthur's guest quarters were located directly above the kitchen. From the noises reverberating through the ceiling, Crown Hill's visitor was up and about. No doubt in minutes he would be downstairs, asking for his morning pot of tea with milk and sugar. Efficiently, the housekeeper set water to boil while cleaning up the remnants of her meal preparations.

Within minutes Agnes was pouring steaming water through a wire infuser into a ceramic teapot. Immediately the fragrance of Sir Arthur's favored brew saturated the humid kitchen air. Tea sipping was part of the famed author's morning ritual and he brought along his preferred black tea spiced with jasmine and a touch of lavender wherever he traveled. As if drawn to the scent, Sir Arthur promptly appeared in the kitchen doorway.

"I say, Agnes. You are a bit of all right having my tea ready. I was just about to ask if you would brew me a pot. You must have read my mind"

While Agnes liked the famed author well enough, his reference to mind reading made her uncomfortable. In fact, a lot of what was going on at Crown Hill since Sir Arthur's arrival was bothersome, like the recent broken vase. It was not possible that the vase simply fell off of the sideboard. It was early morning when it happened and no one was in the dining room. No one, other than herself, was even downstairs. Nothing was taking place that could have caused its crash to the floor. It was the strangest thing and, for the life of her, Agnes could not figure out how or why it had happened.

Then there was the work that the world famous author was undertaking with young Rose Jennings. Agnes wasn't quite sure what that was all about but she knew she didn't like it, even if everything seemed above board and in order.

One thing Agnes did know was that anytime she walked into the Randall's hilltop home these days, she felt an immediate knot in her stomach that would not release until she left Crown Hill at day's end. The thing about Agnes' gut instincts was that they never failed her. It was only a matter of time until she figured it all out.

Edward was next to appear in Agnes' sauna-like workspace, following closely on Sir Arthur's heels. Their dual presence caused Agnes to issue an edict that breakfast would be served directly, on the porch. She instructed the two men to go and wait for their meal there.

Tact was definitely not the housekeeper's strongest trait, but her delicious food persuaded the men to overlook her quirks and her brusque directives. Heading off to the porch like properly schooled boys, Edward and Sir Arthur settled into their now-regular seats and exchanged early morning pleasantries to pass the time.

It was Sir Arthur who eventually addressed the subject silently looming between them.

"So my dear fellow, in the light of the new day, how do you feel about young Rose and this whole spirit business?"

Edward was caught off guard by the direct line of questioning. He had come downstairs early, hoping that they could enjoy one of Agnes' hearty breakfasts before tackling the worrisome topic. Yet since nothing untoward had occurred on Rose's first visit, Edward's concerns had lessened.

"Well, Doyle, I have to admit yesterday was quite a relief. And after reflecting on all that did *not* happen, I am inclined to lean your way. Perhaps whatever appeared in the mirror to my family may have been an anomaly. An apparition now departed."

While Edward's words were positive, Sir Arthur sensed the lack of conviction in his friend's tone. The astute author understood that Edward was disturbed by the possibilities of all that had transpired in his cherished summer home. However, as an experienced spiritualist, Sir Arthur was fully aware that dealing with supernatural activity required a strong character and a resolute mind. At the moment, he felt that his host possessed neither.

Just as the Scotsman was about to broach the topic of Edward's frame of mind, Agnes appeared with a tray of luscious breakfast treats. She began by serving the men individual steaming pots of tea. Next came bowls of sliced cantaloupe adorned with fresh-picked raspberries, followed by plates of scrambled eggs topped with cheddar cheese and coarsely crumbled bacon. Finally came the breakfast piece de resistance, Agnes's secret recipe, sticky buns, dripping with caramel and nuts. Confirming that the gentlemen were content, Agnes left them to delight in the summer morning repast.

At the end of every breakfast, the two men had developed a tradition of pouring a second cup of tea and discussing and debating whatever topic inspired them. On this steamy summer morn however, both men agreed to forego their favored hot beverage and instead take a stroll to the pond. There, Edward suggested that they could enjoy a lazy row in the boat, should they be so inclined.

During their leisurely walk, the two men became completely engaged in literary conversation. Upon reaching the pond, rather than rowing, they chose to continue their chat seated upon a bench alongside a marsh of thickly clustered cattails.

The two became part of the rural landscape and time drifted, becoming meaningless. It was only a menacing black cloud of driving rain and powerful thunder that forced Edward and Sir Arthur away from the pond and hurriedly back to the porch. There, under protective cover, the two realized the morning had passed and the time was just short of noon. Rose would soon be arriving.

The duo made a quick change of clothes, from damp to dry, and returned to the dining room for lunch. Considering that they were still rather full from breakfast, the men declined Agnes' rosemary chicken salad on garden greens and instead chose to eat only the bowls of her summer specialty, chilled tomato-basil soup. To complement the light lunch, the dedicated housekeeper served fresh berries accompanied by a basket of her sweetened biscuits and a side plate of freshly-whipped heavy cream.

The gentlemen's enjoyment of the deliciously cold soup kept them completely unaware of Rose's quiet presence as she slipped into the room.

"Good Afternoon Sirs," the young girl offered in a softly respectful voice.

"Well, well, Edward, see here who has joined us." Sir Arthur replied with a chuckle. "Good afternoon to you, my dear. I see that our work yesterday did not discourage your return."

"Oh no sir. In fact, I know that I am a bit early again, but I just could not wait any longer."

The girl's innocence never ceased to touch Edward's heart. In fact, he was coming to view Rose much like one of his own.

"Come and join us at the table young lady. Agnes has prepared a most special dessert of fresh berries and cream over biscuits. There is more here than Sir Arthur and I need. Please serve yourself and enjoy."

It did not take extra encouragement for the usually shy girl to follow Edward's directive. Assuming the exact place she had occupied the day before, Rose eagerly scooped and devoured a generous portion of the sweet summer treat, happily licking every last morsel from her spoon. It was a moment blissfully focused on the joy of food all around the table.

"Thank you very much sirs. Now may I please begin my work?"

"Of course child," Sir Arthur answered. "Everything is just as you left it on the sideboard."

For the first time since Rose had entered the room, Edward's conscience triggered an alarm throughout his being. The simple pleasure the innocent girl had displayed in eating the berries and cream had melted Edward's heart. He would not be able to manage it if anything unpleasant happened to this sweet child.

"Doyle, can I speak with you on the porch a minute?" Edward nodded toward the screen door. "Rose we will return shortly."

Puzzled, the Scotsman followed his host into the sultry midday air.

"I can't continue this, Doyle. We must escort Rose home and meet again with her mother. This time we will honestly explain what has happened here and why we would like her daughter to spend time with us. There really is just no other way that I can manage having Rose here at Crown Hill."

"That would be absolutely fine, old man. Whatever you think is best. I really don't have…

Doyle's response was cut off by a wail unlike any the two had ever experienced. To add to the shock, the piercing scream seemed to be emanating from the dining room.

In tandem, the two men pushed through the narrow screen doorway into the house. There they found Rose, no longer peacefully seated at the dining room table. Rather, she was standing stiffly before the sideboard, staring at the mirror. Although Edward and Sir Arthur saw only their reflections, it was clear that Rose was envisioning something other than herself and seemed to be engaged in conversation with whatever it was.

"You don't belong here. You need to go away NOW. And what have you done with her? You must let her come back!"

As Rose spoke out, Edward carefully moved toward her. Independently, Sir Arthur drew closer to the sideboard to inspect the mirror. Again, there was nothing to see, but his image and the reflections of the others. As Edward stood by Rose's side and tried to comprehend what was happening, the entranced young girl lashed out in anger yet again.

"I am not afraid of you. No matter what you say, I will find her and help her. You cannot stop me."

The two men looked across Rose's tense body, unsure of how best to proceed. The fact that they had been outside on the porch when Rose's transformation began left them unclear idea as to what was happening; how or why it all began.

Their confusion became further compounded as a scent of roses filtered through the room. Both men noticed the sweet smell at the same moment that they realized a further transformation in the young girl. Suddenly her person took on a forceful aura as she turned to Edward and spoke in a voice unknown to him.

"I have been waiting for you for such a long time. Now that you are finally here, you must help me."

The pleading voice clearly did not belong to the child, but if not Rose, then who? Edward's years of séance experiences with Emily French allowed him to realize that the speaker was most likely a spirit possessing Rose's being in an attempt to directly communicate. His first inclination was to try and identify the voice.

"You say you've been waiting for me. Who are you? How do you know me?"

The questions caused Rose to forcefully grab Edward's arms in reply.

"I have been a part of this house for many years. I have watched you and your family come and go, always biding my time. Now, at last, the goodness and light of this child's being has provided me a means of reaching out to you. I have to end my tortured existence; forever cease my forced wandering. Please, you must help me."

Before Edward could reply, Sir Arthur called out in loud warning, "Edward look up!"

Turning toward Doyle, Edward saw the ornate brass chandelier above the dining room table swinging in a wide pendulum motion. The force of the swaying light caused its crystal globes to release into the air like targeted rockets, all of them headed directly toward Edward and Rose.

Without thought, Edward grabbed Rose and jumped away toward the wall, contorting his body as a protective shield over the young girl. At the same time, Sir Arthur took cover beneath the dining room table.

The tumultuous commotion brought Agnes immediately upstairs from the fruit cellar. As she pushed through the swinging door between the kitchen and dining room the housekeeper recoiled in shock. The long-nagging knot in her stomach intensified as the housekeeper witnessed the chandelier arcing over the table and shards of crystal glass covering the floor. Looking further, she became aware of the defensively curled body of Sir Arthur under the table.

In the far corner of the room she saw Rose up against a wall; Edward Randall seemingly forcing his body against hers. Clearly the child was struggling as she called out again in a distorted voice.

"This cannot happen," she wailed. "He cannot be allowed to do this. Not now. Not when I finally have a chance. Please, help me."

Agnes rushed toward the girl, intent on answering her pleas.

"What are you doing?" Agnes shouted at her employer as she aggressively attempted to move him off of Rose.

"What is wrong with you? Why are you forcing yourself on this child?"

Their dispute became instantly irrelevant as with one, last, haunting cry, Rose collapsed into Edward's arms.

"Get away Agnes," Edward chided the belligerent woman. "Give the child some air, for heaven's sake. Doyle come quickly and help me carry Rose to the parlor."

As all rushed to aid the frighteningly comatose child, a strong strike of thunder shook the windows of Crown Hill and a bolt of lightning torched the land all around, as a powerful storm of an unearthly kind continued to rage within.

So it began, as disturbingly as I feared, and more frightening than I ever imagined.

I had never experienced such an occurrence in my century and a half of existence. Even when Mary's spirit first came into me, I never lost control of my being. Yet in those moments when Rose became entranced, I was nothing more than an observer of all going on within me.

Seeing Rose as she lay limp on the floor was distressing, but it was the echo of the voice flowing from within her that was most concerning. I knew that voice. I recognized it immediately.

"Mary where are you? You must talk to me. Why did you do that to young Rose?"

Nary a response did I receive. Poor Rose had only just come into my shelter and already she was suffering the consequences of her trusting nature. I couldn't let this continue. There had to be some way to connect Mary and Rose without such trauma. Then I heard the voice.

"Leave the child alone. She does not matter. And stop trying to aid Mary. Her spirit will remain here forever, and you have no power to change that."

The words shocked me like an electrical current. It was the same voice from the previous day that had warned me to stay away from Rose. Only this time there was more. There was a threatening edge to the words that felt intimidating, actually evil.

"Who is it speaking?"

"I owe you no explanations House, other than to give you this final warning. Mary is destined to remain here on earth as I deign. She has no choice in the matter, nor do you. You can allow her to be within you or I will place her otherwise. It matters not to me. Just understand that if you continue to interfere in my plan I will destroy you, as surely as I caused the vase to shatter and the chandelier's crystal globes to rain down upon you.

Fear, dread, and confusion combined to cause hesitation in my response. By the time I gathered my wits and could answer, Rose was awake, the evil within me, gone…and Mary still nowhere to be found.

CHAPTER FOURTEEN

Upon her collapse, Edward gathered Rose and placed her limp body on the settee in the parlor. At the same time he barked at Agnes to bring him some cool water and a washcloth. If nothing else, the task would keep the housekeeper out of the way long enough for Edward and Doyle to quickly assess what had happened, and how best to proceed.

"Well my friend, I would say that we bloody well have the answer to our question," Sir Arthur spoke first. "There is definitely a spirit present within Crown Hill. And whomever it may be, they have clearly chosen young Rose as their medium."

Edward tried to process his experienced friend's words while gently loosening the collar of Rose's dress and brushing sweat-soaked strands of hair from her eyes. He agreed, the events of the last few minutes proved that there was a spirit present in Crown Hill. The issue now became identifying that spirit and understanding what it wanted.

"What do we do now, Doyle?"

"Well it would seem that young Rose is the key to connecting with this spirit. What I find most startling about this entire episode of events is that the spirit channels through the child without any formal connection--no séance or conjuring of the spirit world. In all of my years I have never been witness to anything quite like it."

Edward too was struck by Rose's ability to directly connect with the other side; although his wonder was offset by concern over the intensity of the spirit who was clearly manipulating the delicate girl. What did it all mean? Where had this spirit been for years previous, when he and his family had summered at Crown Hill? And what of his family? How would he ever assure them that they were safe to return, once they learned of this haunting event?

Questions shuffled through Edward's mind more furiously than he was able to process them. His thoughts became short-circuited however, as Rose began stirring and Agnes returned to the parlor.

"Here is the water and cloth as you asked." Agnes set the items on the table next to the settee where Rose still lay, unconscious. "I also opened some smelling salts."

Accepting the uncapped bottle, Edward slipped one hand under Rose's head and raised her toward the ammonia nitrate wafting into the air. With one inhale, Rose was awake and railing against the pungent gas. Edward quickly set the bottle down and gently elevated the weakened child to a sitting position. Judging by her grayish tone, it would be some time before she was fully recovered.

As Rose struggled to regain consciousness, Sir Arthur stepped into view.

"Hello my dear child. I am sure that you feel a bit disoriented at this moment, but all that has happened is that you fell faint. As you are able, take a few deep breaths and slowly let your mind return. You are safe and in good care."

Rose's unfocused glance toward Sir Arthur made it clear that while conscious, she was far from coherent. In fact, Rose's disjointed motions were such that Edward feared the child might relapse into an unconscious state. He turned to request that Agnes prepare one of her medicinal tea mixtures, but the housekeeper had disappeared. Frustrated, Edward turned instead to Doyle with instructions.

"I am going to the kitchen to brew Rose a cup of tea. Stay by her side and, perhaps, place a cool cloth on her forehead to help restore her wits."

Edward set off to the kitchen where he prepared a pot of mint tea. He seemed to recall Maria serving it whenever the girls were upset. As he allowed the tea to steep, the gently fragrant leaves ministered their calming effect upon him as well. No doubt the events of the afternoon had been disturbing, but with Sir Arthur's help he was resolved to find a way to deal with the invasive spirit, ensure Rose's well-being and restore Crown Hill as his family's beloved summer home. Edward had to believe that all of these things were possible.

Pouring the tea into one of Maria's sturdy porcelain cups, Edward momentarily pondered Agnes' whereabouts. His thoughts transformed as he delivered tea to the parlor, and found Rose greatly recovered.

"Well young lady, you are looking much improved. Here, I have brewed some tea for you to sip."

"Thank you Mr. Randall, but might you have a piece of chocolate?"

"Actually, old boy, she has been asking for candy since you departed the room," Sir Arthur remarked as he gently raised the cup to Rose's lips.

"I do have chocolate as a matter of fact," Edward replied. "But I'm not really sure if it's the best thing for you at this moment."

"I really don't think it could hurt old boy," Sir Arthur chimed in. To which Rose added, "Actually, my mother allows me a chocolate whenever I have a spell like this. She says it helps me to recover."

Edward was about to question Rose more closely about such, "spells" when a loud commotion engulfed the house. At first sound, it was like a maelstrom of arguing women. As the turmoil advanced, Edward recognized one of the voices as Agnes, in concert with another familiar but not quite identifiable female. It was only seconds before the additional person became known, as Elizabeth Jennings burst into the parlor with Agnes close behind.

"Rose, what has happened to you? What have these terrible men done?" Without pause, Elizabeth pushed aside Sir Arthur, swept her daughter into her arms and venomously turned toward Edward.

"You lowlife, self-important miscreant. You have the audacity to call yourself a gentleman, respectfully devoted to your wife and daughters. Yet as soon as you have an opportunity, you make improper advances on my innocent child? Just because you think we are a lower class than your fancy-dan, high falootin' society friends, it's all right to do unspeakable things to my little girl?

Edward and Sir Arthur stood stunned, frozen in place by the woman's venomous barrage.

"Thank goodness Agnes came to the Spauldings to tell me what happened here today Mr. High and Mighty, Edward Randall. How dare you hold my daughter against a wall while she cried to be released. And you, *Sir* Conan Doyle, you worthless excuse for a nobleman, hiding under a table and allowing my daughter to be ravaged. You both disgust me."

"Mother, please, stop. Stop!" Rose sobbed as her mother's anger overflowed the room. The young girl desperately tried to intervene, but in reality she could not speak the truth of what had happened. Rose couldn't admit that she had endured another of her awake-dreams in front of Agnes, Mr. Randall and Sir Arthur. Elizabeth had drummed it into her daughter's head to never admit such a thing publicly. Other than pleading with her mother to stop accusing Mr. Randall of unspeakable actions, Rose was powerless.

"I am taking my daughter out of here and I tell you, as God is my witness, she will never return. And if I ever hear that either of you have made any attempt to see her or contact her, I will call the police and have you arrested and charged. And Agnes, I fully expect and demand that you will attest to all of this."

The housekeeper was as immobilized by the situation as both men. Hearing her name she blankly nodded in hopes that her accord would help end the unfolding nightmare.

Elizabeth made her way to the parlor doorway with Rose tucked tightly in her arms. Before exiting, she turned directly toward Edward one last time. "You will *never* speak of this to anyone. Do you hear me? *No One!* Nothing ever occurred here with my daughter but some note taking. Do you understand?"

Edward knew that a question was being asked, but his thunderstruck brain was unable to process or produce a reply.

"Randall. I say Randall, I believe that she is looking for a response," Sir Arthur whispered. "I suggest you at least nod."

The barrister bobbed his head once in affirmation and with that singular motion, Elizabeth and Rose were gone, Agnes following in lockstep behind.

Neither Edward, nor Sir Arthur spoke as they moved from the parlor through the dining room and out to the porch. Their shared silence continued as they settled into their chairs and stared out at the Lake Erie shoreline. As moments turned into hours, the two men found themselves facing the setting sun with volumes of questions, but no answers, no explanations.

All that remained were resounding echoes of Elizabeth Jennings' horrible accusations and the vague knowledge that a spirit had been somehow been involved in the chaos. And, in time, a slowly evolving realization that their lives would never again be the same.

Darkness and silence.

It had been my existence for many years following Mary's death-- until the Randall Family came into my world bringing joy and light to my being.

Now here I was, once again, plunged into the blackened world of despair and isolation.

In the days after Elizabeth's enraged exit, Edward and Sir Arthur made a number of attempts to channel Mary's spirit. I added my support to their efforts as well, but as we soon discovered, my sweet Mary was gone. To where, I had no idea.

After days of uneventful séances, both men agreed that their spiritual endeavors were in vain. With little hope, Sir Arthur departed Crown Hill for the nearby spiritual community of Lilydale. Before leaving, he offered Edward a promise to stay in close contact. He also extracted a pledge from Edward to remain faithful to the hope that one day my rooms would again be filled with his family's love and laughter.

Edward deeply pondered that promise in the days following Sir Arthur's departure. With his wife and daughters fully settled at Bear Lake and Agnes no longer willing to work in his employ, a return to normalcy within my shelter seemed increasingly impossible.

While Edward loved my natural beauty and the peaceful wonder of my being, he found the deep silence now pervading my every room to be disorienting. The onerous circumstances also clarified the extent to which he valued his family, above all else. No matter the strong connection that had once existed between us, I no longer mattered in Edward Randall's world.

Resolutely, Edward set in motion a plan that transported his family's valued possessions back to Buffalo, and would bequeath all that remained to the next person to become my owner. He then met with Janina Dent, Eden's sole real estate broker. He set a low market price and signed all the necessary paperwork to facilitate an immediate sale. I was to be sold as quickly as possible in order to become a disenfranchised part of his past.

On Edward's last morning in my care, he arose early and thoughtfully wandered through each of my rooms, traversing every floor and strolling across my grounds. Ultimately, he ended on my porch, a setting that this special man had always cherished. Together we shared the morning sunrise as it came to fullness in the blushing sky.

"Crown Hill, I shall miss you," Edward spoke to me as an old friend. *"I wish that I could understand the secrets you hold deep within your comforting walls and beneath your protective roof. But despite my best efforts, I cannot. So I leave you today, in fond farewell for the gracious life you have provided my family and myself. Know that you will always hold a sacred place within my heart and, as well as any person can, I will always feel an abiding love for you."*

The sight of Arthur Smith turning into the driveway gave Edward notice that his departure time was at hand. Passing through the dining room, Edward collected his suitcases and briefcase. There he stopped for one last look around the room where his life had forever changed.

"Whoever you are and wherever you may now be, I wish you peace, and the ability to find your way to the light."

It was a melancholy moment, amplified by Edward's departure and the fact that Mary was nowhere within me to hear his final wishes.

Over the ensuing months I once again became mired in darkness and silence…without anyone, including my beloved Mary, to enliven my shelter.

BOOK THREE

MEG

CHAPTER ONE

June 3, 1995

Meg took a deep breath hoping that a blast of fresh air might help jump-start her brain.

The documents on the desk before her were filled with endless legalese, all of it appearing like an unintelligible foreign language. Despite her attorney's droning attempts to simplify the legalities, Meg could feel herself spiraling into numb brain syndrome.

It happened whenever she was deluged by details, that disorienting sensation of being frozen in place, unable to comprehend exactly what was happening. Yet as Meg turned to the document's final pages, the ones with the signature lines representing both an end and a beginning, the legal ramifications of what she was doing became clearly black and white.

Meg hesitated.

What in the world are you waiting for? She silently scolded herself.

There was no doubt that Meg wanted this divorce. She had wanted it almost from the beginning of her tumultuous marriage to Cal. She also needed somewhere to begin her life anew. Instinctively, she knew the old farmhouse on the hill would be the perfect place. It made sense to her to sign the papers for both at the same time. A clean sweep, out with her old life and in with her new.

Still, she hesitated. Why wasn't she signing on the dotted lines? Why wasn't she going after her dreams?

"Meg? Hey Meg, you alright?"

The baritone drawl of Jethro "JT" Tull jolted her senses.

JT was an eccentric attorney who worked as a lawyer by day and sang as an Elvis impersonator by night. Meg had hired JT in a weak moment, after hearing him perform a particularly soulful rendition of, *Are You Lonely Tonight*. Somehow, she thought, he would be an understanding legal advisor

As it turned out Tull was extremely understanding, mostly about his feelings toward Meg. Throughout the eleven months it had taken to earn her divorce, JT proposed at least once a week. Not marriage, mind you. Rather, an arrangement that he regularly and suggestively described as "putting our best parts together."

Meg found her lawyer's suggestion disturbing, with imaginings of such a relationship even more unsettling. Ultimately Meg endured by staying focused on the new life she envisioned in her hilltop home. Once settled in, both Cal and JT would be out of her life. Once settled in, she would be able to get on with what her mother always called, "heartmending."

With a few quick pen strokes Meg signed her name and initialed every required line. It was done. She was now once again, officially and legally, Margaret Rose Flynn and the new owner of Crown Hill.

Literally drooling in delight, JT leaned across his cluttered lawyer's desk to bestow a congratulatory kiss upon his client. Realizing his intent Meg jumped up, offered a quick "send the bill" farewell, and bolted from her attorney's shoebox office. *No sense giving the man an opportunity for a mauling embrace,* she thought.

Escaping into the glorious June morning, Meg felt the sun's warmth embrace her like a much-needed hug. Flipping her sunglasses off of her luxurious auburn curls onto the bridge of her nose, Meg took a long look around the Eden Township.

"So this is where you are going to begin again," she spoke softly to herself in a habit that was becoming routine. "Let's see: a post office, a bank, an insurance agency, a newspaper office, a bar, a combination hardware/craft store, a grocery store and, of course, the prerequisite diner."

Meg's growling stomach acted like a magnet, drawing her towards the aroma of the grease-laden diner exhaust fan. The dysfunction and trauma of her life for the last 20 years was finally at an end. Meg was free and moving forward. And she was definitely hungry.

Stepping into the red-ginghamed Four Corners café, Meg took a quick survey of her seating options. The counter--good place for a single, but usually staked out by town regulars. Tables--comfortable but chancy, in that someone might try and join her. Booths--clearly too spacious for one and again, room for the uninvited. Making a quick assessment, Meg decided to try out the counter. Moving away from the door she slid onto a cracked-edged, red leather stool, set at the farthest end of the restaurant.

"Order whatever ya want, but I'm not making milkshakes today."

The terse announcement came from a gum-chewing, uniformed waitress, complete with the requisite pencil jutting out of her red, lacquered hair-do. The surly server completed her pronouncement by dropping a vinyl-coated menu on the counter.

As the woman sauntered away, Meg had one thought. *Milkshake?* She couldn't remember the last time she'd indulged in such a dairy-rich treat. But now that it was forbidden, Meg suddenly had a real thirst for a thick, chocolaty malt.

Inspecting the four-page menu, Meg decided to opt out of a late-day breakfast and instead order mid-day lunch. "Farm Hand's Special of the Day" was featured on a bright yellow strip of paper clipped to the top of the menu. Meg's mouth watered as she read the lineup of meatloaf, mashed potatoes with gravy, green beans, applesauce, and cherry pie alamode. When the waitress reappeared in all of her gracious glory, Meg was more than ready to order.

"So, what'll it be, honey?"

"I'd like the meatloaf dinner please," Meg replied, purposely avoiding the "daily special" title. "One farmhand special," the snarky waitress yelled out loud enough for the entire town to hear. Meg felt a mortified glow creep up her neck and across her fair Irish complexion. *Great,* she thought to herself. *Just what I need in a town where no one even knows me yet; a reputation as a woman with a farm worker's appetite.*

"And what'll ya have to drink?" Her server's cranky attitude tempted Meg to order a milkshake. Yet not wanting to add to her newly established "big eater" reputation, she instead choked out, "Just water, thanks."

As the waitress plopped down a pint-sized canning jar of clear, cold water, Meg noticed a newspaper trapped under a nearby stack of dirty dishes. Deftly extracting the paper from beneath the china, Meg was delighted to discover a recent edition of the town weekly, *The Eden Sun.* Glancing through the single-section publication, Meg came across articles highlighting an upcoming concert in the town park, details of the latest town board meeting, and a story about Miller's Hardware and Craft Store celebrating its 50th anniversary.

Knowing little about her new community, Meg was pleased to have this glimpse into Eden's routines and traditions. Life here seemed simple and pleasant, exactly what she needed. Simple and pleasant was what she had longed for through the 20 years of her precarious marriage. Simple and pleasant was what she now hoped for, after walking away from the only adult life she had ever known.

Meg wasn't sure why she chose the upstate New York community for her starting-over place. She didn't know anyone in the area; had never been any closer to the rural Eden Township than the string of New Jersey cities she had inhabited throughout her life.

In the end, that was part of the attraction. Meg relished the idea of moving someplace where she was unknown and could carve out her own private little corner of the world. She decided to try her luck by combing through want ads from newspapers in the New Jersey, New York and Pennsylvania areas.

Meg found a database of tri-state publications at the New York University College Library. When she came across the Eden "Farm for Sale" ad in the classified section of Buffalo's Courier Express, the description of the hilltop home with wraparound porch view of Lake Erie captured her imagination. She called and made an appointment to see the property and a short thirty days later, she submitted the offer that made it her home. As of today, she was officially the owner of Crown Hill.

"Ok, you're either readin', or eatin'; pick one."

The waitress's challenge jolted Meg from her thoughts. While the woman's attitude was infuriating, Meg's grumbling belly trumped her Irish temper. She put the newspaper aside and greedily accepted the oversized plate of food.

Meg dug into the steaming meatloaf and gloriously lumpy spuds with unpracticed zest, cleaning her entire plate in minutes. *If people are going to think I'm a big eater, than I'm darn well going to enjoy the reputation*, she thought, soaking up the last dribbles of gravy with a buttermilk dinner roll.

Pushing her plate aside, Meg turned to the nearby piece of cherry pie etched with rivers of melted ice cream. With fork in hand, she was about to enjoy a luscious bite when a sudden movement at her left elbow distracted her attention. Instinctively, Meg realized someone had invaded the space beside her. Trying to ignore whoever it was Meg re-focused on her dessert, but the invasive individual would not be denied.

"Hello there." The words were delivered in such a gentle tone that Meg felt forced to acknowledge the speaker. Swiveling her stool Meg encountered a woman with a sweet face haloed by snow-white hair, accented by brilliant, sapphire eyes.

"Hello," Meg responded with more warmth than she intended. It wasn't that she was unsocial, or against making friends in her new hometown. Meg just wasn't quite sure she was ready to start divulging the personal details required to establish her identity--over and above that of her newly acquired truck driver appetite!

"My name is Clara. Clara Johnson. And you are?"

Meg felt an odd sense of fear rise up into her throat, but she kept the feeling at bay with a simple two-word reply. "Meg Flynn."

Well Meg Flynn, I saw you walking over from Jethro's office. Are you new in town, or just visiting?" Despite her apparent innocence, Meg surmised that Clara knew full well who she was, and why she had been in JT's office that sunny June day. Yet not wanting to start her new life on a bad note, Meg took a deep breath, released the tension from her body and allowed her self-protective armor to loosen.

"Yes, as a matter of a fact I am new in town. I just bought a place on the outskirts of Eden. That's why I was at Mr. Tull's, to sign the purchase papers." As the words spilled out, Meg admonished herself. *What's the matter with you? This sweet little woman is no threat. She isn't going to hurt you. Lighten up. Just be yourself.*

As if reading her mind, Clara reached over and gently patted Meg's arm. "Well, I am pleased to welcome you to Eden, dear. I've lived here all my life, sixth generation of my family to do so. It's a wonderful town, filled with people who will easily become your friends."

Before Meg could respond, Clara rose from the stool and departed with a wave and an open invitation, "If you need anything, give me a call, dear. I'm in the book. I'll be happy to help, when you're ready."

When I'm ready? Meg pondered the gentle little woman's parting words. *Ready for what?*

Bewildered, Meg returned her attention to her cherry pie. While chatting with Clara, the waitress had dropped the bill alongside her plate. Its appearance encouraged Meg to forego her now-soggy dessert.

Quickly calculating a reasonably generous tip for her gracious server, Meg left money on the counter and slipped out the diner door, relieved to have escaped the cafe without further inquisitions.

With a buoyant sense of freedom, Meg climbed into her trusty old station wagon and headed toward the hills outlining the southern edge of Eden. Toward the rambling white farmhouse set on the town's highest hill. Toward the place she was ready to call home and where she would begin her new life, begin her heartmending.

It took years for life to return to my being, years of oppressive silence and darkness.

In that time there were those who considered assuming my deed and owning my title, but none could transcend the damaging rumors that defined me upon Edward's departure.

Stories of hauntings, séances, ghosts, and evil endeavors swirled around and within me. The town of Eden and its people created false scenarios to justify Sir Arthur's arrival, and cruel innuendos to embellish all that was rumored to have followed.

True to her word, neither Elizabeth nor Rose ever publicly spoke about their experiences within my walls. In fact within weeks of Rose's disturbing experience, Elizabeth packed up her daughter and their possessions and left Eden, never to return.

During very public, alcoholic binges Agnes would occasionally hint at bizarre occurrences that she claimed to have witnessed in my shelter, all of them involving young Rose, and the work she undertook for, "...that fancy-dan author-friend of the Randall man." Thus, in much in the same pattern that followed Mary's death, I became branded as a place of unhappiness, viewed by many with suspicion.

Ultimately, in February of 1925, Edward relinquished my deed to The People's Bank of Buffalo. The astute lawyer understood that the absence of a potential buyer countermanded the financial loss he would incur by allowing the bank to assume my ownership. Truth be told, Edward's decision was equally based on a strong desire to erase the disturbing memories of our final days---days that continually haunted him.

So it was on a snowy Valentine's, that Edward Randall turned away from me one last time, setting me adrift in a sea of businessmen disconnected from my being and wholly indifferent to my spirit. Their collective focus centered instead on the recovery of their financial investment.

Despite all such difficulties, hope did eventually flicker within me, lovingly rekindled by my Mary. My friend found her way back to me in a reuniting forever imprinted upon my being.

The sun was setting on a glorious autumn day. Shades of amber and violet cast a warm glow across my roof and walls. Within their radiance I felt a touch, an unexpectedly tender caress, followed by the sounds of a voice; her voice.

"Dearest Crown Hill, I am here with a profound hope that my presence will be welcomed. I know that my absence has been long and unexplained. Please understand, leaving you was not of my choosing. Further, I have remained away, disconnected by fear that my unexplained absence would forever impede your desire for my return. Yet, my deep yearning to be once again with you encouraged me to try, hoping that your kind heart would allow me to at least offer an explanation of my actions."

It was the moment of which I had dreamed, to hear Mary's voice, to again feel her presence, to capture a gentle trace of her sweet rose scent. Yet my love knew me well. Her absence had caused a rift between our souls that I was unsure could be healed. Reflective moments passed before I could give voice to my emotions.

"Mary, my heart is filled at this moment with passions of both joy and anger. I truly am unsure of how to proceed, what I can allow."

"Sweet friend, I understand only too well your reaction. Please, out of the joy that you feel, try and allow me a space where I can share with you the truth. Allow that chance so that our spirits might reunite, our souls again become one."

My muddled perceptions continued to inhibit my thoughts and words. Try as I would, I was unable to fully open my being to Mary in a spirit of love and forgiveness. Yet my soul compelled me to try.

"Mary, I cannot fully embrace all that you offer at this moment. Yet I know somewhere within my being is the essence of the love we once shared. So, I offer you a place within me, asking that you allow me time and space to try and release the bitterness created by your absence and perhaps therein allow my love to return."

"Of course Dear Heart. Anything. Anything to be with you once again. Crown Hill, I have missed you…missed my home. Thank you from the depths of my being for allowing my return."

And as with all who have ever truly loved and been loved…Mary and I began again.

CHAPTER TWO

"Hello, hello, hello, anybody in there?"

The words came to Meg as if she were in a dream. Still, the continual barking of her best friend and canine protector, Goldie, forced Meg to open her eyes and realize that it was an actual person, not a fantasy, calling out.

"Hello, hello, hello, I'm here at the back door."

Meg rolled toward the nightstand and tried to focus on her Big Ben alarm clock. It took three tries before she could comprehend it was not quite 7 o'clock in the morning. The only thing worse than the ungodly-hour was the relentless pounding on the back door by someone clearly demanding an answer.

"Hello, hello, hello, I know you're in there I can hear your dog barking."

This is nuts, Meg thought as she considered pulling the covers over her head until the person gave up and went away. However, Goldie's persistent yelps made it clear that whoever was trespassing on Meg's privacy had no intention of leaving unanswered.

Finally, in frustration, Meg threw back the covers and stomped down the stairs to the door, giving no thought to her rumpled-nightgown appearance. Passing through the kitchen to the back porch entry, Meg was astounded by what she saw standing on the other side of the locked screen door.

On her back patio stood a man, slight in stature, wearing a sweat-stained, burgundy-colored Eden Raiders baseball cap. The cap was complimented by an outfit of a well-worn denim vest atop a pair of tan bib overhauls and a frayed black tee shirt. The odd little man's "look" was accessorized by thigh-high yellow rubber boots. In his weathered, gnarly hands he held a rectangular wire basket filled with straw and a variety of brown and white eggs.

Struggling to identify this peculiar person before her, Meg blurted out the first words that came to mind. "Who in the world *are* you, and *why* are you knocking on my door at this ungodly hour of the morning?" Without pause or breath, the elf-like man launched into a breakneck patter that only confused Meg further.

"My name is Franklin B. Jones, B for Buckley, which was my father's name, from his father and his father's father before him, but most people just call me Frankie-B. I'm your neighbor from the red house at the bottom of the hill; you know, the one you pass by as you drive out of town. I've lived there all of my life, just like my father and his father and his father's father before him; well we were all born in that house which, I guess makes it a pretty special place. Anyway, I raise chickens there, like my father and his father and his father's father before him, but I couldn't possibly kill them or sell them so instead I sell their eggs every morning; I go door-to-door, up and down the hill, and sell my fresh eggs to everyone. So I was just wondering if you would like to buy some eggs?"

Meg was completely dazed by this individual, and instinctively reacted to his breathless sales pitch by laughing--and laughing, and laughing. Meg laughed so much that tears ran down her cheeks, and she became acutely aware that she hadn't yet gone to the bathroom and was dangerously close to peeing her pants. At the same time, Frankie-B engaged in his own wave of giggling hysteria that literally dropped him to the ground.

Quickly unlocking and opening the screen door, Meg stepped outside to help the prone man to his feet. Goldie, however, beat her owner to the punch, slipping past Meg and swarming Frankie-B, excitedly barking and licking his face. As Meg scolded her usually well-behaved, pet and tried to pull her away, Frankie-B quickly intervened. "Oh, please don't yell at her; she was just playing, and didn't hurt me at all. In fact I love animals, especially dogs, and I think she is just beautiful."

Frankie-B's non-stop delivery set Meg giggling once again, although this time she managed to blend some conversation with her laughter. "So let me get this straight, Frankie-B. You're going to come to my door every morning at the crack of dawn to sell me fresh eggs?"

"Oh no; well yes. I guess; I mean, I don't know if it will always be this early. It depends on how early the hens lay their eggs, and then in the winter sometimes the snow keeps me from getting out as early as I want, and then there are always those days when I have to go into town to visit my mother. But yeah; I guess. Most every day I will be here."

As Meg began to adjust to Frankie-B's rapid speech pattern, she found that she could listen to him without bursting into laughter. And while she did find the diminutive man utterly charming, she was very sure she did not want him serving as her daily alarm clock.

"You know what, Frankie-B? I think we should make a deal. You see, I would really love to have fresh eggs, but I also want to be sure that I don't waste your time coming to my door when I might not need eggs that day. So how about if we agree that I will stop by your house anytime I'm low on my egg supply. If you're not there I can leave a note telling you how many eggs I need and you can deliver them the next day. How does that sound?"

"Oh, I think it's great; gee I wish more of my customers would come to my house to buy eggs. You know, I'm not getting any younger, and there are days when by the time I'm done with my egg route I'm pooped, but then I guess that as my father, and his father, and his father's father before him always said, "hard work never did a body harm." So I guess it's all, fine, and don't worry; I'll make sure that if you leave me a note, I'll get your eggs to you bright and early the next morning, unless there's a snow storm, or I have to go and visit my mother. Did I tell you that she's at

St. Michael's in town; she's been there since my father died. She was so sad, and so she moved to St. Michael's so they could make her happy again, but anyway I have to go now; I've got lots of eggs to sell. See you soon."

With that, Frankie-B turned and was gone, leaving Meg breathless from her first neighborly encounter. "Well Goldie, if Frankie-B is any indication, our life here is going to be pretty interesting." The doe-eyed Golden Retriever softly nudged her owner, as if in agreement.

Meg relied on Goldie. Over the last year, through her separation and divorce, Goldie had become her best friend, her confidant, her advisor and her confessor. There was no doubt in Meg's mind that Goldie was the single most important part of her divorce settlement. She was grateful that Cal had not punished her by demanding custody of their special pet.

As Meg wandered into the kitchen to scavenge for a decent breakfast, she realized that Frankie-B had left without selling her any eggs. *Darn. Scrambled eggs and toast sounded pretty good,* she thought. However, even toast was impossible as Meg had failed to grocery shop amidst the flurry of moving into her new home the day before.

Moving in. Yeah right, Meg thought. *A bed, a few pieces of furniture and some boxes with assorted clothes, linens, books, and gram's leaded-glass bookcase.* It was hardly enough to settle the rambling, old farmhouse.

Meg went into her marriage with few possessions and came out pretty much the same. A tidy divorce settlement was the most significant result of her legal wrangle with Cal, and Meg was fully intent on safeguarding that money in secure investments. No way was her ex-husband's prediction ever going to come true; that in five years she would be out of money, begging him to take her back.

Meg had to admit though, the possibility haunted her.

Fear had been a prime motivator all of Meg's adult life, as she struggled to live in a marriage of few good times and many sad. From angry tirades to abusive threats and actions, Meg had endured two decades of fear, which at this point was a tough habit to break. Yet here in this house, in her own space and sanctuary, Meg was committed to changing, to replacing her long held fears with courage, and confidence, and a true belief in herself.

"Ok. First things first, Goldie." The faithful pet perked up at the sound of her name. "I'm going to grab a shower and then we'll go grocery shopping so we have food in the house. How about that?" Wagging her tail in agreement, Goldie bounded up the back stairs with Meg following close behind. The cheerful canine claimed a spot on her owner's bed while Meg showered and dressed. It felt like a good start to their new life.

Giving a quick brush to her auburn curls, and putting a dab of her favorite cinnamon perfume behind each ear, Meg headed to the bedroom door and called Goldie to follow. An unexpectedly deep growl returned from her, always good-natured, pet. Turning around, Meg saw Goldie sitting guardedly on the bed, her body fully tensed.

"What's wrong girl?" More deep throated growls along with a warning bark returned in answer. Meg watched in astonishment as Goldie's fur rose in a solid ridge along her back, an unmistakable sign of her sweet companion's angry fear.

Meg had never seen Goldie act aggressively and was somewhat unsure how to react. While she trusted the loyal dog with her life, there was something intimidating about the irate intensity the golden retriever was exhibiting.

Disturbed, Meg turned toward the direction of Goldie's agitation--a carved four-panel bedroom door, partially closed, with a long mirror attached to the back. There was nothing around the door, or by it. Nothing that appeared bothersome in any way. Nonetheless, Goldie's distress continued to increase, her barks escalating into what sounded like loud and angry forewarnings. Suddenly she sprang from the bed toward the mirror.

Looking again in that direction, Meg saw nothing but her reflection and the distraught image of her usually calm pet. From all that Meg could glean, Goldie's reactions were completely unwarranted and they were starting to border on annoying.

"Goldie, stop *now*," Meg called out with all the authority she could muster. Upon hearing her owner's stern voice, the well-trained dog hesitated, looking away from the mirror towards Meg. In that split second Meg saw something, a shadow, a movement, something that hadn't been there before. Then just as suddenly, whatever it was disappeared. Nonetheless, Meg was sure that she had seen something unusual in the mirror, if only for that moment.

The apprehensive woman stood completely still and tried to comprehend what was going on, what had just happened. Goldie came and sat alongside her, whining softly. Meg couldn't help but think how much her whimpers sounded like a human cry.

A strong chill traveled through Meg's already tense body.

"Ok, enough of this," Meg shook off the odd feeling. "Come on Goldie. Let's go downstairs." The loyal dog responded by immediately heading out of the room, Meg following close behind.

Moving past the mirrored door Meg found herself immersed in the unmistakable sweet fragrance of roses. They were her favorite flower and she found the scent at once glorious and hauntingly odd.

Suddenly the perfect beginning to Meg's day felt completely off track.

Cautiously, I allowed Mary into my being. True to her word, she respected my need to proceed guardedly.

In time our days evolved into gentle conversation, our nights into accepted silence, with nary an utterance of Mary's lengthy disappearance between us. Still my abiding sense of darkness continued.

Yet another prospective buyer rejected me, defining my being as "unsuitable" for his family's home. Such continued condemnation increased my worry. Would my unsettled spirit forever prevent anyone from finding goodness within my shelter?

Upon reflection, I recognized that the only way to lighten my being was to address my lingering sadness. I needed to understand what had taken Mary from my care and why.

I began directly.

"Mary, I have a need to ask something of you.

"Of course dear friend, whatever you wish."

"You have told me over and again that you did not leave my shelter of your own accord. I find your words implausible, but at the same time I cannot imagine that you would purposefully speak untruths. Setting aside distracting emotions, can you more fully explain the powers that forced you from within me?"

With her opportunity at last at hand, Mary began.

"Crown Hill, in our life together as homemaker and home you were immersed in the turbulence generated by Owen. You witnessed the many ways in which my husband callously treated me."

"I did, my gentle friend. Owen was a brooding man who attained his power by diminishing yours. It saddened me deeply to witness the spoken and physical mistreatment you endured at his will."

"Dearest, while Owen's merciless ways many times overwhelmed me, the most wretched measure of his mistreatments was that he never considered me more than chattel, a possession to be owned and used at his whim. That is why contemplation of a life, any life, away from Owen was impossible. Escaping my husband's cruel reach was a torturous dream that I understood I would never realize. I had no doubt that Owen would desire my death over my freedom."

The misery woven through Mary's memories was heartbreaking. I could feel my anger dissolving with her every word.

"So dear Crown Hill, while the end of my life was violent, you can understand how, in a strange way, it was also a blessed relief. I was finally free of Owen's cruelties."

Mary paused and in the space of that silence I was returned to the moment of her agonizing death. Shock waves again passed through me as I envisioned her twisted and bruised body choked in the thickly woven rope hanging from the woodshed rafter. I knew Mary was feeling the intense pain of her demise as well, and I extended the comfort of my being to her spirit. It was some time before she was again able to speak.

"The true sadness in my passing was that my respite was short-lived. Owen's malevolent nature continued to control me following his own death, three years after mine. Due to the wickedness of his earthly life, Owen's spirit became trapped in this world, much the same as my desperate passing imprisoned me. Realizing our shared destiny, Owen's intent became to seek my spirit and again control me, just as he had in our life together. In his search, he became a presence and a force within you."

My immediate reaction to Mary's account was disbelieving rage. *"How is it that I was unaware of Owen? How long a time was he in my shelter? What pain did he cause you?"*

My demanded answers returned from Mary, void of emotion. *"You never knew of Owen. I shielded you. I connected with him only in the space of the woodshed. In fact, that is how you came to find me there the day you, Edward, and Sir Arthur first engaged with Rose."*

Recalling the occasion, I instantly understood the sadness I had sensed in Mary's spirit that day. She continued to explain, her words further aiding my recall.

"As I had haunted Owen to his grave, he blamed me for his eternal condemnation. Accordingly, he decreed that I would now be forever responsible for ensuring his comforts. So, in the pattern of our mortal lives, my spirit became entrapped within his dominating self-indulgence. My only saving grace, as always Dear One, was my ability to hide away from Owen within your protective embrace. As long as I appeared in the woodshed whenever he bid, I could keep his spirit separate from you. And so I became dedicated to ensuring that you were never aware of his presence, nor my plight."

The impact of Mary's words upon me was strong and direct. I could not imagine all that she had endured in keeping Owen outside of my being, while still answering his demands. I clearly understood it as a pattern from their married life. Yet I found myself wishing that instead of protecting me, Mary had shared her torture--particularly as she continued to explain her circumstance.

"Wretchedly, everything changed when Owen realized your intent to release my spirit from this world, relying on young Rose as your guide. Owen was enraged by your plan, and his fury made it impossible for me to keep him contained. Forcefully he entered into your being and silenced my spirit, just as he did when we were alive.

Mary's descriptions triggered memories that I had tucked away, hoping to never again recall. My senses streamed with painful recollections of those final moments with Edward, Sir Arthur and Rose. I could feel Mary's despair as well, as she described parts of the experience that I never knew.

"In the depths of my enforced despair, I watched Owen overpower and prevent you from drawing close to young Rose. I saw him challenge the innocent girl as she valiantly railed against his evilness, trying to aide me. And all the while I heard you. Yes you, Dear Crown Hill, calling my name, searching for me. But I could not respond. I could not come to you. Owen's power would not allow it. So I did the only thing possible, I went away from your care, drawing Owen with me."

As I struggled to comprehend all that Mary was describing, she detailed the final part of her story.

"I continued within Owen's control for these many years, only able to finally elude him upon his union with a collective of shadowers--discontent spirits whose sole intent is to haunt the living. Their united purpose now keeps Owen distracted, and each day I pray that his spirit will remain so, allowing me to stay separate from him and safe within your caring space."

Mary's words offered the truth that I had longed to hear, illuminating all that had transpired on that long ago day when her spirit disappeared from my shelter. It also distilled her absence to one factor.

Owen.

Owen was the one who had threatened me and forced me away from Rose. Owen was the one who controlled all of the spiritual activity around the innocent young girl. Owen was the one who had forced Mary to abandon me.

At that moment a burning anger rose up within my rafters against Owen and his evil ways, matched equally by my deeply contrite love for Mary.

The combination of strong emotions roused my being. No matter the challenge or difficulty, I would punish Owen for his malicious actions. I would find the means to help Mary's spirit pass, leaving Owen forever trapped in the isolation of his evil nature.

I was unsure how, but I knew that I would do all things possible so that he would never again have power over my loving Mary…on any level, in any way.

CHAPTER THREE

Brady dropped the heavy tailgate and started transferring groceries from both shopping carts into the bed of his dually truck. The ruggedly handsome man hated shopping and did his best to avoid, or at least postpone, the task whenever possible. That's why it had been four months since his previous trip to Eden's Super Fine Market.

As always, the quiet farmer made it a point to do his shopping early to try and dodge conversation. However, today his plan failed miserably. From the moment he parked his truck and headed to the store, people stopped to say hello and find out how he was doing.

Brady was born and raised in Eden, a fifth generation farmer who embraced tilling the land as a valued, family responsibility. He learned the art of agriculture from both of his grandfathers, as well as his father, a process that had strongly bonded the men. Theirs was a family well-known and respected in the Eden Valley and throughout the surrounding towns. From the day he was born, everyone knew Brady Callahan.

"Why Brady, hello. It's so good to see you dear. How are you managing?" Brady recognized the voice before the person even came into view. It was Ruth Montgomery, the town gossip. There wasn't a story or an event going on in Eden that was unknown to Ruth. That was why, behind her back, most Edenites called her, "Motor Mouth Montgomery." Brady desperately wanted to keep walking and bypass the nosy old woman, but his proper upbringing forced him to turn and politely smile.

"I'm doin' fine m'am. Thank you for inquiring." Brady hoped that he could escape further conversation by flashing one of his charming smiles, but Ruth was long past the age of flirtatious flattery.

"Now Brady, you can tell me. Your mother and I were childhood friends after all. How are you really doing on that old farm all by yourself? It has to be so lonely without Julieann and Colin.

Her words jolted Brady like an unwelcome shock of electricity. It was one thing to reflect on the deaths of his wife and baby boy in his own mind, but to share those thoughts with anyone, no less Motor Mouth Montgomery, that was pretty much beyond impossible. Rude or not, Brady was done.

"I appreciate your kindness, Miz Montgomery, but I really have to get my groceries and get back to the farm for an important appointment. You have a good day, m'am."

Leaving the woman in an unusual stunned silence, Brady made his way into Super Fine, grabbed a shopping cart and began loading up. When he filled that cart, he parked it by the checkout and started filling another. In all, it took the determined farmer less than 20 minutes to amass several months' provisions. His shopping frenzy also helped him avoid all but the briefest of encounters with other townspeople.

Paying the bill, Brady wrangled the shopping carts through the parking lot to his truck and started offloading his groceries. He was one bag away from a safe escape when an over-packed sack of stewed tomatoes gave way and cans began spilling out in every direction onto the black top. Brady started corralling the errant cans while doing his best to dodge drivers entering and exiting the Super Fine lot. *Not exactly the best way to avoid attention*, he thought to himself.

On the far side of the Super Fine Market, Meg Flynn was pulling into the parking area. She and Goldie were on a mission to stock up the pantry and refrigerator in their new home. Meg had a lengthy shopping list running through her mind. She was also still slightly distracted by the rose scent from her bedroom that lingered in her senses. As a result, as she parked her car, she never saw Brady scrambling through the lot.

"Alright Goldie, you stay here while I get some groceries. I'll leave the window rolled down for you and I'll be back shortly." Opening the door, the preoccupied woman didn't realize that as she stepped out of the car, a can of stewed tomatoes was rolling underneath her. When Meg's foot made contact with the errant can, her body went flying out of control.

"Yaaawwwwoowww!" Meg cried out in surprise as she slipped and skidded to the ground. "Damn! Double damn!" was her next exclamation as her knees and elbows brush-burned along the parking lot's unforgiving surface. Goldie's fervent barking in response to her distressed owner's tumble brought Brady to the rescue.

"You ok?" he asked as he bent down to help the unknown woman to her feet.

"I guess so," Meg answered as she pushed back the stranger's hands and pulled herself up. Seeing the cause of her spill, Meg bent down and grabbed the canned tomatoes. "What the heck?"

"Ah, yeah. That's mine. I'm sure sorry."

"Well, I never imagined that on my first day in Eden, I'd be bowled over by a can of stewed tomatoes."

Brady was momentarily caught off guard. He wasn't sure if this unknown woman was annoyed or teasing. However, his concerns quickly became irrelevant as Goldie leapt forward through the open car door. Hackles raised and growling, it was clear that the loyal pet was determined to ensure her owner's safety.

"Goldie, stop! Stay!" Meg's commands echoed across the parking lot. Yet her pleas fell on deaf ears as the protective pet jumped towards Brady with teeth bared.

"Goldie, No!" Stop!" It was no use. The devoted dog had only one purpose in mind, to protect her owner. Meg could only imagine how much worse this situation was about to become when, to her amazement, everything changed.

"Hey there, girl. Hey, Goldie. Are you trying to take care of your mom? That's a good girl" Brady's soothing words brought immediate results. The golden retriever came to a quick stop, obviously impacted by his tone. With controlled power, Brady dropped to Goldie's level and offered his hand for her consideration. Carefully, the perceptive canine inched her way toward Brady until she got a good scent of him. Slowly she began wagging her tail, drawing closer to the stranger. A gentle lick of his palm ultimately ended their standoff.

"Seems you have a way with animals." Meg's remark caused Brady to stand and make his way to her, hand extended.

"My name is Brady. Brady Callahan. I don't believe we've met. Did you say you're new to town?"

Meg extended her delicate hand into Brady's oversized grasp, which caused her Irish complexion to spike to a full-bloom color.

"Um, yes. Yes, I am new actually. I moved to Eden just yesterday." A girlish giggle escaped from Meg's heart.

Her reaction caused Brady to break into a full-out grin. "It's nice to meet you, but I don't believe I caught your name."

Meg pulled her hand away from Brady's, but as she opened her mouth to speak, another giggle escaped. Now fully scarlet with embarrassment, Meg finally formed the words to answer.

"Meg. Meg Flynn."

"Well Meg Flynn, you have a wonderful protector here in Goldie. She's a pretty special dog."

Meg's reply was immediate and direct. "Thank you. But now I really have to grab some groceries and get home. Goldie, in the car, right *now*".

Both man and dog reacted by looking at Meg in a way that made her seem like an outsider. Nonetheless, Goldie quickly responded to her owner's command and obediently returned to the car.

Soundly slamming the door behind her dog's wagging tail, Meg spun around toward to the grocery store and lost her balance, almost falling again. This time Brady saved her in his tanned and muscular arms.

"Oops, careful there!" he said with another full dimpled grin spreading across his handsome face. "Wouldn't want to make more brush burns on those already tender knees."

Doing all that she could to right herself from Brady's grasp, Meg mumbled a reply. "Well, it was nice to meet you, I guess."

Flashing one more infectious blue-eyed grin, Brady stepped back allowing Meg to move toward the Super Fine entrance.

"Actually I enjoyed meeting both you and Goldie, even if it did take a hazardous can of stewed tomatoes to make it happen. Welcome to Eden. I hope you like it here."

With that Brady turned and sauntered back to his pick-up, while Meg found herself riveted in place, appreciating the farmer's muscular physique and what her girlfriend Robyn would describe as, "his good lookin' buns."

Ok. Enough! Meg grabbed an empty cart from the middle of the parking lot and focused on the grocery-shopping task at hand. And as she moved through the store, the suggestion of sweet roses continued to affect her senses.

Upon my reuniting with Mary, my spirit was heartened and my soul was again filled with joy and lightness. Accordingly, when next an Eden farmer considered purchasing me, the goodness within my walls moved him to add his name to my deed.

My renewal continued as the farmer and his wife moved under my roof and extended their family with the birth of a daughter. Their shared happiness overflowed my being, as neighbors and friends from Eden and beyond once again began crossing my threshold. It was a wondrous pattern that continued for more than a decade.

Still, sadness made a return to my being when the father of this young family died unexpectedly. The loss of his love drained the lives of his grieving wife and daughter. It also made them determined to remain within me, close to his memory. It was a challenging life, which they met with resolve.

When the upkeep of the lawns became unmanageable, the two purchased goats to keep short the grass. They made further use of their livestock by selling milk produced by the goat herd. Mother and daughter planted and harvested vegetables, raised chickens for meat and eggs, and took in sewing jobs, all of which made it possible to sustain their valued Crown Hill world.

Life then again changed for the two women as nature took its course and the maturing daughter fell in love and made plans to begin a wedded life of her own. Although mother and child briefly considered joining their families together under my roof, they wisely realized the best course was to move on to their individual futures.

On a cold blustery January day, the two devoted women walked through my rooms one last time before passing ownership to another family---this one defined by a rousing brood of ten children.

For the ensuing 30 years, this active clan and their many friends filled each and every inch of my space. To my great pleasure, all school events and many town celebrations were followed by a party of people streaming through my entryways.

My good standing in the Eden Community continued, as the children worked with their father to raise a two-story barn behind me, next to the wood shed. A variety of horses and dogs occupied the barn's main level, while a basketball court took center stage on the floor above. Life literally flourished within and around me, as each family member brought their own unique energy into my being.

As for Mary and I, we entered peacefully into a world where she did her best to accept her continued existence on earth, and I offered my most nurturing power to soothe her discomfort. We spoke not of Owen, other than an agreement that Mary insisted upon...that I would no longer try to aid her in passing. She believed that our pact would prevent Owen from ever again forcing her from me. Although unsure, I made a promise to abide by her wishes.

Remarkably, in accordance with Mary's plan, Owen's evil did not resurface within me. And though I was aware that Mary continued to deal with Owen's darkness outside of my being, that knowledge never came between us.

We were together and seemingly safe and that was all that mattered...for now.

CHAPTER FOUR

From her place at the kitchen sink, Meg could hear the unknown visitor navigating around Crown Hill's circular driveway. She couldn't imagine who would be calling. She really didn't know anyone in town yet.

Truth be told, the idea of someone driving up to her door was a bit unnerving. Her life with Cal had conditioned her to stay in the background where he was in charge and she was safe.

You can't stay in that place anymore.

Her inner voice counseled her regularly these days. Meg was not quite sure if the thoughts running through her mind were her own or perhaps those of a guardian angel, but she was learning to listen and rely on the helpful thoughts.

Whoever alights from that car, you need to welcome them into your home and into your new life. It's time.

As Meg worked at bolstering her confidence, she moved to the back door. Looking out she recognized the car as belonging to Kathryn Winston, her real estate agent.

Meg had randomly connected with Kathryn through a "house for sale" ad. What she didn't know from the ad copy was that Kathryn was the ultimate authority on Eden real estate. It was not only that she was a third generation Eden resident, but also that Kathryn possessed an amazingly complete recall of details. She never forgot a name, a family history or the particulars of a property, all of which consistently allowed her to make perfect matches between owners and homes.

Meg watched as Kathryn parked her car at the end of the curved brick walkway leading to the house. A classic white picket fence and rose-covered arbor accented the sienna path winding to the farmhouse door. Orchards of trees, flowering shrubs, and well-established perennials perfectly accessorized the surrounding 14-acres of Crown Hill land.

As the realtor alighted from her car, Meg offered a tentative welcome. "Hello Kathryn."

"Meg, so nice to see you," came the realtor's genuine reply as she started up the brick walkway. Yet before Kathryn could reach the picket fence, a burst of yellow canine fur came bounding past Meg out the back door.

"Goldie! Goldie! Stop. Come back!" Meg called out in her best commanding tone.

The retriever had no intention of obeying her owner's commands. Instead, she went running directly to Kathryn, stopping just short of knocking her over.

"Hello you sweet baby girl! I haven't seen you in a month of Sundays," Kathryn drew close to Goldie. "Sit down here and let me give you a nice scratch behind the ears."

Without hesitation Goldie planted herself directly in front of Kathryn, anticipating the special attention.

"Oh Goldie, for heaven's sakes, you're going to get Kathryn's lovely suit all covered with dog hair." Meg headed down the walkway, fully intent on breaking up the evolving love fest between her dog and her realtor. Kathryn was a nice enough person, but Meg was still unsure of her true colors.

Since her earliest memories, Meg had categorized people by color. It was a youthful diversion that, as she matured, became more of a self-protective process. Her first recall of connecting a color with a person traced back to a soft and comforting blue luminance that always surrounded her mother. The glow became such a natural part of her mother's appearance that Meg never questioned it. Neither was she surprised when, as a teenager, she began to detect colors around others.

The color game was not something that Meg could play at will. She couldn't look at someone and imagine or command a color to appear. Rather, hues would randomly materialize as she became familiar with people. Once she began to understand how the power worked, she realized it as a reliable way to classify people's characters.

Generally, blue meant kindness, green--peace and healing, purple--spirituality, yellow--joy, orange--an uplifting or inspiring nature.

Whenever she saw colors of red around someone Meg protected herself and expected the unexpected. Such people were often materialistic, focused on getting only what they wanted, no matter the cost.

In the same way, colors of brown or black indicated a person of violent or negative character, much like Cal. She had seen browns and blacks surrounding her ex-husband from their first meeting, but deluded herself into believing they didn't matter. Never again, Meg promised herself. Never again would she ignore a person's true colors.

"Oh Meg, it's alright. Really she's fine." Kathryn spoke earnestly hoping to engage the clearly tentative woman. "I'm at the end of my day and just thought I would drop by to see how it's going, now that you've moved in. Honestly, I'm not worried at all about Goldie's hair on my suit. She's such a sweet dog."

Try as she would, Meg could not allow Kathryn's charm to soften her defenses. She was unsettled that the woman had dropped by unexpectedly. The fact that her dog was clearly thrilled with the realtor's appearance didn't help, especially after Goldie's affable parking lot encounter with Brady Callahan earlier in the day.

"That's kind of you Kathryn," Meg's words hit the air like rivets shot from a gun. "But Goldie has been a bit out of control lately. I really need to rein her in. Goldie, come over here, *now!*"

The force of her owner's voice caused the loyal dog to jump and scoot to Meg's side in an almost singular motion. Her instant reaction startled both women into smiles that helped lessen the tension between them. Kathryn realized the opportunity and proceeded gently.

"Meg, I know that I probably should not have stopped without calling, but you have been on my mind for the last few days. I heard that you moved in and I wanted to be sure that everything was ok. The fact that you're living here at Crown Hill is just so special. It was really meant to happen. I felt it from the moment I first saw you on the property. So if there is any way that I can help you get settled, I would be most happy to do so."

For some reason, every sentence Kathryn spoke raised red flags in Meg's mind. Yet when she looked at the realtor, there was a complete absence of color around her, no way to really know whether to trust this woman or not. Meg hated when she had to rely solely on her gut as a people guide.

"Thanks Kathryn, I do appreciate your checking in." *That felt ok*, Meg thought. *Maybe try another step.*

"It's interesting that you say that I am meant to live here at Crown Hill. What makes you think that?" It was more of a giant leap than a step, but Meg couldn't help herself. She had experienced the same feeling about buying the farm and had wondered about it. Perhaps, she thought, Kathryn possessed some wisdom that could help rationalize her thoughts.

"Actually it's something that I experience quite often in my real estate work," Kathryn replied with casual caution. "It's a bit hard to explain exactly, other than to say I've been selling houses for a long time in this town. My experiences have taught me pretty much all there is to know about Eden's homes and properties. Add to that everything the job has taught me about people and human nature, and I guess it all adds up to me having sort of a sixth sense about these things. I hope it doesn't sound too weird or spooky to you. It's not as if I'm some kind of psychic. It's more a combination of knowledge and experience that guide my thoughts. Anyway, there was no doubt in my mind that you and Crown Hill were a match and I am so glad it has all worked out."

Kathryn's explanation made sense to Meg, which made it a bit easier to consider the realtor's visit as a neighborly gesture. Maybe she should invite Kathryn in for a cup of tea, if she could even manage to find tea bags and mugs in which to serve her guest.

"Kathryn, I'd love to invite you in, but truthfully the house is littered with boxes and unpacked debris. Perhaps we could make a date in a few weeks when I am a bit more settled?" It was the best Meg could manage.

"Oh Meg, I completely understand. And I didn't come to intrude. I truly just stopped to check in and see if you needed anything. I tell you what. I'll call you later this month and we'll figure out a date and time that works for both of us."

Kathryn extended her hand toward Meg to say goodbye. In response Meg moved forward, which released Goldie from her mistress's side. The loving pet sprang toward Kathryn, eagerly nudging her hand for attention. The two women again shared a smile, this time radiating a warmth between them.

"By the way Meg, did you know that your home has twice been purchased as a wedding gift?"

The question was innocent enough and Meg was quite sure that Kathryn had no ulterior motive in asking. Yet something about the query caused an immediate knot in Meg's gut...not a good sign.

"Why, no. I never heard that before. But then I really don't know that much about the history of the farm."

"Yes, in 1866 Owen Southwick proposed to Mary Stickney. When she accepted, he purchased the farm and gave it to her as a wedding present. Then again in 1930, Henry Miller bought the farm as a wedding gift for his fiancé, Julia. Just a couple of romantic stories I thought you might enjoy."

Still somehow uncomfortable with the conversation, Meg simply smiled and nodded.

As Kathryn turned and walked to her car Goldie playfully kept pace alongside. The realtor paused and reached down to bestow one last scratch.

"You be a good girl for your mom, Goldie." Then looking up, Kathryn added, "And you take care, Meg. Don't put too much pressure on yourself to get unpacked and settled right away. There's always time. And if you decide that you want help, give me a call. I'm a pretty good room organizer if I do say so myself!"

From Kathryn's view, Meg's lithe figure was perfectly framed within the arbor's drape of sweet-scented roses.

"That arbor is so gorgeous, Meg. Mary Southwick, one of the women who was given the farm as a wedding gift, she started those roses over 100 years ago. According to some of your neighbors whose families have lived on this road for generations, Mary planted most every tree, shrub and perennial still growing here at Crown Hill, but she especially loved roses. I bet she's smiling these days with all the blooms on that arbor. Anyway, take care!"

With a wave Kathryn was in her car exiting the driveway, leaving Meg to process all she had just heard about Mary Southwick. Once again on their own, dog and owner made their way along the brick path to the house, pausing as they passed under the blooming arch.

Kathryn was right, Meg thought as she marveled at the archway, *These roses are beautiful.* Luxuriating in the lush blossoms, Meg tried to imagine a vision of Mary Southwick. Instead, her mind became entranced in the realization that she was once again immersed in a rose-filled fragrance, the same scent that had filtered through her bedroom earlier that day.

Unnerved, Meg herded Goldie into the house and locked the door behind them, wondering if she was locking her concerns outside, or in.

During this time that we were together, Mary was often silent within me. I was troubled by her withdrawal, but I understood that she was stilled by her constant struggle with Owen and by her deep desire to pass that she continually suppressed.

Eventually, I accepted the need for Mary's quietude and gave my energies to simply loving her more.

Ultimately, to our shared delight, this time of stillness ended with the arrival of new owners on my doorstep. The previous family of ten children had grown and moved on to their own lives, their parents no longer in need of my eight bedrooms, my oversized kitchen and dining room. Thus, they sold me to a commune, a community dedicated to creating a life of spirituality and peace.

The presence of the caring commune members re-invigorated Mary. I often found her in their community meditation room where followers gathered daily, or outside in their purification lodge where cleansing ceremonies were held. My sweet Mary was not present to haunt, but rather to gather strength and blessings from the many graces the commune members created and shared.

The commune's dedication to spiritual renewal gradually wove a protective layer over my walls and across my eaves. The purity of those within the community drove away all evil and allowed none to enter in to me. It was within that space of goodness that Mary and I cautiously began a return to our life of conversation and laughter, music and joy

"Oh, Crown Hill, I have need of you in a way that we have not shared in many years. I am so grateful to once again be part of you in a place where we can truly share our spirits and again become one.

"My Mary, only you can know the strength of our love that has kept us together through so many darknesses, and which now again connects us within this goodness. While I know your spirit holds a continued desire to pass, for now let us celebrate this sense of renewal and hold close these joyful feelings. Let this time be the light that you seek, for as long as it can be.

Mary and I remained in this place of goodness for years, magically suspended in time, innocently unaware of the changes that one day would take place, upon the commune's leave taking…and the arrival of Meg Flynn.

CHAPTER FIVE

Meg hurled the emptied cardboard box down the back stairs. She took immense satisfaction watching the oversized carton bounce off the walls and fall atop the growing stack of boxes on the landing. Every room, upstairs and down, was now unpacked and settled with all of Meg's worldly possessions. Once she dragged the collection of boxes out of the house and to the road for garbage day, she and Goldie would officially be in-residence.

Meg suddenly realized the significance of the moment. For the first time in her adult life she was completely free to do whatever she pleased—make her own decisions, create her own life, be herself without fear, or ridicule, or punishment. Most importantly, Meg knew that she was safe, safe in a place where no one had control over her, or could force her to do anything against her will. She was finally, home.

"Let the *heartmending* begin!" Meg shouted out as she danced through the upstairs, waltzing into her bedroom. Goldie had been napping at the foot of Meg's bed when she heard the commotion. Seeing her owner bounding with joy, the playful pet jumped up to join in the fun. Around and around they danced, Meg singing and Goldie howling until finally the two collapsed onto the floor where the affectionate dog began lavishing her owner with kisses.

"Goldie, Goldie, enough girl. Enough!" Meg could barely get the words out, she was laughing so hard. And the more she laughed, the more Goldie showered her owner with affection.

It took a ringing telephone to short-circuit their celebration. Meg jumped up to answer the call. Actually this was the first time since Meg and Goldie had moved in, almost a week earlier, that the phone rang. To be truthful, Meg couldn't imagine who was calling. She didn't recall giving out her new number.

"Hello?"

"Yeah. I'm lookin' for Margaret Flynn."

The sound of her full name caused Meg to pause.

"Hey, ya there?"

"Ah yes, I'm sorry. This is Margaret."

"This is Jake. Jake Kelly. I'm the owner of Kelly's Construction Company here in Eden. Jethro Tull's a friend of mine. He said ya might be lookin' for work."

Meg was immediately sorry that she'd answered the call. With her legal work completed, she figured Jethro was pretty much out of her life. She couldn't believe that he had recommended her for a job, especially without talking to her first. Plus, knowing JT, Meg could only imagine the character of Jake Kelly. However, the reality was that she did need to work.. She just hadn't started looking at want ads or filling out applications.

"Exactly what kind of a job is it?" Meg reluctantly inquired.

"Well, that depends on the day. Some office work, some fieldwork, some writing, maybe even some travel. Pretty much anything I need ta help run my company and get my construction work done."

"Well, to be honest, I really don't have experience doing some of those things. So I'm not sure that I'm the employee for you."

"Listen here little lady. From what JT tells me, you're one sharp doll. Anything ya don't know I can teach ya. And I'd rather teach someone the way I want things done. A lot easier trying ta make somebody who's smart, smarter, than trying ta make somebody dumb not as dumb, if ya get my drift."

To her amazement, Meg did understand the point Jake Kelly was making and she found herself drawn to the rough and tumble-sounding man.

"Well, Mr. Kelly, exactly what are the hours and pay for this job?"

"Ok, let's get somethin' straight right outta the gate. My name's Jake. Mr. Kelly was my old man. As for the hours of the job, they're whenever and wherever I need ya, Monday ta Friday. And the pay, I'm figurin' I can afford eight bucks an hour plus mileage if ya go on any jobs. So whaddya say?"

Meg was caught off guard. She had planned on taking a couple of weeks to get settled in her home and get a feel for the town before worrying about a paycheck. She definitely needed a regular income though, and she also was pretty sure that Jake Kelly was not the type to offer twice. Life was happening and for the first time it was *her* life. As Meg was quickly realizing, she was completely in charge.

"Um, well, I guess. Yes. No, *yes*! I will come to work for your Mr. Kel...I mean Jake."

"Ok. Can ya be here tomorra', 7am sharp? I got paperwork pilin' up everywhere 'round this joint. "

Another curve ball. *Ok Meg, time to start learning how to trust your gut,* she thought. *Just make a decision. Ready. Set. Go!*

"Yes. I can be there," the words flew out on command. "But just exactly where is there?"

"Hemlock. Offa the main drag. Come down Sandrock to Main St. Turn right and then take the first turn ya see...ya can only go one way. Look for a big green buildin' on the right...got a sign out front says, Kelly and Sons. Ain't no sons no more, I'm the only one left since my old man died and my brother Mike decided he was too damn important to run a construction business. Be there. 7am sharp."

With a loud click echoing in her ear, Meg found herself standing with her hand tightly wound around the receiver. It felt as if a hurricane had just barreled through her world. Then, the mental gymnastics began.

What did I just do? What kind of a job is this? I didn't even ask about a lunch break or vacation or sick days. And what am I supposed to wear?

Panic started to rise in Meg's body, and with it a reaction that had betrayed her emotions from the time she was a child. Whenever she was caught up in a situation highly stressful or embarrassing, she would turn bright red. Not just a sweet blush that added color to her cheeks. More a full out, head to toe, rosy red flush that blanketed every inch of her body. The first time it happened, Meg's mother explained it as, "the red spread," a condition experienced by generations of Flynn woman before her.

The worst part of the disorder was that it carried with it an intense heat. Meg literally felt as if her body's thermostat was cranked up to wide-open, full throttle mode whenever the red spread occurred. Over and above the uncomfortable sensation, the increased warmth caused Meg to perspire. No ladylike glow, but a drip from the forehead, across the upper lip, from the armpits down the arms, watery release that fully compounded the embarrassing reaction.

As Meg grew from child to teen, her red spread experience occasionally included fainting spells. It would happen whenever her body transferred from hot and sweaty to cold and clammy at a pace that would leave her dizzy and, ultimately, passed out on the floor.

To deal with the curious condition, Meg learned to recognize advance notice of the red spread as a tingling in her toes and a burning sensation along the bottom of her feet. Whenever she felt those warning signals, Meg did her best to find a place where she could privately endure the hot-blooded torment.

The good news was that the red spread had quieted as she matured. The intense reaction was now a random occurrence that usually lasted only a moment or two. A quick trip to the nearest bathroom or a short stroll around her house or office, and the annoying condition pretty much disappeared.

With only Goldie around as a witness, Meg was unconcerned with how she appeared at the moment. More importantly, she needed to prioritize the tasks on her to-do list. She started by noting the household chores that were absolutely essential and eliminating those that could wait until after she settled into her new job.

New job? *YIKES,* she thought. Just the idea of going to work in the morning started Meg's toes tingling all over again. To circumvent a red spread replay, the focused woman took pen and pad in hand and began writing

I need some suitable clothes to wear...at least a few things clean and ironed. I need to make sure that I pack a lunch. And snacks-- gotta have snacks.

Meg was a stress eater. Whenever life presented challenges, her immediate reaction was to rip into a bag of chocolate. It was a habit that escalated during her marriage. After one of Cal's heartless rants or when he would overpower her physically, she would find sweet solace in milk chocolate of any form, baking chips to expensive truffles. In consideration of her health, Meg was learning to modify her snacking habits, somewhat! She now often substituted granola or energy bars that were only laced with chocolate. *Hey, it's a start,* she thought. Ultimately, no matter the food choice, whenever Meg was stressed, she snacked.

The only other concern Meg held about starting a job was Goldie. She hated to leave her favored pet alone every day, but she also had to face the realities of this new life. No longer was she part of a two-person household where there was always a way to ensure that Goldie would be fed, or let outside on schedule.

"Goldie, girl, don't you worry. Momma will make sure that you are ok while she's gone to work. And every day when I get home, we'll go outside and run around the yard and play tug of war with your rope toy, I promise."

The sensitive pet responded by wrapping herself around Meg, as if sharing a big hug. It was a special trick Goldie first started as a puppy, when she was only big enough to get halfway around her owner's leg. As a full-grown dog, Goldie had perfected the technique to the point that Meg actually felt as if she were being embraced. The devoted owner loved these moments and always responded by reaching down and gently scratching Goldie behind her ears.

The loving connection between owner and pet at that moment was powerful, bringing a swell of emotion to Meg's heart. Without effort or thought, tears began cascading down her face and onto Goldie's thickly furred body. Looking up, the tenderhearted canine gave out a soft whine, as if offering comfort. That loving response further encouraged Meg's tears, to which Goldie unwrapped her body, sat down and placed her paw directly onto her owner's leg. Again she offered a tender whine.

"Oh Goldie, I love you too." With her declaration Meg sank to the floor where Goldie snuggled close in furry comfort. But as invariably happened, within seconds the two were tangled in a rough and tumble game of tickle, something they had been playing for years. As Goldie bound back and forth nudging her owner from head to toe, Meg reached out to try and tickle her playful companion. Barks of excitement and shouts of joy filled the house as the two eventually played to exhaustion, dropping flat to the floor, side by side, both panting for air.

Meg was just about to roll over and give Goldie a big hug when a loud crash from the first floor caused both woman and dog to jump. Goldie ran quickly ahead of her owner, taking the stairs two at a time to investigate. As Meg followed, she found Goldie in the dining room. There the dog was exhibiting the same aggressive behavior that she had shown previously at the mirror in Meg's bedroom. Goldie's hackles were up, her ears laid back and she was growling.

"Goldie, quit! What is wrong with you?" As Meg spoke, she gave a quick look around the room. Searching for the source of the crash, her eyes stopped at the glass book cabinet. It was one of the few pieces of furniture that Meg owned and it was a treasured antique. It had belonged to her grandmother--her father's mother...and was uniquely constructed of a wooden oak frame that encased beveled and leaded glass panels, an intricate and expensive detail. Although Meg had never met her grandmother, she felt connected to the woman through this specially crafted piece of furniture.

Meg's heart dropped to her stomach as she saw glass shattered all around the cabinet. Her pain increased dramatically as she realized that there was a gaping hole in the antique where the glass door panel should have been.

Despite her distress over the cabinet's damage, Meg's immediate thoughts turned to Goldie. She didn't want the dog to slice open a paw on one of the pointed glass shards littering the dining room floor.

"Goldie, come on girl. Let's go to the kitchen!" Clapping her hands to grab the dog's attention, Meg started to run toward the adjoining room as if playing a game. Although the dog was unsure of which instinct to trust, her owner won out as she bounded after Meg.

Once in the kitchen, Meg turned and gently took hold of Goldie's collar. The trusting canine followed easily as her owner led her to the back porch.

"I'm sorry to do this, girl, but I'm going to put you on the porch for a bit while I clean up the glass. I'll be back."

As Meg closed the door behind her, Goldie began barking in vehement protest. However, the concerned woman was already back in the dining room, surveying the book cabinet more carefully, trying to figure how in the world the glass panel had broken. There was nothing wrong with the cabinet that she could see. The glass panels on either side of the door were in place with not a mark on them.

Stepping closer, Meg assessed that the hole in the broken door panel looked as if something had been thrown through it, from the inside out. Then she spied one of the larger books, an encyclopedia on gardening that her mother had given her years ago. It was on the floor beside the bookcase. Meg was sure that she'd unpacked all of her books and placed them inside the cabinet in an orderly fashion. And yet the third shelf, where she had placed all of the oversized books, was in disarray, as if someone had been searching for a specific volume.

Meg went to the kitchen pantry for a broom and dustpan, thinking that perhaps by walking away she would see something different upon her return.

She did not.

Slightly dazed, Meg began the task of cleaning up the fragmented glass panel that was almost equal in size to her 5 foot nine inch frame. It was while sweeping that Meg first heard the unfamiliar sound. *A voice? Someone speaking softly?*

Meg stopped and looked around the room wondering if another unannounced visitor had stopped by. No one. The she heard it again. Meg felt fear knotting her body as she definitely identified the sound as a voice.

"Who is it?" she blurted out in frightened reaction. "What do you want?"

Meg stood completely still and silent. Nothing but the sound of Goldie softly scratching at the back porch door returned.

"Ok. Enough of this," Meg said out loud, trying to calm herself and take control of whatever was going on around her. "I'm going to vacuum up the glass that is left and then I'll call around to see what it will to cost me to fix this. Good thing I'm starting a job tomorrow."

The clean-up work gave Meg some confidence that whatever just happened was one of those unexplainable things that can occur when moving, nothing more. As long as she didn't dwell on it, she would be fine. She just needed to get the bookcase glass repaired.

"No big deal," she said out loud as one last test. Again silence, but also something else. Something familiar.

The sweet scent of roses was once again surrounding her.

Without hesitation, the determined Irishwoman headed for the phone. Meg was going to call Kathryn Winston and invite her for lunch. She needed the knowledgeable realtor to return to Crown Hill. She needed to talk to her about Mary Southwick. She needed to learn more about this woman who once lived in her home and about her roses--

and the rose fragrance that was becoming a haunting part of Meg's world.

"What have you done?" I knew my tone was harsh, but I was stunned by Mary's actions. After so many years of relative calm within me, it felt as if we were sinking back into the terror of her past hauntings.

"Mary, answer me. We need to talk about what has happened."

"Crown Hill, I know that you are angry, and you have every right to be. But know that the book cabinet was an accident. I didn't mean to shatter the glass. I was trying to arrange a few of the books inside and I errantly crashed one through the glass in the door."

"Arrange the books? But why? Why would you do such a thing?"

"You know how I loved to read, Crown Hill, and how much I valued my books. I have been over a century of worldly time within you, without any physical possessions. That beautiful cabinet filled with books entranced me from the moment Meg put it in place. I thought perhaps by arranging a few of the volumes in a special way, I could welcome and comfort Meg. Then it would be easier to engage her and make her aware of my presence. You see, Crown Hill, I believe that Meg has the ability to help me pass. I know this is something that we were never again going to speak about, but Meg carries within her the same powers that young Rose possessed. I can feel it. I need to try and reach out to her, dear heart. It is time."

The thought of Mary's spirit becoming active within me once again was both startling and exhausting. We had come so far over so many years simply by being; simply by accepting circumstances that were less than perfect, but which allowed us to remain together. Now Mary was taking steps to destroy all of that.

"Dearest Mary, I love you. From the depths of my being I love you, you fully know that. But I cannot begin to think about returning to the traumatic life linked to your desire to pass. And what of Owen? What of his hold on you and his rage that we both know can harm and even destroy. Truly, Mary is this what you are choosing to bring into our world again, now, after so much tranquility? I cannot even begin to fathom your decision."

Silence like a thick velvet shroud fell between us. I could neither feel Mary's emotions, nor sense her thoughts. There were only the echoes of my frustration passing through my being, allowing me to realize how my words must have impacted my tenderhearted friend.

At the same moment, I felt fear burning like the singe of a finely sharpened razor. While the time may have come to reach out to Meg and assess if she could truly help Mary's spirit pass, such change could only mean the dreaded return of Owen's evil...and the stark reality of Mary's departure, forever from me.

CHAPTER SIX

Meg tugged on the rusted door handle. The early morning chill embedded into the corroded metal transmitted through her fingers and into her body. Once, twice, even with a third pull Meg's chilled hands could not get the door to budge.

Shivering at the edge of dawn outside Kelly and Sons bright green building, Meg was unsure of what to do. Jake Kelly had clearly stated that she needed to be at his office at 7am sharp. And even though she was 10 minutes early, the truck in the nearby parking lot and the lights on throughout the buildings assured her that her new boss was inside, no doubt impatiently awaiting her arrival. She was also pretty sure that he had *not* locked the door behind him. So what was the trick of entry, she wondered?

Preparing to yank on the door again, Meg heard a sound that was about to become part of her morning routine. It was the melodic tones of a man singing, terribly off key, but nonetheless singing. *What was the song though?* Meg wondered as she listened through the closed door.

"Good mornin' to youoooo, mornin' glory! Kissed and caressed by the dewwwww. Beautiful mornin', glory. Good mornin' glory to youuuu!"

As the soulful refrain continued, the soloist was joined by a voice that Meg quickly defined as a dog, howling in pained response to the distorted performance. *Well, at least I know there's someone in there,* Meg thought.

Rather than continuing to grapple with the seized handle, Meg pounded forcefully on the door, calling out as she did, "Jake. Jake Kelly. It's Margaret Flynn. I'm here to start work and I can't open the door."

Hearing rumblings within, Meg stepped back and in seconds got her response. The heavy metal door burst open to reveal what Meg could only classify as a rugged mountain man--tall, stocky but solid, sporting a flaming red beard that flowed out and over his suspendered coveralls.

"Well whaddya doin' standin' out there in the cold'? Time's money ya know."

With that hospitable welcome, Jake Kelly turned and made his way back into the building, leaving Meg to follow.

"And don't forget ta shut the damn door!"

It all happened so fast that Meg had no time to think. She quickly grabbed the door, slammed it closed and followed behind Jake, proceeding down the hallway into a large open space.

In the overhead glare of buzzing fluorescent lights, Meg identified three office desks with chairs and a long narrow table, much like those she recalled from school cafeterias. At least that's what she thought was in place admist the chaos looming before her.

Kelly and Sons was exactly as Jake had described. From desk to desk and across the long table top, papers, notebooks and catalogues were strewn everywhere. Telephone and electric cords looped from wall outlets to desks suggesting locations of phones and faxes completely buried beneath unfiled piles of invoices and bills.

Computer screens were barely visible behind misshapen stacks of file folders braced by keyboards shoved up against them. Banks of cabinets lined the outer office walls, many with open drawers supporting mounds of precariously balanced folders.

In the center of the room sat the larger-than-life Jake Kelly himself. Positioned in the midst of an overloaded oak desk, the business owner appeared much like a Nordic warrior battling an unrelenting army of paperwork.

Within the small workspace to which he claim, Jake had arranged a hoard of yellow pads and a ceramic cup filled with pencils. Meg thought that she could also make out a calculator beneath some crumpled fast food wrappers along with an elegant brass and onyx clock partially concealed by a box of Cheezee snack crackers.

On the floor beside her new boss's desk sat a large, oval wicker basket filled with an oversized denim pillow. Atop the pillow sat a droopy-eyed Bassett hound, thumping his tail in rhythmic welcome.

Meg felt the room whirring around her as she attempted to assess the fiasco. The office was undoubtedly a nightmare and she had a pretty strong feeling that by staying, she would become a main character in the horrific dreamscape. Meg's instinct was to turn and bolt, go as far away from Jake Kelly as possible. It was a fight or flight response she had cultivated during her life with Cal.

In the early years Meg railed against what she believed to be unacceptable behavior from her husband. Sadly, the life lesson she learned was that the more she spoke, the more Cal would abuse her, mentally and physically. And so flight became her life-preserving option of choice.

You can't hide anymore. It's time to speak without fear--once again become your own person.

Meg knew the voice was right. What good did it do to make all the changes of the last year only to live the same life of fear? She knew exactly what needed to be said. The question was, could she find the courage? As it turned out, Jake Kelly provided Meg with all the bravado she needed.

"So whaddya standin' there gawkin' for? Can't ya see there's work to be done? I'm not paying ya for my health, ya know."

It was the perfect prod to ignite the gentle Irish woman's fuse.

"Work to be done? Are you kidding me? This isn't a work place, it's a disaster zone waiting for a dumpster!" Meg's comment flew from her mouth without restraint. She was shocked to shaking at the bluntness of her words, but truthfully, at that point, Meg really didn't care. She was quite sure that going home and starting a new job search would be better than working at Kelly and Sons.

Jake's face turned red in a tone to match his beard, an outward sign that Meg assessed as an explosion ready to happen. Instead, the big man erupted in gales of laughter that shook his entire body.

"JT said ya was a quiet one, but you're a little spitfire ain't ya there missy?" Kelly raised his ample body out of the chair and came around the desk to where Meg was standing. Extending his bear paw of a hand, the massive man radiated a natural charm.

"Welcome to Kelly and Sons little lady. Sorry 'bout my kinda gruff beginin'. It's been a while since I've had someone workin' in this office with me. Guess I kinda' forgot what it's like."

As Meg interlaced her hand with Jake's, a soft yellow glow outlined the sturdy man. *Perfect,* she thought to herself. *This guy is filled with joy.*

Meg inhaled a deep relaxing breath and took another shot at speaking honestly. "I appreciate your apology Jake and I can understand how being alone can change a person. So, let's start over. My name is Meg, not Margaret and this office is a disaster zone. What has been going on around here? Or should I ask what *hasn't* been going on?"

The two spent the next hour in coffee and conversation as Jake explained the past years of his life that included the death of his father, the irreparable fallout with his brother, the string of office workers who came but never stayed. Jake finished with a surprisingly open-hearted and emotional plea for Meg's help.

"I know that this place is outta control. Most days it's pretty tough for me ta even make sense of what's goin' on around here. But all's I need is someone ta make some order. I got jobs to do, work and money comin' in. And ta be honest with ya Meggie girl, I just can't give up. I can't let this place go. Somehow I gotta keep it goin'. This business is everything my old man worked for and dreamed about all his life."

The break in the strong man's voice and the singular tear spilling into his bushy beard was all Meg needed. There was no way that she could walk out of that office and leave the lovable grump to fail. She also knew that she had to stay strong in her resolve and set clear terms and boundaries, or Jake Kelly's dysfunctional world could easily overwhelm her life as well.

"Ok Jake Kelly. Here's the deal. I'll stay for one month, but you're going to pay me $10 an hour plus mileage, working Monday through Thursday, 7am to 5pm. On top of that, I want an hour lunch break every day where I can be gone from the office. In that month I guarantee you that I will get this place in order. Then, I'll let you know if I'm willing to stay longer or not. And if at any time in those 30 days you're rude or nasty or inappropriate to me in anyway, I'm outta here, no ifs, ands, or buts. Take it or leave it."

Meg was proud of herself. It took all of her courage to set such terms and yet she didn't let her fear show. At the same time, the thing about Jake Kelly was that even as she spoke openly and directly the soft yellow glow around him continued. Meg trusted that glow and felt as if her strong words would not cause problems. Although she was keeping an eye on her proximity to the door, just in case she needed to make a quick exit.

In the end, Meg was never sure if it was talk about his father, or the overwhelming condition of his office, but Jake Kelly's response to her terms was immediate.

"Ok, Meg Flynn, I'll give ya all ya ask for, but at the end of the month, this office better be in tiptop shape. Oh and one more thing, makin' coffee in the mornin' is part of your job. As you can taste from this stuff we're drinkin, I stink at it…end up brewin' something more like sludge." Again with a touch of tenderness in his voice, the straightforward businessman added, "And I won't budge on that one. A man's gotta have some pride ya know."

Meg couldn't help but smile seeing Jake accept terms of someone else's making. It was hard on him, but he was in a tough spot and realized that Meg might be his best and last chance for survival. It was his half-hearted demand for morning coffee however, that allowed Meg a glimpse past his gruff exterior and into his heart. She was hooked. No doubt Jake Kelly and his construction business were about to become a significant part of her life. But she wasn't ready to let him know that.

"Me make coffee every morning? Really? That kind of thing disappeared from office rules about 20 years ago, Jake."

Taking great delight in the pained expression on her new boss's face, Meg made her way over to the stained metal pot and rusted warming tray that defined the office coffee station. "And speaking of 20 years ago, I'm guessing that's about when you bought this old thing."

Turning back to the tortured man, Meg forced herself not to giggle as she delivered her final salvo. "Tell you what Jake. I'm going to get started cleaning up the office today, but I'll be leaving an hour early. In that hour, I'm going to go into town and buy a new coffee brewer and some new china mugs. And you're going to pay for all of it. Then I'm going to set it up tomorrow, nice and neat, and teach you how to use the brewer. That way we can both make coffee whenever we want it."

Meg enjoyed each delicious second of Jake's reaction to her coffee speech. This was a man who would never succeed at playing cards, as his every emotion showed in his expressive face. Meg could tell that Jake absolutely hated the thought of buying anything new and fussy, but he knew he was past the point of protest.

"I'll tell you what Meg, ya may think you're pretty damn smart sashaying in here and makin' lots of big talk about cleanin' up this office. Well, ya just better be good ta your word, cause in 30 days, if the office ain't in order, ya'll be paying me every penny that ya're gonna waste buyin' that fancy schmanzy coffee maker and them damn china mugs."

Taking pity on the little boy in a man's body before her, Meg softened her approach and offered her hand in good faith.

"Deal, Jake Kelly."

Reaching out, Jake's hand engulfed Meg's as he gave it a sound shake. "A deal it is Meggie girl. And now if I was you, I'd be gettin' to work. You've only got 29 and a half days left." To which Meg turned on her heels and headed to the nearest bank of disheveled filing cabinets.

"Meggie girl indeed!" She muttered as she began the task.

With Meg off to work and my rooms empty of all but Goldie, the time was at hand to push aside the sharp words and hurt feelings that had passed between Mary and I. We needed to share our thoughts, hear our fears, and again become of one purpose.

"Sweet Mary, I know that you are lingering, waiting for better feelings between us. And I too want the same. Please accept these words of apology for my hasty reactions yesterday. Please return and allow us to fashion good will between us."

Silence.

It was Mary's way that I had come to understand. She needed space to come forward, not be forced by someone demanding of her. So I waited, comforted by the strength of our love. In time, she responded.

"Crown Hill. I hear your words and know them to be true; yet I cannot in good faith begin unless I know our intent is shared. I am going to reach out to Meg and call upon her righteousness and inner strength. No matter yours, or Owen's, or any other power within my world, I will use Meg to find a way to pass. I am determined to pass."

So many thoughts filtered through me...the years Mary spent as my keeper, her agonizing death, the struggles her spirit had endured within me. Among all those thoughts wove threads of fear over the consequences of Mary's decision to reach out to Meg. There was also a great sadness in realizing that by reaching out, Mary could forever leave me.

"My dear Mary. For so long you have dreamed of release from this world, and few times has that dream ever seemed possible. I understand, more feel, your pain in being trapped in a time and space that is so torturous. All that said, I would be less than honest if I did not admit that a part of my hesitation in joining with you is my own selfish desire for you to remain here, with me. While I love you deeply enough to want the best for your spirit, I love you selfishly as well, wishing for us to be together always. The intensity of my selfish desire is something I have only just realized and it is both surprising and concerning to me."

From the depths of my being I felt joy rising, followed by echoes of laughter resonating through me. There was no doubt...it was Mary's delight I was experiencing. Yet happiness was not the reaction I had anticipated.

"Oh my, Crown Hill, you are most the loving reward in all of my troubled existence. Every moment we have shared has softened the cruelties and absorbed the sorrows that I have endured. Yet what delights me at this moment is your admission of selfish intent. Did you really think I was not already aware of your feelings? Even more amusing, did it not occur to you that I would feel the same? With another lilt of laughter, Mary exclaimed, "Oh dearest, we are surely of one heart."

Mary's joy was infectious and I could feel her delight envelop my being from rooftop to rafters. It was a wondrous moment so very much like those we had shared when Mary was alive.

So it was that the memory of such treasured moments rekindled within me a deep desire to help Mary's spirit in whatever way she desired. My feelings of dread and sadness over her passing lingered no longer.

"Sweet Mary, as you well know me, you can be assured that I will help you with whatever is needed to reach out to Meg. Regardless of any evil consequences or the great sadness that will follow in your absence, I am renewed in my dedication to your will."

From the depths of my being I felt Mary's joy again rising…and I fully understood that my words had been heard.

CHAPTER SEVEN

Meg delicately navigated the stairs, balancing the Irish linen tablecloth over her shoulder, the matching napkins across her arm. It was mid Saturday morning and the new homeowner was happily preparing her first official Crown Hill luncheon.

The table linens had belonged to her mother's great-great-grandmother, Brigid Julia McCormick. They were part of the dowry for her 1851 marriage to Padric Joseph O'Shea. Immediately following their simple country wedding, Padric and Julia departed Ireland for America amidst the strife of Gorta Mor, or the Great Hunger, as the Irish called their potato famine.

The new bride took particular care in packing her few heirloom possessions for the ocean voyage. Three full sets of her mother's table linens and her grandmother's emerald and diamond lavaliere comprised the greatest part of the luggage she carried. Throughout the many challenges of her married life, Brigid fiercely protected those valued family treasures, determined to continue the tradition of passing them on to the generations of McCormick women to follow.

Meg clearly remembered the day that her mother gifted her with a set of the cherished linens. It was the morning of her marriage to Cal. Gently peeling back the layers of yellowed tissue paper, Meg burst into tears upon discovering the gorgeous tablecloth and matching napkins embellished with Brigid's delicate needlework. Little did either woman realize that Meg's intense emotions were as much related to her apprehension over becoming Mrs. Calvin Becker, as the import of the special gift.

As she smoothed the tablecloth perfectly into place, Meg added two place settings of her mother's English bone china, rimmed in silver and accented with delicate pink roses. Alongside the plates, she placed Brigid's embroidered napkins, topped by silverware embossed with roses on the handles. Next came crystal water glasses and china teacups to complete each place setting.

Meg felt a serene joy in viewing the blended arrangement of her family's cherished possessions, as they accented this special place that she now called home.

Today was the first time that Meg had invited anyone to Crown Hill. She had to admit, she was a bit nervous. The fact that the social engagement was coming at the end of her first full workweek only added to the pressure.

Fortunately, the work schedule she had negotiated with Jake allowed Meg all of Friday to clean and prepare the house. She then rose early Saturday morning to shop for just the right groceries for her luncheon menu. Now all that was left was to finish the table and prepare the food.

Meg filled the house with vases of peonies, deep rose to light pink, gathered from Crown Hill's lavish gardens. She even snipped a few roses from the walkway arch, enough to fill an antique cut-glass bowl she had recently purchased at an estate sale. Walking through and inspecting each room, Meg was at once moved to joyous laughter and bittersweet tears.

"Alright Goldie, no time for this. We have a lunch to prepare. Come on, girl." The two set off for the kitchen, where Meg assembled plates of fresh baby spinach, topped with dried cranberries, mandarin oranges, lightly toasted and sugared walnuts, thinly sliced red onions, and some crumbled chevre cheese. Setting the salads aside, Meg sautéed two boneless skinless chicken breasts and left them to gently simmer in heavy cream, white wine, chopped shallots, and rosemary.

Finishing up, she mixed together an old family recipe for buttery blond brownies, which she knew by heart. Popping them into the oven, the only tasks that remained were to slice the bread and fill the glasses with ice and water.

Meg checked the clock on the stove. *11:15. Just enough time to take a quick shower and get dressed.* "Let's go Goldie." Meg headed upstairs to the bathroom while Goldie settled into her usual place at the foot of Meg's bed.

As the restorative water cascaded over her body, Meg allowed events of the last five days to tumble through her mind. She had managed her first week on the job at Kelly and Sons with reasonable success. Her worries about working for Jake Kelly were calmed as the two settled into a comfortable office pattern--Meg making order of the chaos and Jake desperately trying not to undermine her progress.

It took a few days for the gruff owner to adhere to putting invoices in the inbox, billings in the outbox, and submitting receipts with all expense sheets. But by week's end, Jake was getting the hang of the new office order with a minimum of complaint. In addition, the two discovered that despite their differences, they enjoyed working together. Every time Meg thought about Jethro Tull recommending her for the job, she couldn't help but laugh. Who would have thought?

Reluctantly leaving the comfort of her steaming shower, Meg toweled off and slipped into her favorite pair of black capris, topped by a crisp white blouse. Choosing a pair of quilted red flats to complete her outfit, Meg took a quick look in the mirror. *Not bad for a woman recently turned 40,* she thought. "We're doing just fine, right Goldie?!"

Hearing her name brought the loving pet to her owner's side. Sharing a quick hug, Meg and Goldie set off down the stairs just as a knock came on the back door.

"Hello. Anyone home? Meg, it's me Kathryn."

Meg passed through the kitchen and onto the back porch to greet her guest.

"Hello Kathryn. Your timing is perfect. Welcome."

Meg opened the door to allow Kathryn Winston to step inside the house, but Goldie immediately moved forward and separated the two women.

"Hey there Goldie girl. How are you today?" It was hard to tell who was happier at the reunion, realtor or dog. Either way, Meg quickly took hold of Goldie's bright green collar and gently guided her back from the doorway.

"Thanks Meg, but not to worry, she's really fine." Extending a beautifully bowed basket to her hostess, Kathryn added. "So nice to see you both. Thank you for inviting me to Crown Hill today."

Meg released her hold on Goldie and accepted Kathryn's gift. The basket was filled with an assortment of picture-perfect homemade muffins and cookies. "Oh Kathryn these look delicious, but you didn't need to bring anything."

"It's my pleasure. I love to bake. However, when you empty the basket, you have to refill it with treats of your choice and share it with someone else. I've been doing this for years and it's become sort of a tradition around town, especially with my real estate clients. I always bring them a basket once they are settled."

The thoughtfulness of Kathryn's gift made Meg immediately comfortable with the businesswoman. Suddenly she felt that lunch was more of a coming together of friendly neighbors than business acquaintances.

"What a wonderful idea Kathryn, and I will definitely refill the basket and share. Please come in."

Meg led Kathryn through the kitchen and into the dining room.

"Oh Meg, I have to say, Crown Hill feels like a whole new space with your energy. And this table setting is gorgeous. Where ever did you find such beautiful linens?"

As Meg served lunch, she shared the story of her family's treasured handiwork, along with additional Flynn history that she knew. Kathryn's genuine interest encouraged Meg to impart some of her own life details and before she realized it, the women had finished lunch and were ready for dessert.

"Kathryn, I'm afraid that I've monopolized the conversation today. I'm so sorry. I rarely chatter away about my life like this. Let's move out to the porch and enjoy some iced tea and brownies. Then we can chat about you and your world."

Settling into Meg's newly acquired white wicker chairs, nestled among planters of delicate green ferns, the women continued their pleasant conversation well into the afternoon. Kathryn regaled Meg with anecdotes of Eden families and their real estate transactions, interspersed with tidbits of her personal life. It was enjoyable company that became more significant to Meg as she noticed a color materializing around Kathryn. Purple was defining this woman as someone of passion and spirituality; a personality revealed through her words as well.

The longer they conversed the more Meg found herself drawn to Kathryn and engaged by her charm. Yet no matter the pleasantness of the afternoon, Meg kept close the memory of the broken glass in the book cabinet and the prime reason she had invited the busy realtor for lunch.

"Kathryn, I know it's getting late and no doubt you have other places to be today. But before you go, I wonder if you could tell me a bit more about the history of Crown Hill?" Hesitant but determined, Meg continued. "The other day, when you stopped by, you mentioned a woman named Mary, I believe. Do you know background information about her, or details about her time at Crown Hill? I would love to know more, if you do."

Kathryn laughed softly as she considered the question.

"Oh my Meg. This house has been written about and photographed for local newspaper and magazine articles many times over the years. Mostly the stories have focused on its historic presence in the Western New York area. But articles have also been written about the commune that existed here before you arrived. Also there are vintage photographs showing previous owners raising sheep and growing crops. You know, human interest kinds of details."

Meg sensed that Kathryn was measuring her words and she wondered why. She instinctively decided to encourage conversation about previous owners. "What about stories of the people who have lived here, such as the Mary that you mentioned?"

Kathryn paused in thought before answering.

"Well, as you can imagine in the almost 150 years of its existence, many people have called Crown Hill home. I don't know about them all, but I can tell you that the early dwellers settled onto a much different property and into a much different house. The first tract of land was over 50 acres and the house was a one-story residence with two rooms and a luxury outhouse attached to the back!"

The two women laughed over the bathroom accommodations suggested by Kathryn's description.

"Over the years, the property was divided and sold off for one reason or another and the house expanded, both out and up. I don't know that I can tell you the names and stories of everyone who has ever lived on this property, but yes, Mary and Owen Southwick were two people who I specifically remember."

"So when did they live here?" Meg asked, anxious for more details.

"Back in the 1870's into the mid 1880's as I recall. As their story is told, Owen was a farmer and Mary worked right alongside him. She kept the house and the gardens in order, and Owen well fed. Actually, Mary was well known throughout Eden for her gardens and for the interesting herbs that she cross-propagated. I've never seen photographs of either she or Owen, but they are prominently featured in one of the volumes of the History of Eden."

"There's a history book written about Eden?" Meg was surprised by this information, as she never imagined anything of great historic impact happening within the tiny, rural town.

"Oh yes," Kathryn assured her. "It was compiled and written 50 years ago by the town historian, Doris Walsh. She basically edited information that she had been collecting for years into three soft cover volumes. The books highlight those who first established Eden in the early 1800's and those who played prominent roles in its development through the late 1960's.

"How interesting," Meg responded. "So what did she write about Crown Hill and the Southwicks?

Kathryn proceeded with care.

"Actually, Doris wrote about the Southwick's life at Crown Hill primarily because of something unusual that happened here.

"Oh, you've got me interested now Kathryn. Do tell."

"Well, according to all that I know, Mary Southwick died here. Or perhaps more accurately I should say, she was found hanging from a rafter in a woodshed here. Actually, it's the woodshed that still exists on the back of the property--that small building right next to your barn."

The summer sun awakened me gently, warming my roof, expanding my rafters, filling my rooms with light. It was a much needed and soothing beginning after all that had transpired within me.

The shattered glass of the book cabinet definitely caused Meg to become more aware of Mary and to question the signs of her presence. Her resultant lunch invitation to Kathryn Winston brought with it the specter of life-changing revelations for Meg, as well as for Mary and me.

I observed Meg carefully as Kathryn revealed the truth of Mary's death. Her expression initially was one of shock and some fear. But as the two women continued to discuss Mary's wretched passing, I could see an empathy developing within Meg. Her trepidation over someone living at Crown Hill more than one hundred years earlier was dissolving into compassion for a woman who had suffered many of the same uncaring life circumstances as her own.

As Kathryn continued, she shared Mary's story including the town-wide rumors and innuendo about her spirit remaining within me after her death. Meg's body once again reacted with fear. Yet I could see in her eyes an inner calm coupled with a desire to know, to understand.

Ultimately, after Kathryn satisfied all of Meg's questions and departed, we were left together Meg, Mary and me. It was then that Mary reached out.

"Crown Hill, did you hear, did you understand? It is exactly as I felt. Meg is of a nature and strength to help me. When the time comes, she will be there to aid me, I know it. I can feel it."

"Yes, dear Mary, I did hear and I do understand. Meg's character and spirit are strong. Yet we must also be aware of the strength of Owen, of his ability to drive Meg from our world. We are going to have to be thoughtful in the ways that we reach out to her. We will need to maintain a façade within me that will not alert Owen's evil spirit, which we both know is ever-lurking."

"I understand your wisdom, Crown Hill. I dedicated much of my life to acting in ways that kept me protected from my husband. I am aware of all that is needed to ensure Meg's safety and my deliverance."

Amidst her anticipation, Mary declared her intent. "We have not been blessed with someone of this goodness and ability since Rose came to us. We both know that such individuals are not easily found and I will not let Meg slip away as did Rose."

"Agreed, dear friend, but how is it that you would proceed?"

"*I will continue to embrace Meg by encouraging the scent of my roses throughout your being. I will also appear in her dreams so that my vision becomes part of her thoughts. It is my hope that such experiences will encourage Meg to further engage in conversation with Kathryn and with others, leading her to a greater awareness of my plight. When that stage is set, I will then reach out to Meg in a way that I know will allow my soul to finally journey toward the light. And nothing, not even a being of Owen's power and evil, will stop me.*"

While my heart was breaking over the specter of Mary's absence, there was no doubt in my mind...the time had come.

CHAPTER EIGHT

Meg woke up feeling as if she were immersed in a fog. She knew where she was. She was aware of her surroundings, but she couldn't quite focus on the day or, for that matter, on what plans she might have.

Slowly, the hazy-headed woman rolled over to face her nightstand and the ever-looming Big Ben. It was a relic, she knew, especially when compared to the fancy digital models that did everything but serve a hot cup of coffee. But the clock had been her mother's and Meg treasured it for the many memories it inspired.

Struggling to read the timepiece's luminescent dial, Meg rubbed her eyes and tried again. *That can't be right*, she thought to herself. *There's no way that it's 8:52 in the morning. I never sleep past 7am.*

Untrusting, Meg made the effort to roll herself out of bed and shuffle to the bathroom, bequeathing a quick pat on Goldie's head in passing. A paltry tail thump let Meg know that her faithful companion was awake, but not overly excited about rising and shining either.

A splash of water on her face and a brush of her teeth encouraged a bit of clarity within Meg's brain. The day was Sunday. She had nowhere to go, or anything that absolutely had to be done.

It was a start.

Heading back to bed, Meg again checked Big Ben's illuminated dial. It was now 9 o'clock.

What in the holy hell happened to me yesterday that I'm just waking up?

Dropping down onto the edge of the mattress, the auburn-haired woman faced the age-old dilemma: to flop, or not to flop under the beckoning covers? The decision was made for her as Goldie snuck her head under Meg's arm and gave her face a quick lick, her tail thumping a steady rhythm on her owner's back.

"Ok girl. I hear ya. Come on, I'll let you out."

Cruising on autopilot through the house, Meg released Goldie out the back door. While waiting for her return, Meg headed to the kitchen, plopped a tea bag into an oversized mug of water and slipped it into the microwave. As her morning wake-up beverage warmed, Meg served up Goldie's kibble breakfast in her favored red bowl. When the happy pet returned from her morning rounds, the two settled in the kitchen and savored their breakfasts.

After a few sips of her Irish Breakfast tea, Meg determined that her first order of the day should be simple. She needed some time to emerge from this brain-numbing stupor.

It had been a long week beginning a job and then hosting Kathryn for lunch. Was she really getting so old that a few changes in her schedule could throw her that far off track?

Taking a couple of deep breaths over the steaming mug, Meg felt the cobwebs of her mind slowly clearing. With their retreat came a memory of her conversation with Kathryn about Mary and Owen Southwick. Meg's brain registered the fact that it was a pretty bizarre exchange of information, especially the details of Mary's gruesome death in the shed-- the shed still standing and visible through her kitchen window.

The mere thought of the tragedy spun Meg to the window her body fully facing the antiquated outbuilding. "I wonder how it really happened?" she pondered, replaying Kathryn's words that a definitive cause of Mary's death had never been determined.

According to Kathryn, the known fact was that the town doctor had ruled Mary's passing a suicide. Yet from stories handed down through generations, most townspeople of the day felt the physician's prognosis was influenced by his close friendship with Owen. Kathryn added that local lore, shared publicly and privately throughout Eden, intimated that Mary was not the type to take her own life, but Owen was reprehensible enough to kill her.

Imagining the scene inside the shed that long ago day entranced Meg. "So which was it, Mary Southwick? Murder, or suicide?"

The question was a simple one for Meg, more general curiosity than a burning need to know. Yet as quickly as she imagined the thought, an answer came directly into Meg's mind.

"I was always a happy woman by nature, yet anger and violence became a part of my life through my husband. It was his brutal nature that eventually caused my death. I tell you this because I know you understand such harrowing treatment. That is why I am grateful that you have come here and are with me now."

Goldie's wet nose nuzzling her hand startled Meg from her deep thoughts. The unexpected touch caused the daydreaming woman to shriek, equally startling the affectionate dog. Goldie jumped back from Meg and barked loudly in reply.

"Oh Goldie, sweet girl. I'm sorry to have scared you. But you scared me as well! Come here and let me give you a big hug."

The gentle dog returned to Meg's side and lingered as her owner indulged her. While soothing her favored pet, Meg distractedly refocused on the voice that had just echoed through her head. Was she going crazy? Had Kathryn's stories from yesterday skewed her mind toward unstable imaginings? Suddenly, in a flash revelation Meg recalled the dream from her previous night's sleep.

She was in the midst of a gathering of people in her home, some familiar, others total strangers. The event seemed somewhat like a party as she recalled, but it also appeared like some kind of review of her life. Meg was seated in an oversized chair by the fireplace in the living room, with guests approaching one at a time to share their thoughts and wisdoms.

As Meg struggled through her subconscious, the details of the dream became fuzzy with vague words connected to random people. Frustrated with the hazy scenario Meg finally gave up trying to define her sleep-filled memories.

"Come on Goldie. Time to get dressed and figure out what part of our to-do list we should tackle today." Meg headed to the sink to rinse out her teacup just as the phone rang.

"Hello?"

"Good Morning Meg. It's Kathryn. How are you on this gorgeous summer day?"

For a moment, Meg thought about sharing details of her fuzzy mindset and the troublesome dream, but decided against it. "I'm well Kathryn. You certainly sound bright and cheery."

"Oh I've been up for hours actually. I have a client coming in from out of town. He's looking for a specific piece of property and I'm doing quite a bit of research to find just the right place. But I called this morning to thank you again for yesterday's lovely lunch. The food was delicious and your table was perfection! I could have stayed the entire summer on that wonderful wrap around porch of yours! I'm almost beginning to regret not buying Crown Hill myself!"

Meg was touched by Kathryn's genuine sentiment and returned the same. "It was my pleasure to have you here as my first official guest. You made the occasion special and very enjoyable. Thank you for your company. We'll have to do it again soon"

"That sounds wonderful Meg. I'll look forward to it. Oh and I hope that I didn't disturb you yesterday with the story of the Southwicks. Some people find that kind of information a bit eerie."

"Actually, I'm glad that you told me about them. I know that a house of this age is going to have a history and I've always been intrigued by such things. I guess maybe the fact that I don't know that much about my own family's background encourages my interest in others."

"Well that certainly sounds like a conversation we need to share on another lovely summer afternoon. In the meantime, enjoy your beautiful home and good luck with your new job. Talk soon."

Before she could reply Kathryn was gone, leaving Meg feeling more disoriented than before she picked up the phone. Whatever was lingering in her mind from last night's dream, it felt annoying. She needed to get to work, to do something physical. That would help clear her mind. It always did.

Deciding to tackle her list of outdoor tasks, Meg threw on some jeans and an old t-shirt. Heading to the back porch, she grabbed her sneakers, laced them up and headed out the door with Goldie in close pursuit.

Pruning the recently blossomed rhododendrons seems like a good place to start, Meg thought. The waxy green perennials covering the length of the wrap around porch were in need of a good cutback.

Meg didn't have much in the way of garden tools. She had managed to slip a pair of hedge trimmers, a pointed shovel, a rake and a bushel basket into her car the day she packed her worldly possessions and drove away from Cal. The question was, where had she put all that stuff when she moved to Crown Hill?

The barn, of course! Meg remembered that she had driven the car past the house and down to the barn to unload her meager tool assortment.

As she approached the white, two-story outbuilding, with vented towers across its sharply angled roof, Meg's attention was distracted, her motion literally halted. It was as if something was blocking her from going forward.

She was definitely being redirected to the nearby shed.

The same woodshed where Mary Southwick's life had ended.

"*Crown Hill, do you see? Meg is near.*"

Mary's excitement drew me immediately to her. "Yes, I am aware, but what will you do if she enters the shed?"

"I am not sure. It would be possible to materialize in the human form in which I last existed there. That way she could witness the end of my life. To see me in that state might help her understand my plight and my inability to pass...my need for her help."

"*It might also frighten her away. Mary. I know you are impatient for this chance to draw close to Meg, but you need to find a middle ground between your intense desire and her ability to manage such connection.*"

"I hear and respect your wisdom dear friend. Yes, perhaps it would be better to allow my spirit to be present within the shed in a gentle way. Simply be, so that Meg will be aware of my being and all that transpired there."

Watching Meg move cautiously toward the shed while listening to Mary's words brought clarity to my thoughts. The only way in which Meg could help Mary was if she felt connected to her...comfortable with her spirit.

"I believe your instinct is true, Mary. Allow Meg to enter into the shed and experience your spirit, not in the form of the woman who was found hanging, but rather as a women of a shared heart. You both have endured anger and anguish at the hands of loved ones in your lives. That is the place where you can meet and join without fear. Hopefully, that is the reasoning that will encourage Meg to push away any misgivings and help you."

As I finished my words, Meg approached the shed and lifted the tarnished latch on the aged wooden door. Stepping back to allow the door to swing open, she became overwhelmed by a surge of hot summer air escaping the outbuilding. The intensity of the heat caused Meg to step back and gulp for breath. I watched as she regained her balance and again stepped forward to peer inside. The contrast between the bright exterior and the dark, windowless interior made the shed appear like an endless black hole.

As Meg took tentative steps past the door, I quickly searched for Mary. Was she within the shed? Would she appear? Was she going to frighten Meg or bond with her? I tried with all the care in my heart to reach out to Mary and encourage her gentle nature.

"Please, sweet Mary. Do what is best and proceed with care."

Response to my encouragement came immediately as Meg stumbled backwards out of the shed...shrieking in cries that punctured the tranquil Sunday air.

CHAPTER NINE

Goldie was off in a field tracking a woodchuck when she first heard her mistress's frightened cries. The loyal dog quickly ran toward the sound of the ear-piercing shrieks to see her owner running from the shed towards the house. Barking in pursuit, Goldie stretched her stride to catch up with Meg, finally reaching her at the edge of the picket fence walkway.

"Oh Goldie. I'm so glad to see you. You have to come with me. We're going in the house right now."

The obedient dog followed on the heels of her owner as they passed under the archway and through the back door. Meg headed immediately to the phone and dialed 911.

"Emergency services. What is your emergency?" came the professionally unemotional voice.

"I need someone to come to my farm. I need help."

Replying with practiced patience, the dispatcher continued. "Ok m'am. Just stay calm. Let's start with some information. What's your name and location."

Annoyed by what she deemed the responder's patronizing attitude, Meg shot back. "My name is Margaret Flynn. My address is 1396 Sandrock Road."

"Ok, now what seems to be the problem Mrs. Flynn?"

"It's Ms. Flynn actually. And the problem is there's some kind of wild animal in my shed. I went in there to look for something and it leapt out at me, hissing and growling. For all I know it's some kind of rabid crazy creature that could hurt me, or kill my dog. You have to send someone up here. You have to do something right away."

"The panic in Meg's voice let the dispatcher know that the call was not a prank. Still he found the nature of the emergency somewhat amusing.

"Alrighty there, Ms. Flynn. When this animal leaped out, did it land on you or injure you in anyway?"

"No. No, I was able to jump back and avoid it. And then I ran out of the shed and slammed shut the door, so it couldn't escape. It's trapped in there and you have to send someone up here so it can be captured and destroyed. I have a dog and I don't want anything to happen to her."

"Ok Ms. Flynn, just take it easy. I'll have one of the animal control officer's head up to your place. Being that it's Sunday, it might take a bit before I can locate one of them. So you just sit tight. Don't go back to that shed until somebody gets there. Ok?"

Meg could almost hear the chuckle in the dispatcher's voice as he issued the directives. What she wouldn't give to see his face when that animal control officer captured the dangerous wildlife lurking in her shed.

"Fine, but please tell them to hurry. I don't want this animal to somehow escape and be free to roam around."

"Yes ma'am. I'll do my best. You have a good day."

Even though the dispatcher had already hung up, Meg shouted at him through the phone. "Yeah, you better do your best. You do not want to have to deal with me if you don't."

Slamming down the receiver, Meg realized that she was trembling and, in fact, suddenly felt the red spread tingle in her feet. *Oh no*, she thought, *What if I pass out? That would be all that I need, for the rescue squad to have to come in addition to an animal control officer. That son of a gun dispatcher would have a field day telling everyone in town if that happened.*

Attempting to avert such embarrassment, the overwrought woman chided herself. *Ok, Meg, just walk around the house for a few minutes. Take a couple of deep breaths. Get a grip. You know the drill.*

With Goldie trailing in confused concern, Meg followed her own advice. In moments the red spread tingling had passed. Determinedly, she moved to the kitchen sink for a glass of water. Taking small sips, the shaky woman reviewed the events of the past hour, trying to figure why they felt linked to her already-murky mindset. Mid-thought she was interrupted by the sound of a diesel engine in the driveway.

Moving to the back door, Meg saw a large dually truck parked at the end of her walkway and a man alighting from the driver's side. It only took a moment for Meg to realize that it was the guy from the Super Fine parking lot. *Oh damn, what was his name? More importantly, what was he doing at her house? And had she bothered to comb her hair and brush her teeth this morning?*

Running her hands through her unruly curls, Meg straightened her tee shirt and put on her best smile as she stepped out the door. "Hello." The word had no more than left her mouth when Goldie sped past her owner toward the approaching man, wagging her tail in full welcome.

"Hey Goldie! How are you girl? Come here and let me give you a big ole pat on the head." As man and dog easily engaged, Meg was reminded of their Super Fine parking lot meeting and how the two became fast friends. It was a scenario that Meg was not overly happy to witness again.

Breaking away from his love fest with her dog, Brady Callahan looked up at Meg and broke into one of his impossibly charming smiles. "Well, we meet again, Ms. Flynn. How are you today? Or perhaps I should say, how are you doing now?"

Unsure of his meaning, Meg chose to turn the question around on the smug man. "Regardless of how I'm doing, what brings you to my home?" She knew she sounded rather curt, but there was something about this guy's self-assured charm that made Meg nervous, uncomfortable.

"I'm here because you called me to come."

"Well you're mistaken somehow. I don't even have your phone number to call you, nor do I even remember your name." Meg knew she had just passed from curt to crabby, but she really didn't care. This guy was getting under her skin and she didn't like it.

"Well you may not have telephoned me directly, but I did receive a call from Joe Henry, the town dispatcher. He gave me your name and address and said that you reported a rabid animal attack. Actually he said you sounded on the verge of hysteria and he wanted me to get up here as fast as I could."

"You mean *you're* the animal control officer in town?" Meg knew the answer to her question, but was hoping against hope for a different reply.

"Actually, I'm the emergency ACO. It's not really my job. I just volunteer to cover some of the weekend and late night shifts so that the other officers can have time with their families."

Oh perfect, Meg thought. *Not only was the guy handsome, he was good-hearted as well.*

"And by the way, my name is Brady..."

"Callahan." Meg finished the man's words, recalling his name as soon as he started to speak.

"Right, Callahan. Nice to know I'm not completely forgettable. Now, let's get to the reason I'm here. Where is this rabid, wild animal?"

"I didn't exactly say that it was a rabid wild animal" Meg quickly countermanded the sure-willed man. Somehow in his calming presence the whole incident seemed a bit less intense, making Meg feel slightly foolish. But none of that discounted the fact that the incident had happened and there was some kind of crazed animal in her woodshed.

"I stepped into the woodshed, out back by the barn, and I heard this wild hissing and growling coming from a back corner. It was very dark in there and having stepped inside from the bright sunshine, I couldn't see all that well. So I stood still for a moment and waited for my eyes to adjust. In that moment the hissing and growling intensified and without any provocation, I felt this swell of air move toward me. Out of the darkness, I made out the image of a large furry animal leaping at me, eyes bulging, teeth barred, as if it wanted to shred my throat. Obviously I didn't wait around to give it that opportunity. I ran out of the woodshed, slammed the door shut and called the police for help. And here we are."

Appearing respectfully interested, Brady opened an official looking notebook and began filling out a form. "Let's begin with the required information. Name?"

"Margaret Flynn."

"Really? I didn't know that Meg was short for Margaret. Does anyone call you by your full name?"

The unexpected personal question caused Meg to answer without reserve. "Only my mother ever called me Margaret, mostly when I was in trouble."

The genuine reply caused the two to laugh in shared acknowledgment.

"Yeah. When my mom was angry with me, I got the full name treatment as well. Brady Michael Patrick Callahan, she would shout at me. For some reason when she did that, it made me laugh. And that made my mom even angrier, which made me laugh more. It wasn't that I disrespected her. It was just that she looked so sweet when she was trying to be stern; I couldn't help but be tickled. Do you have more names that go along with Margaret?"

The unaffected nature of his question again kept Meg from putting up her defenses.

"My full name is Margaret Rose. It's a family name. I'm not sure from which side though. My mom never talked much about family, so I don't know very much about my history or heritage, other than that I am Irish."

"Obviously, I can relate to the Irish part," Brady answered in an easy patter. "But my family is big on history and our ancestors and I know quite a bit about my family's genealogy. Anyway, back to the official questions."

Finishing up the required information, Brady asked Meg to show him the woodshed.

"You might want to put Goldie in the house, just to keep her safe while we deal with whatever is down there."

At least he's being respectful of my experience, Meg thought as she led her distrusting pet into the house. Goldie did not want to be left out of whatever was about to happen with Brady Callahan. She tried to wrest herself from Meg's firm grasp, but to no avail. As Goldie barked in protest, Meg firmly shut the back door on her pet and set off to the woodshed in step with Brady.

As the two stood before the rusty-latched door, Meg could feel that tingly feeling in her feet. "Oh no. Please not now," she silently begged her body. "Don't let the red spread happen here and now in front of Brady. Come on girl, you can control this."

"Meg, you ok? You're looking kinda red."

"Yeah, sure, I'm fine. Let's get the door open and catch this thing, whatever it is."

Brady carried with him a sturdy net attached to a long pole, a pair of thick oversized leather gloves and a helmet with a facemask. Donning the protective gear, Brady told Meg to stand over to the side of the woodshed. Lifting the latch and letting the door swing open, the practiced animal trapper stepped just inside the small building. Standing perfectly still, he allowed his eyes to adjust to the darkness.

Watching him intently, Meg waited for the wild animal screeching to begin. She also found herself wondering if Brady were attacked would she run to his aid or run to the house? Annoyed with her girlish mindset, Meg admonished herself, *Come on woman. Get some backbone and be ready to help this man if he needs it.*

Meg's resolve was immediately tested as howling cries ricocheted out of the woodshed. She wanted to yell for Brady to be safe, but everything happened too quickly. One minute she could see the sturdy man standing in the woodshed doorway and the next he was swallowed up in the dark echoes of the screeching animal. Then, only silence.

Meg's gut twisted in fear as she neither heard nor saw any sign of life from within the woodshed. Regardless of her fear, she moved forward to try and verify that Brady was all right. Forcing each step, Meg approached the doorway and softly called, "Brady? Brady? Are you ok? Do you need help?"

Her answer came as the helmeted and gloved man emerged from the darkness. In his protected grasp he carried on old wooden crate. Looking inside, Meg saw the object of her fears: a snarling mother cat and her 5 baby kittens.

Mary was despondent. She had held such hope for connecting with Meg once the inquisitive woman entered the woodshed.

While I identified with Mary's dejection, I was also enlivened by all that the woodshed had kindled between Meg and Brady.

It had been many years since sparks of romance had danced around me. And while they were far from in love, the attraction between Meg and Brady was undeniable. It was that breath of new life and love that I broached to Mary

"My sweet, come close and let us share kind words and soothing feelings. I know you are hurt, but there is much goodness in this day as well. Let us be together as we have long done. Let us be for each other."

Mary's response was not immediate, but when it did return, the tender nature of her soul shone through.

"Dear Crown Hill, it is true. I am disappointed that Meg and I did not bond. It seemed as if the circumstance was perfectly designed. But I have faith that my time is near. I will continue to remain a gentle force within Meg's world and await her awareness."

As we joined and shared our innermost thoughts I was fully reminded that soon, these tender moments would be no longer.

"Beloved Crown Hill, what troubles you? I can feel the sadness within you and it influences my spirit as well. Talk to me. Tell me what it is that cloaks you in such melancholy?"

"Kind heart, I am challenged to explain the gloom that you feel within me, other than to tell you that no matter when your spirit passes, I will always hold a special place for you, a place of deepest love and devotion, never-changing, never-ending. And should you return to this world, know I will recognize your heart, no matter the appearance of your person. I will be yours always and forever. "

Within that comforting thought, Mary and I nestled into the approaching summer's eve, ignoring all that we knew would soon transpire, reveling in all that we felt in the here and now...at peace within that place.

CHAPTER TEN

Meg crawled her way into bed. She felt like pulling the covers over her head and staying there for a week. It had been an incredibly long and exhausting day, salvaged only by the fact that no one was hurt. Well, at least not physically. The truth was, Meg's ego had taken a pretty lethal hit.

Reviewing all that had transpired, Meg still could not believe that a wild barn cat had been the source of her intense fear within the woodshed. She was mortified that she had raised such a ruckus over an uber-protective mother cat and her kittens. The only thing that salved her embarrassment was Brady Callahan's kind reaction.

When he came out of the woodshed and set the wooden crate down in the sunshine, Brady stepped back and admonished Meg to do the same. "I wouldn't get too close, Meg. This momma is a barn cat and that makes her wild right off the bat. Add to that, she's got five little ones to protect and, as you found out, she'll jump out with claws bared for just about any reason."

"So you're not going to tease me mercilessly over my rabid animal report?" Meg queried the humane man.

Flashing another one of his heart-stealing grins, Brady stepped toward Meg and placed his hand on her shoulder. "Meg, the last thing I would do is pick on you. Actually I tussled with a momma cat once when I was young and I've got the scars right here on my hand and wrist to prove it."

Brady turned his wrist and proudly displayed his war wounds while continuing to detail his feline battle. Meg heard none of it. Her mind and body were completely transfixed by the lingering sensation caused by Brady's touch. Her feet were definitely tingling, along with the rest of her body and Meg was sure that the feeling had nothing to do with the red spread.

"So I don't blame you at all for being afraid, especially when you couldn't see what was coming at you in the darkness of that shed."

Brady's reference to the woodshed brought Meg back to reality before he could realize her absence. To ensure that she stayed functional, Meg took a step apart from the ruggedly handsome farmer, allowing distance to clear her thoughts. She barely knew this man and was certainly in no position to entertain romantic feelings about him.

"I'm going to take this crate to the barn and put the momma and her kittens in a stall where she can feel safe, but where you'll also be able to come and go without any worry of harm." Brady finished his sentence with a gentle laugh that Meg understood was not directed at her, but rather at the situation. His easy-going approach affected her almost as much as his touch.

"Great. Thank you so much Brady. I truly appreciate your help with this. I also appreciate your kindness in not making me feel foolish, misjudging a barn cat with kittens for a rabid animal."

Once again reaching out and lightly touching her shoulder in reassurance, Brady smiled and then turned his attention to the crate of kitties.

Completely undone by her attraction to this virtual stranger, Meg decided to put some space between them. "Ok. Well, I'm going to head up to the house. Goldie is no doubt beside herself by now, so I need to check on her."

Brady was focused on the task at hand, but replied that he would stop to say good-bye before he left. The thought of his departure formed words in Meg's mouth that flew out before she could stop them.

"Would you like some iced tea before you go?" Meg hoped that her invitation sounded more relaxed than her pounding heart.

"Sure. I can stay for a few minutes." And with that Brady secured the crate in his gloved hands and made his way to the barn, leaving Meg once again staring at his well-defined torso.

Oh man, oh man, oh man. Get a grip girl, Meg admonished as she forced herself to turn away from Brady and move toward the house. There was no doubt that Brady Callahan was a good-looking man. And he seemed to have a caring heart to match. But in reality, Meg knew nothing about him. He could be engaged, or married with kids for pity's sake.

The sound of Goldie's plaintive howls quickly ended Meg's daydreaming. Reaching the house, she opened the back door and immediately blocked the entryway. Gently pushing the anxious retriever back, Meg soothed her pet with loving words and a few strokes on her head. The attention was enough to encourage Goldie to happily trail after her owner into the kitchen.

Gathering her thoughts, Meg pulled out her best milk glass pitcher and two tall drink glasses. She filled the pitcher with iced tea that she had brewing in the refrigerator and added a mixture of lemons, limes and oranges for a kick of citrus flavor.

As an extra treat, Meg plated some of the blond brownies she had made for her Saturday luncheon. Recognizing how strongly she was trying to appeal to the local farmer, Meg quickly banished such thoughts with the rationalization that she was only being hospitable, as she had been with Kathryn a day earlier.

All of her anxieties quickly became secondary as Brady knocked on the door and strolled into the kitchen. "All taken care of. You shouldn't have to worry about those kitties at least until the babies get mobile and start crawling around the barn. Then you might have some issues start up again with that momma."

Capping off his statement with a beguiling wink, Brady moved easily to the sink to wash his hands. Reaching for the towel from the nearby holder, the tanned and trim farmer seemed right at home at Crown Hill. Meg was definitely caught up in a spell that Brady Callahan was casting over her heart.

"I have some iced tea and a plate of brownies here. If you'd like we can head out to the porch and sit for a bit. It's the least I can do to repay you for your efforts here today. Besides, it would be nice to spend a bit of time, get to know each other." Meg hoped that her eagerness wasn't overly obvious.

Glancing at the tray Meg had assembled, Brady's eyes clouded and his perpetual smile disappeared. "You know I really need to go. By now I imagine there are other animal calls I need to answer and there's always work to be done on my farm. But really, Meg, thanks anyway."

The sudden chill to Brady's personality caught Meg off guard, sinking her heart. Before she could form an answer, the usually engaging man turned and abruptly departed from the house out to his truck. Meg's reaction was completely instinctive as she flew out the door after him.

"Brady wait, please, just a minute."

His good manners stopped the farmer mid-way into his truck cab. Reaching him, Meg forthrightly asked, "Did I do something offensive just now? I mean one minute you were smiling and the next brooding. I'm not trying to be invasive, but it just seems odd."

Meg's words touched Brady. He stepped away from the truck and drew close to her. It was then that Meg could see tears filling his eyes. Instinctively, she reached out and wrapped her arms around him. The big-hearted man responded by falling into her embrace. The two stood silently joined for a moment, bodies connected in comfort.

Brady was the one to step back as a flush of embarrassment spread over his chiseled face. "I'm sorry Meg. You didn't do anything wrong. It's all me."

"Ok, well then can you tell me what did happen back there in the kitchen?" Meg knew that she was pushing some kind of invisible boundary between them, but anything less felt like quitting on a special chance.

Brady hesitated. Within the awkward silence his eyes registered deep pain. What was it about tea and brownies that disturbed him so, she wondered? Feeling the moment too intense to continue, Meg broke the barrier between them.

"You know Brady, never mind, really. I'm not trying to be intrusive. I just thought that perhaps we could be friends, and as a friend, I was trying to reach out and understand what was going on with you. Forget it. I know you want to get going. Thanks again for your help."

Turning and walking to the house, Meg couldn't decide if she was angry or hurt. Either way, she was done with Brady Callahan. She didn't need another emotionally unavailable man in her life, even if he did have great buns.

As Meg reached the back door, she realized Goldie was missing from her side. Turning around, she saw her favored pet sitting loyally by Brady Callahan, the man himself seemingly paralyzed in place.

Oh no, this isn't happening, Meg thought to herself. "Goldie come, come on in the house." The straightforward command moved both dog and man as the two made their way towards her.

"Meg, please wait. I'd like to explain." Drawing close, Meg could see the sincerity in every part of Brady's being. She also noticed strong hues of blue developing around him, colors of love. She could find no defensible reason to do anything but honor his request.

The two stood face to face on the brick walkway, Goldie between them, as Brady began. "Blond brownies are my favorite dessert and my wife's recipe is the absolute best."

A wife? The information resonated through Meg like a rocket. Now it was making sense. Meg had completely misread the situation. No wonder the guy got uncomfortable. "Brady, really, you don't have to say any more. I had no idea you were married and certainly didn't mean to suggest anything improper..."

"Meg, stop please and just listen. It's hard for me to tell you this and if you interrupt I'll likely not get through it. Seeing your brownies made me think of my wife and my son. They were killed in a car accident five years ago at Christmas. They were on their way to her parent's house in nearby North Collins. I stayed back to milk the cows and was going to join them in time for dinner and presents."

Brady looked away from Meg and gulped several deep breaths before continuing. "Anyway, an inexperienced young driver hit a patch of ice and lost control of his vehicle. He ended up crashing broadside into my wife's car and then driving it sideways off the road, through a ditch and into a power pole. The pole fell on top of the car and literally split it, instantly killing my wife and son. I still harbor guilt over not going with them that afternoon. Every day for the last five years I get up and go to bed thinking that if we had driven together, I could have saved them, or at least died with them. And I obviously still struggle at times, like now, seeing the blond brownies that my wife always made for me. I'm sorry, I didn't mean to act so oddly. It's just hard."

Meg had no words to honor all that Brady had just shared. Rather, silent tears streamed down her cheeks in heartfelt sympathy. In a perfectly timed reaction, Goldie gave a soft whine and nudged Brady's hand with her head. The dog was uncanny in her ability to comfort those around her.

"Goldie, you're such a good dog." Brady dropped to his knees and wrapped his powerful arms around her, as if she were delicate porcelain. The image caused Meg's tears to flow more fully as a silence of sadness and broken dreams descended upon the trio.

Ultimately, it was Goldie who broke the powerful quiet as she began softly kissing Brady's face and licking his ears. The sensation felt much like tender tickles and brought laughter from within the mournful man's heart. Like sunshine breaking through a bank of gray clouds, Brady's smile chased away the intense sorrow that had encompassed them.

Rising, Brady reached for Meg's hands and held them tightly as he spoke. "I don't talk to people about the accident, about losing Julieann and Colin. I can't even remember the last time I said their names out loud like that. So please accept my gratitude for listening, for allowing me to say what I needed to say. I know it's hard to hear and if you would like me to leave now, I would certainly understand."

The intensity of the blue color around Brady stirred Meg's heart. The purity of his spirit and the tragedy of his life made it almost impossible for her to speak. Yet she knew that words were crucial at this moment.

"Brady, I am honored that you would share your sorrow with me. I cannot imagine the pain and loneliness you have endured. As for your leaving, oh my. I think I would struggle for the rest of the day if you were to go at this moment."

Brady gave a soft squeeze to her hands as he spoke, "Then if you wouldn't mind, Meg, I would love to sit on your porch, enjoy your company, and sample some of your delicious brownies."

As Meg drifted to sleep, I lulled her with soft breezes and sweet scents.

It had been a tumultuous day at Crown Hill, which had thankfully ended in quietude.

Brady and Meg settled on the porch and spent the rest of the day nurturing their friendship. Brady talked further of the tragedy that took the lives of his wife and son, softening the pain by sharing sweet family memories as well. Meg listened carefully as Brady spoke, trying to define this man who was surely navigating his way into her heart. And in the silences between Brady's stories, Meg shared bits and pieces of her life as she could.

The strong and loving energy generated by the two spread through me like a welcome resolve. It was as Mary imagined, that the kindness between this man and woman might one day help fill the void of her absence within me. So it was comforting that, even after Brady departed and Meg set about preparing for her workweek, my being remained charged with the sweetness of their afterglow.

"My Mary, how is it that you feel tonight after so many unexpected happenings? Are you settled that you did not connect with Meg in the woodshed? What need do you have of me as you continue to reach out to her?"

"Dear One, I must admit that I am somewhat off-kilter from all that transpired today. The emotions ran from excitement, to fear, frustration, anger, and kindly loving care. And now that all is calm, I know that I must realign with Meg and find a way to bring us together."

While I knew Mary was strong in her purpose, I sensed a reserve in her spirit. From our many years together I knew Mary's strength would, in time, connect her with Meg. But I was also aware of her kind soul's fragility in moments of self-doubt. It was at such times that I would open my heart to Mary and afford good thoughts to encourage her.

"Gentle friend, from all that I saw today, Meg has an inner strength and compassion that should serve you well. I don't think she will lack courage when it is time to realize the presence of your spirit within me. I have great faith that it will all come to be as you hope and wish."

"I agree, Crown Hill, and I thank you for your always-encouraging words. I do worry though, if Owen should become aware of my connection with Meg if her strength will be enough to ward off malintent on his part. But at this point my deepest concern is developing a bond between Meg and myself and I do not intend on losing further chance or time in making it so."

"What is it you foresee, my Mary?"

"I am going to return to Meg's dreams tonight and bring her images and remembrances of my life. She is ready for such things, as her time with Kathryn Winston has prepared her. Then when she desires more, and I have no doubt that she will, I will reach out directly to her, soul to soul. That is when I will need your help, dear one, to bring the many comforts of your being around Meg and allay any fears of me that she may have."

"Mary, you know that I will be by your side. But at the same time I wonder, what is it that you will bring into Meg's dreams? I am curious to know what you deem as important remembrances."

"I have taken heart in the wisdom you have shared with me Dear One. I believe you to be true when you say that the place for Meg and I to connect is in our lives that mirror each other. So, I will bring to her moments of my life within you, when Owen's cruel ways dispirited me. Then I will ensure that her dreams are filled with the many ways that you have cared for me and kept me safe. By encouraging images of you that will be familiar to her and incorporating my life into them, I believe that I will become real to Meg. Thus, she will be willing to connect with me when the time comes."

Pausing in thought, Mary softly added, *"And know dearest Crown Hill…that time is near."*

CHAPTER ELEVEN

How could she have overslept?

Meg was sure she set the alarm for 5:45 am before she drifted off to sleep. Yet here it was 6:30, no alarm and she was just waking up.

Monday morning of her second work week and she had less than 20 minutes to get showered and dressed, take care of Goldie, grab some tea and head out the door. Ugh. Meg hated having to rush first thing in the morning, but she hated being late even more. Somehow she would find a way to get to work on time.

With two minutes to spare Meg drove into the Kelly and Sons parking lot, pulling up next to her boss' tried-and-true pick up. There was as much rust and dirt on the old truck as there was metal, but Jake loved his, "old warrior," as he called the aging vehicle. Truthfully, after seeing the way he abused the truck, Meg thought it a true testament to its durability that it continued to run at all.

Heading to the door, Meg could hear the now familiar refrain of Jake's *Morning Glory* serenade. She was getting used to his off-key delivery and understood that singing got Jake's morning off to a good start.

According to her boss, the song was one he learned while spending time with his maiden aunts from his mother's side of the family. Whenever he would stay overnight at their house, one of the aunts would come upstairs and waken him with "Morning Glory" and a fresh baked muffin treat. Jake came to love the song, to the point that he started singing the ditty at home every morning. He didn't care that his father termed it a "sissy girl" song. He liked the way it made him feel as he belted it out, crooner style.

Over the years, Jake continued his morning song fest, eventually bringing the musical tradition to work, mostly as a means of annoying his father. Meg wasn't sure she would have enjoyed being around the business during those family years. Dealing with one Kelly at a time was more than enough of a challenge.

Her assumption was confirmed as she walked through the door.

"Well, nice of ya to show up Ms. Flynn." Jake enjoyed teasing Meg, and she understood that it was his way of showing affection. However, with the hurried nature of her morning, Meg was not exactly in the mood.

"Morning Jake, and it's 6:59. I am officially one minute early. But I won't charge you overtime…this week." Meg realized that the best way to deal with Jake was to return exactly what he gave. "Sassing back," was the term her mother used to describe it. It was a lesson Meg had learned long ago in high school when the boys would pick on her. It was also a lesson she learned to forget with Cal, who punished Meg anytime she had the nerve to be "sassy."

"Aw, whats'a matter Meggie girl? Get up on the wrong side of the bed this mornin'?"

In the name of peace and quiet, Meg chose to ignore Jake as she headed to her desk of stacked paperwork. The silence that followed gave her hope that Jake would settle down and allow her time to fully wake up and become functional.

"Or maybe you're still recovering from that crazy wild animal attack yesterday, huh Meggie?"

Meg sat stunned, trying to decide if she had somehow misheard Jake or if she was still in an early morning stupor. How could he know? She couldn't imagine that Brady had told her boss. They weren't even friends as far as she was aware. And no one else was around her farm yesterday. No one else could have knowledge of what went on.

"What are you talking about, Jake?" Meg was not about to admit to anything that could give her boss an edge.

"Oh come on Meg. Don't try and deny that ya thought a plain ole' barn cat was some kind of rabid animal trying to attack ya. The whole town knows about it, so ya might as well admit it."

So Brady did betray her.

Frustration started rising up within Meg. She was torn between sinking into embarrassed silence and bolting out the office. Yet her "voice" offered another option. *Don't follow your old pattern of running and hiding just because you are angry and hurt. Stand up for yourself. Set the boundaries by which you are willing to be treated.*

Meg struggled with how to best handle the situation, but she knew that she could not just sit there with Jake Kelly laughing at her. Ultimately she took a leap of faith and spoke her mind. "Well I am so glad that Brady Callahan had fun spreading this story around town. And I hope that you have all enjoyed a good laugh over what seemed like a real emergency to me on my farm."

While her words hung between them Meg focused on her computer, feigning complete disinterest in how Jake Kelly might respond. Yet every fibre of Meg's body felt like a radar system monitoring Jake and his reactions. Would he lash out against her? Would he take action to quiet her?

"Brady Callahan? What are ya talking about Meg? Brady had nothin' to do with your story gettin' around town. The dispatcher put it out to Brady on the police frequency radio. Every police and fire department member hears that, as well as the rescue squad and any of the town busy bodies that have scanners runnin' in their houses."

Meg could not believe what she was hearing. Her panicked 911 call had been reported over a public radio system? This time her reaction came swiftly, without thought or consideration. "Jake are you saying that the dispatcher announced my call publicly?"

"Yep and let me tell ya, that news spread like wildfire. Hell, I heard about it when I stopped at the Legion for a beer yesterday afternoon."

Meg could feel a tingling in her feet that signaled a red spread well on its way. On top of everything going on at the farm, the voices she was hearing both in her mind and her dreams and the fact that she was now the laughing stock of the town, there was no way Meg was going to allow Jake to witness a red spread. She needed to get out of that office if she was going to maintain any slice of self-confidence or pride.

"Jake, I'm going home. I really don't feel well. I haven't slept soundly in several nights. And while all of Eden may be amused at my inexperience with farm life, I don't need to sit here and have you throw it in my face."

Before Jake could object, Meg was out of the office and on her way home. During the short drive she did her best to rationalize the town's behavior, but in all honestly, she could not. Here she was a brand new member of the rural community, barely around long enough to have met more than a handful of people. Yet she was being turned into a town joke for no other reason than she misjudged a wild barn cat protecting her litter?

By the time she pulled in the driveway Meg was in a full-blown red spread and her head was pounding. Walking into the house Goldie immediately came to her side, greeting her owner with a caring welcome.

"Oh Goldie. I don't know what's happening, but things aren't going so great in our world right now."

Without pause, the "girls" moved in tandem to the summer warmth of the wrap around porch. Meg settled in on the wicker swing, suspended from the bead board ceiling in the far corner of the spacious veranda. Goldie tucked herself neatly underneath.

Meg took comfort in snuggling into the lightweight cotton blanket that she pulled off the back of the swing. Although the day was warm, the gentle softness of the coverlet felt like a comforting hug, which was just what Meg needed at the moment.

The turn of her morning made Meg feel as if she were back in school, ostracized by the cool kids who always mocked her. She had experienced a tough life growing up. Her parents, Elizabeth and Michael Flynn, met and married young and divorced shortly after she was born. Even before the ink dried on the divorce papers, Meg's father was gone, leaving her high-school-educated mother to struggle through a life of low wages and short-lived jobs. The end result was that Elizabeth and Meg moved often, continually packing and relocating their few possessions in hopes that the next town would become, "home."

Home. It was a word that Meg idealized, as she really had no sense of its true meaning. It wasn't that Elizabeth failed at making sure that her daughter had a decent place to live and good food to eat. It was more that Meg had been left alone and to her own devices for as long as she could remember. There was no choice. Her mother was always working to make ends meet and there was never any other family around to help.

Meg often wondered about her family, especially at school events when she would witness a stream of grandparents and aunts, uncles and cousins showing up for other kids. Yet try as she would, Meg could never get her mother to share memories or stories about her family. Whenever she brought up the subject, Elizabeth would simply say that she didn't want to talk about it.

Once, on Christmas Eve, Meg pressed her mother for details. Upon finishing off her traditional brandy-laced eggnog, Elizabeth sentimentally revealed a few snippets of family history, in almost sacred-like whispers.

"My grandmother died before I was born, so I never knew her. My mother always told the story that my grandmother was widowed at a young age and had to work any job to make enough money to support the two of them. Guess that kind of tough luck runs in our family, huh? Anyway, one day my grandmother decided that she wanted to move away from her family; pretty much cut all ties to them. My mother never told me why. She just said that my grandmother packed up all their belongings and moved to New Jersey."

As her mother spoke, a million and one questions popped into Meg's mind, but she was afraid that if she interrupted, her mother's storytelling would come to an abrupt end. So Meg sat quietly, listening, committing every detail to heart.

"The really sad part is that my grandmother ended up dying several years after she and my mother moved. My mother was just eighteen at the time and in her last year of high school. Without family, my mother had no choice but to drop out of school and get a job. She went to work as a housekeeper for a wealthy New York City stockbroker and his wife. Eventually she became the nanny for their five children. It was there she met my father, who was working as the family's mechanic and chauffeur. Within a year, they married and continued on with their jobs. Two years later I was born and shortly after that our family moved to Atlantic City for a business opportunity for my father."

At that point, Elizabeth's voice broke and she began to weep uncontrollably. Meg was unsure if it was the brandy or some untold family history causing her mother's melancholy. Either way, she sensed that the family storytelling had come to an end.

Years later, after Elizabeth's passing, Meg went rummaging through a chest of her mother's keepsakes. There she discovered a journal authored by her mother during her teenage years. Meg sat cross-legged for hours reading through Elizabeth' youthful reflections and dreams. The faded blue handwriting, inscribed upon yellowed pages, revealed a wealth of unknown details about her family. Included were two entries Meg imagined as the cause of her mother's tears that long ago Christmas Eve.

In the first, Elizabeth detailed her mother's death from breast cancer and the deep depression suffered by her father after his wife's passing. The next entry was written a year later, to the day of her mother's death. It described Elizabeth's emotional devastation in finding her father lifeless in his bed, an empty bottle of pills seized within his hand.

For months, Meg returned to her mother's journal to read and re-read stories about the family she had never known Yet of all that she learned, the most meaningful discovery related to Elizabeth's mother, Meg's grandmother. According to the journal, she and her grandmother were connected not only by blood and heritage, but by name.

By their shared name of, Margaret Rose.

I observed Mary filtering through Meg's dreams as she had planned, sharing images of the earthly life she had lived within me. There were moments of happiness as well as sorrow, all intended to deeply imprint Mary within Meg's mind.

It wasn't difficult for Mary to accomplish this task. All spirits have the ability to filter through a human's subconscious. The impact of such spiritual interaction however, depends on each person and their willingness to accept their dreams as more than mindless fantasies. From all appearances, Meg was willing.

However, as Mary advanced herself from Meg's dreams into her daydreams, I watched the stalwart woman begin to struggle. Meg was clearly disturbed by the imaginings Mary was bringing into her mind, especially as the thoughts began to consume both her days and nights. Yet I understood that Mary's intent was not to haunt Meg, rather to fully reach into her being and connect with her.

It was a difficult situation and I was caught between my compassion for both women, wondering how I might best aid them. I decided to first approach Mary.

"Mary, can you come near? I would like to speak of something of importance, something of concern to both of us."

"I am always close by dear friend. What is it that you would discuss?"

"I have been observing the ways in which you are reaching out to Meg and I believe that she has become most fully aware of you. I wondered if you feel the same?"

"I do think that she feels my presence, although I am not sure she is quite ready for my spirit. Thus, I continue to permeate her dreams and occupy her mind."

Understanding Mary's intense longing to pass, I proceeded carefully into my next thoughts.

"I know that you are doing all that you believe necessary, but I wonder if Meg is someone more aligned with the spiritual side of her nature than most? I wonder if her knowledge of you is already sufficient and by continuing to engage her, you may be depleting her more than preparing her?"

Mary's reaction to my question was swift and direct.

"How can you say such a thing, House? You know how hard it is for people to accept and engage spiritually. You, above most, understand

how such interaction often requires numerous appearances and almost undeniable proof of existence. I have been but a few weeks proving my being to Meg. And if I should shorten this process and directly connect with her too early and it does not go well, then all is lost. There is no going back to try and rebuild the bond. You and I both know that from our many years of trying to connect with other souls."

Mary's words held truth. I also knew that there were exceptions to every circumstance. From all that I was observing with Meg, she was reaching a breaking point that might push her beyond her abilities and Mary's needs.

"Sweet Mary, please try and hear my words and understand my intent. I am not finding fault. It is just that as I observe all you are undertaking in connecting with Meg, I believe she is ready. I also believe that should you push your connection with her soul much further, you may lose her and your chance to journey into the light."

I finished my thoughts by radiating a strong feeling of love throughout my being. It was my hope that such tenderness would soften the way in which Mary received my words.

The silence that followed indicated that my hope was flawed--- Mary was not accepting my thoughts, and to be honest, I could not fault her. In our time together, there were few who came to us with the clear ability to help her spirit. And while there remained the possibility that someone of such power would come to us again, it had been 150 years of failed tries.

Mary was well-entitled to her silence…and to her plan.

CHAPTER TWELVE

Meg awoke to the sound of someone calling her name. Opening her eyes, she was unsure of her surroundings. Murky-minded, she inventoried her senses.

Sunny. Warm. I'm on the porch. I'm moving. On the porch and moving--ahhh--I'm on the swing.

Meg found the familiarity of her whereabouts immediately comforting, although she still had no idea of the day, or time. Again she heard her name called out and realized that she was not in a dream.

"Meg, hey Meggie girl. Ya in there?"

Meg recognized the voice as Jake Kelly, but she couldn't imagine what he was doing at her home. Taking matters under her control, Goldie jumped up, started barking and headed off the porch in the direction of the back door. She would protect Meg and the house from whoever was invading their summer afternoon.

Guess I better get up and see what Jake wants before he and Goldie get in to some kind of tussle. Meg threw off the cotton blanket, slid off the swing and smoothed her wrinkled slacks and blouse.

Taking the dining-room-through-the-kitchen route, Meg saw the reflection of her sleep-spiked hair in the glass of the book cabinet. *Falling asleep on the porch swing definitely did not help one's appearance,* she thought as she tried restoring order to her thick auburn mane.

"Ok there little lady, just take it easy. I ain't hurtin' nobody or nothin'"

Meg could hear Goldie vehemently addressing her boss with every step she took. Finally rounding through the kitchen to the back door, Meg called off her loyal guardian.

"Goldie that's enough. Come over here." Pushing on the latch, Meg allowed sufficient space for her retriever to step in and pass by her. In greeting Jake though, she brought the door to a firm close.

"Hey Jake, what are you doing here?"

"Well, I wanted to talk to ya a minute. Can I come in?"

Meg's instincts told her to keep her distance from the brawny man. This was her new life, in her new home, and, as Meg was learning, she had the right to decide who could come in--and just how far she would allow them.

"I'll talk to you right here," Meg replied stepping outside the door.

The snub of not being allowed into Meg's home was not lost on the hard-headed businessman. He knew that he had crossed a line with this woman, who had so quickly become a valued part of his world. Now, he needed to make it right.

"Listen Meg, I'm real sorry about this morning. I was just teasin' and I didn't mean to hurt your feelings. And the way ya just left the office, well I was kinda worried about ya. So I came all the way up here to check and be sure you're ok."

Meg could not help her immediate reaction. "All this way? Jake, the office is only 2 miles from my house."

"Ok, ok. So it's not so far, but still, I left all that work sittin' on my desk to come and check on ya. And I am apologizing, which doesn't happen very often, I'll have ya know."

Meg was sure that apologies were not a way of life for the outspoken man, and he did seem sincere.

"Apology accepted Jake. I'm not saying that your behavior was appropriate or excusable, mind you. I'm just saying that I'm willing to let it go, as long as you understand that I won't tolerate that kind of treatment again. Fun is one thing. To pick on someone because they are afraid and trying to do what's right, well that's cruel, and I won't allow cruelty in my life anymore."

The impact of Meg's words on Jake was visible. His face turned red and his eyes softened as he spoke in an unusually quiet tone. "Geez Meg, I really am sorry. I didn't think about teasin' like that. I was just happy to see ya and thought I was bein' funny. Really, I'll try not to do it again. But I can't promise that I won't yank your chain every once in a while. What the hell, a man's gotta have a little fun!"

The childlike innocence of her employer, in contrast with his burly workman's body brought a smile to Meg's heart. He really was a big teddy bear who just needed somebody to keep him in line. At the moment, that somebody seemed to be Meg.

"Ok Jake, why don't you come in? I have some iced tea in the fridge and some brownies that I made the other day. I want to talk to you about something anyway."

With the suggestion of food, everything else became irrelevant to the stocky man. Happily he followed Meg into the house and went directly to the kitchen table. Like a little kid, he pulled up a chair and waited for his promised treat.

Cutting a generous slice of dessert and pouring a tall glass of cold tea, Meg set them both in front of her boss. She then watched in amazement as he devoured the brownie in three clean bites. This was someone who clearly did not get homemade desserts very often.

"Wow, Meg, them brownies are really somethin'. But they ain't brown, they're tan. So why don't you call them tannies?" The question caused the hearty man to laugh out loud which shook his belly as well. Meg couldn't help but join in Jake's laughter. It also made her realize that no matter how frustrating he might be, more than likely she would always forgive her boss's errant ways. While she was hesitant to admit it, Meg was becoming very fond of Jake Kelly.

"So Jake, I want to understand something about living in this town. Why is it that everyone was so busy talking about me and that darn cat in my woodshed? Do they enjoy making it out as if I'm some kind of a fool? Really, I don't understand any of it. Hardly anyone in Eden knows me, so why would they want to be purposefully mean to me?"

Jake's answer was direct and no-nonsense. "Now you listen here Meg, there is somethin' ya gotta understand about livin' in a small town like Eden. Everybody *does* know everybody, whether you've met 'em or not. This ain't no big city where ya can move into a neighborhood and nobody knows your name or who ya are. And that's a good thing."

Meg couldn't keep her thoughts to herself as she blurted out, "I don't think it's such a good thing. I think it's nosy, and mean, and none of people's business who I am or where I came from, or for that matter, what I do up here."

"Well if that's gonna be your attitude then ya better plan on movin' or spendin' a lot of time by yourself, cause you ain't never gonna fit in or be happy here."

Meg was completely caught off guard by Jake's tough words. He was right that she had never lived in a small town community. All the same, she had a hard time believing that knowing everyone's business was a trustworthy way of life.

"Lemme try explain' it to ya Meg. Ya met Brady Callahan yesterday right?"

Meg didn't dare open her mouth in response. She was quite sure that her voice would belie her heart's interest in the handsome widower. Instead, she simply nodded.

"Now Brady's growed up in this town, fifth generation. So in his case, pret near everybody in Eden knows him and all 'bout his life from the time he was runnin' 'round in diapers. Yet I'm gonna tell ya, when his wife and baby died in that car accident, this whole town made Brady their business. They fed him, and prayed for him, and cleaned his house, and mowed his lawn. Hell, Laurie Schwab, the nurse over there at Doc O'Grady's office even went and shaved him and bathed his sweet baby ass in those early days when he was really hurtin'."

The straightforward descriptions created powerful images in Meg's mind. After listening to Brady describe this time in his life, she could clearly imagine all that Jake was recounting.

"Since those days when Brady was nothin' more than a sacka tears, and even as he's got to puttin' his life back together, people in this town have kept on makin' him their business. They keep talkin' about him at the Legion and at church on Sunday and at the Super Fine. And they're not talkin' outta meanness, neither. It's on accouta when ya live here in Eden, ya belong to Eden, plain and simple. Good and bad, right or wrong, don't matter. It's just how it is."

Meg knew she had asked for the sermon that Jake was delivering. She just hadn't expected Brady to be part of it. Using the farmer's tragic circumstances as proof of the town's caring nature was strongly impacted Meg.

"So now, let's move on to you, little lady. Yeah, everyone was talkin' about ya and that barn cat yesterday. Why not? It was damn funny. So it was on the embarrassin' side too. What the hell's the difference? We all do dumb things and make mistakes. Don't mean a hilla beans. What does matter is that if anything had really been wrong up here, them people that were talkin' about ya woudda been up here helpin' ya. Makin' sure ya was ok."

Again, Meg had asked for this explanation, but never thought the answer would soften her heart to tears. Thoughtfully, Jake pulled a red bandana hanky out of his back pocket and tenderly dabbed each of her cheeks. In a kindly voice he continued.

"Ya gotta understand Meggie girl. This old house has been here longer than a lotta people in this town. It's one of them places that people around here grew up playin' in and goin' to parties at. So they feel it belongs to 'em in a way. It's parta the town and its history. Like I said, you're just gonna have to get used to that, or leave, cause it ain't gonna change.

Jake finished his sentence by moving to Meg and gently wrapping her in a comforting hug, the likes of which she had never known. The sense of protective care that Meg felt within this gentle giant's embrace encouraged her to more tears, which turned to laughter upon Jake's final admonishment.

"And next time ya go into town and somebody asks ya about your rabid momma cat…look 'em square in the eye and tell 'em she's just as wild and crazy as ever. And then have a good laugh with 'em. That's all you gotta do."

Drawing apart within a new-found bond, Meg allowed her heart to speak, "Jake Kelly, you are a very special man."

"Aw Meg, quit it now. No need to go getting' all mushy on me. If ya wanna be nice, ya can slice me up another piece a that tan brownie to take with me. I gotta get outta here. Kelly and Sons don't run on its own ya know. And by the way, I ain't payin ya for today and ya better be back at your desk tomorrow, on time and ready to work."

Meg wrapped up the remaining brownies and gave them to her boss with the guarantee that she would return to work in the morning. "And while we're at it, I wasn't late today. Although I have to admit, I came close. I'm just not sleeping well. It's been going on for the last week or so. Got a lot of crazy dreams going on when I'm asleep and sometimes even when I'm awake."

Jake took a step closer to Meg, appearing very somber. It was an unusual expression for the high-energy man, causing Meg to be unsure of what was coming.

"You listen to me little lady. If anything up here makes ya feel uncomfortable or gives ya the willies, you just call me and I'll be here to take care of it."

"What do you mean, Jake?" Meg didn't exactly know how to define, "the willies," but she didn't like the sound of it.

"There' been a lotta stuff happened in this ole house over the years and ya hear tell a lotta tales. I'm not sayin' true or false. All's I know, is some men in this town braver than me been run outta here by somethin' they couldn't explain. It scared the b-jezus outta 'em. So all I'm sayin' is if you're havin' bad dreams, then maybe ya need to have one of them hocus pocus people up here and make sure there ain't no evil gonna hurt ya."

While appreciating her boss's protective attitude, Meg was sure he was going overboard. "Oh for heaven's sake,

Jake, there's no evil in this house. It's a wonderful place. So don't you go scaring me over nothing but a lot of rumor and gossip."

"It ain't all rumor and gossip Meggie girl. You need to talk to Clara Johnson if ya don't believe me. She's been around here forever and her family's been parta Eden for near 200 years. She knows this house, spent a lotta time here growin' up with one of her best friends. She'll tell ya stories, make the hair stand up on the backa your neck."

Clara Johnson. The name sounded familiar but Meg couldn't place it. But it really didn't matter because, as she was starting to learn, Jake was often more bluster than truth. Besides, if anything really creepy was going on here, Meg was quite sure she would realize it.

"Ok Jake Kelly, time to take you and your brownies out of here. I'm still not feeling great and all your jibber jabber is exhausting me."

"Ok. I'm goin'. But don't ya forget what I told ya. You talk to Clara Johnson. She'll set ya straight."

"Ok. Bye-bye Jake." Meg gently guided the burly man out the door and watched as he climbed in his old pick up and roared out of her driveway.

Looking down at Goldie, Meg felt a loving warmth pass between them as the dog gently leaned in to her owner's leg. "Well Goldie, this has been quite the day and it's still not over. I sure am glad that you are here with me. Some days you're the most reliable one in my world."

As Meg bent down to scratch behind her favored pet's ears, a soft breeze came through the screen door carrying with it the scent of roses from the nearby arbor. The gentle fragrance stayed with Meg as she and Goldie made their way through the kitchen and climbed the back stairs to her bedroom. *Time to get out of my dress clothes*, Meg thought. There was daylight left and plenty of work to be done. Those rhododendron bushes were still in need of trimming. Perhaps she could get to them this afternoon.

Digging around for work clothes, Meg noticed the scent of roses that she'd enjoyed by the back door within the confines of her closet. *That's odd,* she reflected.

Meg realized that this was not the first time she had noticed a rose fragrance away from the arbor. In fact, now that she thought about it, there were several instances when she could recall the scent lingering, some of which were connected with an odd phenomena like catching a glimpse of movement, or feeling a presence in the room. Then, there was the broken glass in the book cabinet which, as Meg now recalled, was also followed by a rose scent. How could she have forgotten that? It was the reason she had invited Kathryn Winston to lunch and how she ultimately learned about Mary and Owen Southwick.

So what of it? What possible coincidence could there be in drifting scents from flowers growing right outside the house? Meg felt confused and ultimately decided that she was not thinking clearly. As she had told Jake, she'd been struggling for a few days, and nights with weird imaginings. Maybe she just needed a good night's sleep.

Yet, as Meg turned to walk out of the closet, she felt a chill creep along her spine followed by the hair rising up on the back of her neck. The sensations reminded her of Jake Kelly's words, "You need to talk to Clara Johnson. She'll tell ya stories ta make the hair stand up on the backa your neck."

Ok Jake, maybe it would be a good idea to see if Clara Johnson's phone number is in the Eden directory. After all, what could it hurt to talk to her?

As Meg became more aware of and connected to Mary, my thoughts became singularly focused on Owen.

While I was not aware of his presence within or around me, I had little doubt that his spirit lingered. I was troubled by thoughts of Owen's vengeful return into my being and of Meg filtering into his vindictive awareness. Thus, I turned to Mary.

"Dear friend, while I do not wish to intrude, I am at a place of concern over Owen's looming spirit. Can you draw near and share with me the specter of his presence?"

"Crown Hill, while I keep your goodness protectively separated from Owen's evil, I will tell you that he remains close enough to be connected to my spirit, but not within you. As when I was his wife, I continue to temper his control by assuring him that his will is my primary concern. And now, with the power of the universe guiding me, I will continue to promote that assurance to Owen as Meg helps me to pass from this world."

A pause came into our conversation. After so many years of waiting, and wondering, and hoping, we each fully realized the moment in time. It was Mary who broached the unspoken question between us.

"Dearest Crown Hill, tell me. Do you have doubts about all that is about to transpire?"

I wanted to say yes. I wanted to tell Mary that after so many decades together she would not be happy in any other world. I wanted to impart that she would regret leaving me. I wanted to beg her to stay within me forever.

But I did not.

Instead, I summoned all of the love within me and enveloped Mary with the sweet scent of her roses. I brought forth the echoes of her favored piano music played so long ago. I wrapped her in the protective embrace of my being.

I promised her that I had no doubts…and that all would be well.

CHAPTER THIRTEEN

Meg woke up with a yen for cinnamon-sugar toast. Rapidly, her hunger became a relentless craving that drove the sleepy woman from her cozy bed into the kitchen.

The process of creating the sugary-sweet breakfast treat was a sacred one in Meg's world. She started by cutting two thick slices of spelt bread from a loaf baked at a nearby organic market. Meg had discovered the charming shop during one of her business errands for Kelly and Sons.

Next, she delicately placed the bread upon a wire oven rack, consecrating her breakfast indulgence under a low broil. The fussy cook had long ago determined that broiling gave the toast an added crunch that elevated it to divine perfection.

With the bread grilling, Meg went in search of her treasured cinnamon sugar shaker with the bright red top. The clear plastic container had been a random purchase at a housewares outlet years ago. From the first shake, it had become her favored method for the sprinkling portion of her sweet toast ritual. The problem, at the moment, was that the shaker was missing.

"What in the world could I have done with it, Goldie?" Meg wondered aloud to her nearby pet. Unconcerned, Goldie thumped her tail in half-hearted reply as Meg continued to ravage her cupboards.

Pausing to carefully turn and re-position the warming bread slices, Meg returned to the spice cupboard for one last look. Digging deeply through the various sweet and savory seasonings she finally spotted the red-topped shaker wedged in the recesses of the cabinet, trapped between two oversized containers of ground sage and curry.

Quickly separating the shielding spices, Meg grabbed her treasured cinnamon-sugar mix and swooped to the oven just in time. She seized the perfectly golden slices of toast and placed them on a waiting platter. Next, came the slathering of softened butter onto the steaming bread, infusing luxurious richness into every toasted grain. Finally, it was time. Reverentially, Meg took the shaker in hand and showered the indulgent divinity with a blizzard of cinnamon-sugar sweetness.

Exercising absolutely no self-control, Meg lifted the first slice of golden toast to her mouth and devoured it. The fusion of sweet and spice with buttery crunch bordered on immoral decadence. Slice two tasted equally divine.

On this summer Saturday morn, life was definitely good for Margaret Rose Flynn.

Cleaning up from her cinnamon toast revelry, Meg felt clear headed for the first time in days. Following a good night's sleep, her sense of well-being encouraged the resolute woman to begin a regimen that she'd envisioned since moving to Crown Hill; to rise early each morning and exercise. Meg didn't care what form the physical activity took, she was intent on establishing a regular workout routine.

"So what's your choice, Goldie? Shall we try one of our yoga videos? Or maybe get out the weights?" Again offering nothing but a meager tail thump, Goldie's clear indifference left Meg with only one choice. "Ok, girl, you win. A walk it is."

At the sound of the magic word, Goldie was up and dancing around, yipping in excitement. "Ok, Ok. Calm down and let me get your leash." The smart pooch knew the routine and immediately sat and waited for Meg to attach the bright green braided lead to her matching collar.

"Alrighty, off we go girl. Let's have some fun exploring our new neighborhood." Meg and Goldie had long enjoyed teaming up for energizing walks. However the trauma and stress of Meg's divorce had curtailed their exercise ritual. It had been over a year since the two had delighted in a workout hike. Today's venture felt revitalizing to both woman and dog.

The duo set off heading north, toward town and the rolling hills that lay in-between. The land surrounding Crown Hill still nurtured a few farms and some random vineyards. However, it had primarily evolved into a colony of homes in varying shapes and sizes, with Crown Hill appearing as a treasured gem among them.

Meg and Goldie hit a strong pace as they advanced into the first steep grade of their walk. To their credit, they met the elevated challenge with ease. Yet as they continued, their path became unexpectedly blocked.

"Well good morning! It's nice to see others up and out today. Saturdays can be on the quiet side with walkers taking a break from their weekday schedules."

A petite, dark-haired woman garbed in sleek, black spandex suddenly materialized before Meg and Goldie. She was graceful in her movements as she approached from her home's driveway immediately intersecting the road.

My name is Leigh. Leigh Wilson. I walk along Sandrock just about every day. Nice to meet you."

Without hesitation, Goldie moved toward the athletic woman, broadly wagging her tail in response. Meg joined as well, extending her hand.

"Hello, nice to meet you. My name is Meg Flynn and this is Goldie."

"Hello Meg, my pleasure to make your acquaintance. And hello to you, Goldie. I have a retriever named Missy who could be your twin. Would you two care to walk together?"

Unsure of the distance and pace of Leigh's routine, Meg hesitated. The trim woman's appearance and garb marked her as a walker of serious intent. Meg and Goldie were just getting back on track with a resolve to start out easy. None-the-less, Meg decided to accept Leigh's invitation, hoping it wouldn't evolve into a competitive challenge.

Continuing in the direction that they had started, Leigh launched into an easy patter that matched her stride. "So, tell me, do you live on Sandrock or are you a distance walker on a longer route?"

"No, we live on the road. Just moved in a few weeks ago actually."

Before Meg could elaborate, Leigh excitedly responded." Oh, I know who you are. You're the woman who bought Crown Hill. You're a divorcee, right? No children. From out of town, as I recall. Well, welcome to Eden and to Sandrock Road. And please accept my apology for not yet bringing you a cake or a meal or something to welcome you properly."

Meg's immediate thoughts were that this woman possessed a lot of information about her. At the same time Jake Kelly's small-town admonishments echoed through her mind. Meg knew that she needed to lower her defenses if she was ever going to experience the heart-mending new life of which she dreamed.

"Thank you for your kind welcome Leigh, and please don't think twice about not meeting before now. I've been settling in kind of quietly." That was it. That was all she had. Meg had no idea where to go with this conversation. Fortunately Leigh Wilson was an expert at such chatter.

"Well, still and all, I should have at least stopped by to say hello, and we're going to do something about that this morning. When we're done with our walk, we're going to sit on my terrace and enjoy a cup of tea. That way we can get on track as good neighbors. Goldie and Missy can meet as well and play in the yard while we visit. And I won't take no for an answer!"

Meg furtively searched her mind for reasons to refuse the command appearance. Yet try as she might, there were none. Cautiously, she settled into the idea and accepted Leigh's invitation.

After several miles of hills and dales, the women agreed to reverse and work their way back to their meeting point. As they reached the Wilson's driveway and approached Leigh's house, Meg was impressed with the architecture of the stately residence. The Georgian-style home appeared considerably more gracious than most along the road, causing Meg to wonder about its past.

"Leigh, if you don't mind my asking, what is the history of your home? It's gorgeous, but also seems a bit fancier that the rest on Sandrock; almost more city than country."

"You're spot on with your observation, Meg. This house was the first to exist on the road, built around 1851, I believe, by Cyrus Kulp. Cyrus was a wealthy businessman who made his fortune by brokering and delivering food and provisions produced in Eden to consumers between here and Buffalo. His wealth increased with the advent of train transportation, furthering his reach to urban areas as far as Rochester to the east and Erie, Pennsylvania to the west."

Meg found the information fascinating, as learning about Crown Hill's history had encouraged her interest in such details. She wondered if there were noteworthy connections between the two neighboring homes and their previous owners. She was about to inquire about such possibilities when Leigh opened her backyard gate and a whirling dervish of gold fur spun into their midst.

"Ok Missy, take it easy." Leigh's admonishment was useless. The effervescent retriever swarmed Meg and Goldie in unabashed welcome. To her credit, Goldie accepted the animated greeting with gentle reserve.

"Now see here Missy, you have to let Goldie get used to you. I'm sorry Meg. She just loves playing with other dogs. Why don't you and Goldie relax here on the terrace while I go in and brew a nice pot of herbal tea? I'll take Missy with me and hopefully she will settle down a bit--be better behaved when we return."

"That's fine, whatever is easy," Meg replied as she kept a close eye on the canine summit playing out around her.

Within minutes, Leigh returned with a lovely tray of tea and muffins, and a much calmer dog. This time, Missy approached her visitors respectfully, allowing Goldie time and space to deal with the standard sniffing and posturing required of canine alliances. By the time Leigh served Meg her tea, the two dogs were comfortably strolling shoulder-to-shoulder along the fenced boundaries of the terrace.

"You know Meg, while I was inside I gave more thought to your question about my house. I don't know everything about it, but I do know a few stories relative to Crown Hill."

Leigh's words caused an odd sensation within Meg. It wasn't a red spread. It felt more like some kind of intuitive recognition, almost as if she knew what Leigh was about to share. Trying to shake off the odd feeling, Meg responded, "I would imagine the closeness of the two houses connected them in many ways over the years."

"Exactly. And from everything I know, those in residence in the two houses have always been neighborly. Actually this house was the first to be built, with your house constructed several years later. Crown Hill was originally designed as a small cabin for a man who worked for Cyrus Kulp. Cyrus wanted someone close by so that everything always ran smoothly on his property. Hiring and housing a farm manager was the easiest way to achieve his goal. After Cyrus' death, his house passed to other owners. His property was divided and sold, and Crown Hill became its own domain."

Meg thoughtfully sipped her tea before responding. "Kathryn Winston was the realtor who sold me Crown Hill. She told me that three books have been written on the history of Eden and that my home is featured in one of them. Do you know if your house is written about as well?"

"Yes, it is noted in book one, when Cyrus built it and then in book two, some thirty years later, when a man named Frederick Sandrock assumed ownership, around 1882 as I recall."

"Frederick Sandrock?" The name surprised Meg.

"Yes," Leigh replied. "And yes, the road is named after him. He was quite a prominent man in this area. He was a retired business owner who came to Eden to become a gentleman farmer. He also served as the town judge for three decades. From all stories, he ruled with an iron hand, bringing great order to Eden as it advanced from a rural wilderness to a respectable community."

The time frame Leigh spoke of piqued Meg's interest. "So if this Sandrock fellow was here in the 1880's, that was the same time that Mary and Owen Southwick lived at Crown Hill. Do you know anything of their relationship, if they had one?"

"Actually, I do know a bit about that. Mary was close to the extended family of Frederick Sandrock. Frederick's brother William, his brother's wife Elizabeth, and their children lived here with him. From what I know, Mary and Elizabeth, bonded over their shared love of gardening."

So far, Leigh's information was quite innocent. Perhaps the odd sensation Meg continued to feel was more a side effect of their brisk walk, than anything else.

"It's funny though Meg, now that you mention it, I actually know more about your home from my husband's parents than any other source. My in-laws lived in this house before we did and they often told us stories about their neighbor across the road, a woman by the name of Dorothy George. From what they said, Dorothy enjoyed a strong friendship with the people who owned Crown Hill in the early 1900's. If I recall properly, their name was Randall.

Tales of the twentieth century were much less compelling to Meg, as the era was far removed from Mary Southwick's lifetime. Try as she might to remain engaged, Meg found herself mentally drifting from Leigh's words.

"The Randalls were a family from Buffalo, a lawyer, his wife, and their two daughters, who spent only summers here in Eden. According to my in-laws, Dorothy told stories about this lawyer--Edward, I believe--being deeply involved in the world of spiritualism. She said that he engaged in a lot of mystical activities, you know séances and things like that.

She also told my in-laws that she knew first hand such goings-on happened at Crown Hill and that they were connected to a long-running rumor about Mary Southwick's ghost haunting the old farmhouse."

Bingo! Meg became fully engaged, as the information Leigh shared jolted her brain. Suddenly the odd dreams and unusual happenings in her home were coming into focus. If Mary Southwick had really haunted Crown Hill only 80 years earlier, could it be that some type of spiritual connection was still in force? Meg considered the possibility as Leigh continued.

"The really interesting story that Dorothy often shared with my in-laws involved English mystery writer, Sir Arthur Conan Doyle. She said that Sir Conan Doyle joined with Edward Randall in spiritual activities at Crown Hill. She was actually friends with a housekeeper for the Randall's who witnessed such things."

The odd sensation in Meg's body was now fully bloomed. Her ears were ringing, her eyes were sparkling and her stomach felt ready to launch the tea and muffin she had just consumed. Yet her mind was fully engrossed in Leigh's story and demanded more. "So Leigh, have you any knowledge of, or experience with the supposed ghost of Mary Southwick in my home?"

With a laugh, Leigh responded, "Actually I have never heard anyone talk about a ghost in your house since we have lived here, and that's better than thirty years. So, no, you couldn't prove any of that by me. Why do you ask? Have you ever seen Mary Southwick's ghost?"

Leigh asked the question in a joking tone, but the conversation didn't feel humorous to Meg. At this point, she had heard all of the Crown Hill history she could manage. She needed to get home, by herself, to process all of this new information.

"As far as I know, ghosts are nowhere around Crown Hill, Leigh. And you are welcome to come by anytime to see for yourself. Right now though, I really must get home and attend to some of the chores on my list. Still so much to get settled, as I'm sure you understand."

As the two women rose, Leigh reached out to Meg with a neighborly hug. The unexpected kindness brought a warmth to Meg's heart that she was beginning to identify as belonging, to a town, to a neighborhood, to people who care. Gently returning the embrace, Meg silently thanked Jake for setting her straight about small town life.

"Meg I hope that you will stop by often. And please join me, if you'd like, for walks. It would be nice to have your company. I'm usually on the road around 8 am."

"Thanks, Leigh. I'm sure that we will enjoy many walks to come." With that, Meg set off for Crown Hill, realizing, with an increasing sense, that her life there had a purpose.

"Oh Meg, just one more thing," Leigh called out, stopping Meg and Goldie midway in the Wilson's winding drive.

"You might want to call Clara Johnson and talk to her about your house. Her mother was a friend of Dorothy George and Clara grew up with Dorothy's daughter, Flordie. I'm guessing that she knows more about that story of Sir Arthur Conan Doyle and Mary Southwick's ghost. I'm quite sure that her number is listed in the Eden phone directory."

"Thank you Leigh, I will."

That was twice in the last twenty-four hours that Meg had been told to reach out to Clara Johnson. Again, she knew the name, but could not recall why. She kept rolling Clara through her mind as she and Goldie made their way along the half-mile walk to Crown Hill. It was only as they passed under the arbor and became immersed in its sweet rose scent that Meg finally put a face to the name.

Clara Johnson. That sweet little woman in the diner, who told me to call her when I was ready.

With Meg's return, the air within me became energized. Although she looked the same and acted with no unusual purpose, something had changed within Meg, and it was a change directly impacting me.

Mary and I were settled in the quietude of the morning as Meg's energy swirled around us.

"Mary do you feel that? "

"Yes Crown Hill, I have sensed the infusion of energy since Meg's return. Is it like anything you have known before?"

"There have been moments of extreme energy and emotions…in those early days when you haunted within me and, of course, when Owen isolated us both from Rose. But even the most impactful of those did not measure up to the intensity that is now present within Meg."

"It would seem that there is some kind of power now accompanying her. Do you think it possible that she has become possessed?"

The thought of another life force invading my being was disturbing. While many spirits had passed through me, only one other than Mary had ever impacted me with the power that I was feeling.

"Owen."

"No. It cannot be," Mary answered in despairing tones. "We have taken such care with Meg. And truly, Crown Hill, stop and feel this power churning through you. It has not the evil that accompanies Owen and those like him."

Carefully assessing all that I was feeling, I guardedly became of the same mind. Whatever was happening within me did not carry the darkness of evil.

"It is true, Mary. I do not feel Owen's wicked force as I have other times when he was near. It's more that I dread his return and am always in anxious wait."

"I understand Dearest, as I too balance on a fine line of trepidation where Owen is concerned. But if we are agreed that this power accompanying Meg is not a force of evil, then what? Or who?"

The answer to Mary's wonder became clear as Meg picked up the telephone and placed a call. "Hello, this is Meg Flynn. I'm trying to reach Clara Johnson."

Meg was reaching out to a woman who could reveal much of the life that had transpired within me, as well as Mary's enduring presence.

Instinctively, both Mary and I understood this evolution as part of all that was necessary to deliver Mary's spirit to the light.

"Sweet Mary, let us return to the quiet of the morning we were sharing and enjoy our moments together. "

"Indeed, dear friend. Let us be still and connected so that we will be able to transcend all that is about to come. "

In a bittersweet blending of joy and sorrow, Mary and I became protectively encircled in our love...leaving aside all conscious care.

CHAPTER FOURTEEN

Meg hung up the phone feeling unsettled, although not quite sure why. She definitely wanted to talk to Clara Johnson, but the fact that the kindly woman was not immediately available was frustrating--more frustrating than it should have been.

At the same time, Meg felt energized with an oddly extreme anticipation. It was rather like waiting for Santa Claus and a dreaded report card, all at the same time.

"This is crazy, Goldie. What's happening to us?"

The sensitive Golden Retriever nosed her way under Meg's hand, encouraging some behind-the-ear strokes. The routine of gentle affection was calming to Meg, allowing a space in which she could settle her brain. One thing was certain. She needed to refocus her energies.

"Ok good girl. It's time we got serious about clipping those rhododendrons. Let's go."

Meg and Goldie headed straight for the barn, this time giving no more than a glance to the nearby woodshed. Meg approached the heavy barn door, dug her heels into the graveled walkway, and pulled the iron forged handle with all of her might. The rusted metal track allowed the door to roll open only an inch. Remembering that Brady had been the last one in the barn, Meg realized that his strength probably outweighed hers in sliding the door closed. Refusing to be deterred, Meg repeated the door pulling process over and again until there was an opening wide enough to squeeze through.

Once inside, Meg heard the same primal growling that had launched her backwards from the woodshed a week earlier. The wiser woman's response this time was to forge ahead, peering into the closed stall where the wooden crate of cat and kittens was safely tucked. Brady had created a secure nest of straw into which he burrowed the crate, allowing the mother to come and go while safeguarding the babies. Clearly momma was policing the mice population of the barn, as all 6 felines appeared healthy and well. Unlike her previous experience with this family of cats, Meg found the present scene to be quite heartwarming.

As she lingered, Goldie whined in protest at the barn door, unable to push her way through the constricted opening. "I'll be right out Goldie, just hang on."

About to walk away, Meg noticed increased movement in the stall on the part of the kittens. They were clearly becoming more mobile, much to their mother's dismay. Meg giggled, watching the babies collectively explore the world beyond their crated boundaries. Momma struggled to keep them together, grabbing them individually by the scruff of the neck and dragging them back to the nest, a parental growl of admonishment dispensed to each one.

It was an endless routine that provided Meg a twinge of pleasure. "A little payback there momma? Maybe next time you won't be quite so worried about protecting them!"

"Oh, I wouldn't count on that too much."

The unexpected voice startled Meg into a shriek as she jumped back from the stall.

"I'm so sorry Meg. I didn't mean to scare you." Brady threw back the barn door and was by her side before she could blink. The bad news for Meg, other than once again acting like a screaming mimi around this guy, was that she found him just as attractive as the last time they were together. How was she ever going to handle her strong emotions related to Brady Callahan?

In spite of Goldie swarming Brady's sturdy thighs, his attention remained focused solely on Meg. "You ok? I'm really sorry. I guess I was just so engaged in watching you watch those kittens that my words popped out without realizing they might startle you."

Desperate to appear cool and in control, Meg waved off Brady with a carefree laugh. "No big deal. I'm easy to scare, been that way all my life. Anyway, how are you? And what brings you here today?"

"I'm well, thanks. I was passing by on my way home from the Stockman's down the road. Do you know Justin? He owns a nice little horse ranch about a half-mile from you. He doesn't farm his land, so we have an agreement that I bail his hay and take it for my animals, minus what he needs for his two horses. I keep all the bails at my place and bring him a load every month. It's a bit of work, but Justin and I grew up together and it's always good to spend time with him. I expect our hay deal is as much an excuse to hang out as anything. Anyhow, I saw your car in the driveway and thought I would stop and see how you girls are doing."

All the while Brady spoke, Goldie did her best to garner his attention. Her persistence finally paid off as Brady bent to her level. "Yes, I'm very happy to see you too Goldie!"

Again, Mr. Nice Guy, Meg thought. *Was there anything about Brady that was annoying, rude or mean?* Meg had never been around a man as seemingly goodhearted. She kept waiting for his bad side to surface. At the same time, she secretly hoped that he was exactly as he appeared.

"So are you spending a lot of time down here with the kittens?

Meg laughed in response. "Not exactly. This is the first time I've been down here since you left. It's been a busy week for me. But thanks for coming along and opening the door. I could hardly budge that thing. Must be you slammed it shut when you put momma and her kittens in here."

"Nah, it just needs some oil on the track and then it needs to be used. Have you got any oil handy? I'll be glad to get it working for you."

Meg hated that about Brady Callahan. Every time he was around she ended up feeling like a helpless woman. And she wasn't, at least not completely. She just needed a little support here and there, like anyone. Or so she tried to convince herself as she rummaged through her meager collection of tools and equipment that she'd unceremoniously dumped in the barn hallway on moving day.

"Hmmm, doesn't look like I have any oil. If you would just show me where it goes on the track, I'm sure I could do it myself. After all, it's not rocket science."

Brady looked at Meg with a mix of amusement and compassion, then made her an offer he hoped she wouldn't refuse. "Tell you what. I've got a can of oil up in the toolbox in my truck. You go get a ladder and we'll oil the door track together. That way you'll know exactly how to do it yourself."

"Great idea Mr. White Knight, but I don't own a ladder." *Ugh! There it was again, her sassy mouth. Was there any chance that she could just say thank you to this poor guy who was only trying to be nice?* Waiting for Brady to call her, "rude," or to walk out on her, Meg moved toward Goldie for moral support.

"Funny, my wife used to call me her knight in shining armor. Not exactly in the tone that you just used Ms. Flynn, but your words reminded me. I hadn't thought of that in years.

"Oh Brady, I am so sorry. Obviously I didn't know that what I was saying would bring up memories of your wife. Truly, I'm an idiot and you should probably leave now and just stay away. I would completely understand and not blame you in the least."

"First of all Meg, there's not much you could say that wouldn't remind me of Julieann or Colin, and that's ok. They are a part of me forever, but they are also part of my past. I have to find ways to move on. It's time. And as for staying away from you, I am not easily dissuaded when I find something, or someone, I like. And Meg Flynn, I definitely like you."

As he finished the sentence, Brady stepped closer to Meg and slowly matched his lips to hers. It was the perfect first kiss, tender, with a strong edge of passion that let Meg know this man was determined.

As he stepped back, Meg felt as if a favored blanket was being taken away. Oh how she longed for the comfort of Brady's body, to experience the full promise of that kiss.

"Tell you what. I'll pull my truck down to the barn and we can stand on the tailgate to reach the door track. Then when we're done with the door, I have something to ask you. Come on Goldie, let's go get the truck."

With that, Meg was left standing alone in the barn hallway, breathless and dazed.

Oh Lord, what are you getting me into? Though raised in the faith, Meg was far from a devout Catholic. Yet she prayed, and believed in the power of prayer. It was that belief that got her through some of the darkest nights of her marriage to Cal, and what helped her take the first steps to her new life. Still, no matter how much she had prayed for someone to come into her world and love her truly, the promise of that man standing before her in the person of Brady Callahan was unbelievable. Almost unmanageable.

The sound of the diesel truck nearing the barn forced Meg to refocus. *Ok, it was just a kiss. It's not like the guy put a ring on your finger, for goodness' sake.* Moving to the barn door, Meg issued a self-directive. *Just relax and be natural…whatever that means,* she chided in self-mockery.

Dropping the tailgate, Brady turned to Meg and offered a hand up. "Thanks. I can get there on my own," she said, firmly planting one foot on the tailgate and pushing off from the ground with the other.

Hopping up next to her with Goldie close behind, Brady pulled a small can of oil from his back pocket. "Ok, now if you take a look at the door, you can see that it rides on a wheel that slides on this metal track."

Meg needed to move closer to Brady in order to view the door's mechanics. However, she was pretty sure that she didn't need to be within touching distance of the appealing man, as long as the memory of that kiss lingered.

"Uh, Ms. Flynn, if you want to learn about fixing your barn door, you're going to have to get close enough to work on it." Brady taunted her with a knowing grin as he beckoned with an outstretched hand.

"I can see it from here and I'm not totally unfamiliar with such doors. I understand what you're talking about, so just go ahead and oil the track." Meg wasn't going to be undone by Brady Callahan's charm.

"Suit yourself." Brady turned his attention to the door track. After liberally applying the oil, he hopped down from the truck and began working the door back and forth across the metal guide rail. Within seconds, it was gliding like a sharpened skate on ice.

Meg was grateful, and impressed. She was also thinking about the list of farm repairs looming on her kitchen bulletin board. No doubt Brady could handle every one of them.

"Ok, the only thing you have to careful about is to not slide the door too fast and hard. It moves easily now and if you put too much muscle into opening it, it could come off the track."

Meg felt a sense of embarrassment as Brady continued to guide her through the repair project. She really was being ridiculous in not standing next to the man while he was trying to teach her. To obliterate her girlish actions, Meg jumped out of the truck, landing close to Brady. The electricity between them was immediately re-established like a jolt from a faulty wire. However, their connection was tempered by the airborne arrival of Goldie from the truck bed onto the ground between them.

Brady knelt and wrapped his arms around the tail-wagging dog. "Hey Goldie, what's up girl? Are you helping fix the door? Such a good girl."

To her shock, Meg realized that she somehow resented Goldie for stealing Brady's attention.

Oh for heaven's sake, stop! You are absolutely wound up over a two-second kiss that probably was no big deal to this guy. Settle down and get a grip, would you!

"Thank you for fixing the door." Meg tried to get back into a comfortable rhythm with Brady. "I appreciate your help, as obviously I am not prepared with the proper tools or the knowledge for such repairs. But now at least I know how to take care of it myself, once I get better organized."

Trying some humor to lighten the moment, Meg added, "Also, I'll do my best not to throw the door off the track with my Wonder Woman muscles!"

Grinning in response, Brady replied. "Not a problem, Meg I'm happy to help. And if other things come up around here that you can't manage or don't know how to fix, just give me a call."

"That's a great offer Mr. Callahan, or would be, if I had your phone number!" This time, Meg's sass provided her a certain sense of security. *Nothing like a protective wall of smart retorts,* she thought to herself.

"Is that so, Ms. Flynn? Well, we can fix that right here and now." Grabbing a pen and paper from the console of his truck, Brady scribbled away and then ripped the sheet of paper from the pad.

"Here is my phone number with my name as well, just in case you forget who I am again." Brady had his own style of sassiness that he liked to share. It had just been a long time since his heart had felt playful.

"And now I need to get back home. Still have a few chores to tend to before I call it a night. But I have something I'd like to ask you first, Meg, before I leave.

Unsure whether to be nervous or excited, Meg simply smiled and nodded. Going mute was akin to being sassy in her arsenal of self defense mechanisms.

"I'm sure you know that Monday is the 4th of July. I was wondering, if you don't have plans already, if you would like to picnic together?"

Images of fried chicken and red checked tablecloths filtered through Meg's mind. An invitation to a summer picnic was something she had not received in years and she was pretty sure that her heart had skipped a beat as Brady asked.

"How nice, Brady, thank you. Actually, I had no idea that Monday was the 4th. I guess I've been too wrapped up in getting settled and starting my job. So where would this picnic be, exactly, and would it involve other picnickers?"

Brady chuckled at the question. "Well I kinda thought that we could figure that out, that is if you say yes."

Meg wasn't sure that she was ready to debut at some big holiday picnic on Brady Callahan's arm, but she also knew that she didn't want to refuse his invitation.

"I'd like to picnic with you on Monday, Brady, but to be truthful, I'm not quite ready for a public outing with a lot of people. I'm still getting settled in Eden and trying to figure out how a small town operates. It may sound silly, but I'm just not used to people being involved in everyone's lives, as seems to happen around here. "

A broad grin broke across Brady's tanned face, firing his eyes into an intense blue glow. Meg found their color almost iridescent and their pull on her heart quite powerful.

"Meg, I was born and raised in Eden and sometimes I can't figure out the folks who live here. And I totally agree, I don't need an outing with a lot of people either. So how about we plan a nice picnic dinner and enjoy it here on your farm, or at my place if you like. Then, if we want, we can go into town at dusk and watch the fireworks at the Legion field. They set them off there every year and the whole town goes, but we can park my truck in a far corner of the Legion lot and watch the fireworks from there. That way we don't have to talk to anyone and hopefully no one will start talking about us."

"That sounds pretty perfect to me," Meg replied with a gentle flirtation.

"Good, because I think you're pretty perfect, Margaret Rose Flynn."

Such a sappy line. And who ever called her by her full name but her mother? While her mind was logically dissecting Brady's words, her heart was completely adrift in their sweetness. Again Brady moved to her and connected their lips, this time with more power and passion. Once. Then again. It was Meg who finally stepped back and disconnected their magnetic field of attraction.

"Didn't you say you had work to do at home. Mr. Callahan?" Meg delivered the question teasingly, but with an awareness that she needed to get away from this man before she abandoned the small shred of self-control keeping her clothed and vertical.

Brady winked and gently caressed her cheek. "I did indeed, Ms. Flynn. That's what I said. But there are times when work can wait."

"Oh no you don't Brady Callahan. You're out of here. Go home. Go on. Git!"

The playfulness in Meg's tone caused Goldie to bark in chorus. As she bounced between them, Brady and Meg shared a glance of newly realized emotions. It was a moment that both understood as rare and deserving of protection.

"Alright ladies, I'll go. But we at least need to talk tomorrow about our picnic. How about I give you a call, once I'm done with chores and church."

Ah yes, the perfect man and his perfect Sunday, Meg thought.

"Talking tomorrow would be great. By then we should both have an idea of what foods we want to make. I have a pretty awesome fried chicken recipe that isn't really fried but tastes like it, so it's yummy and healthy too."

"What foods we both want to make? You're expecting me to cook, Meg? Why do you think I asked you to picnic? I'm expecting you to layout the whole deal…fried chicken, potato salad and, of course, homemade pie!"

Brady lost the end of his menu description in good-natured laughter. The happiness regenerating in his heart was invigorating. Sorrow had been his life pattern for so long that Brady believed it was all he would ever know. Now, without forethought or plan, he was becoming involved with this beautiful woman who was reminding his heart how to once again smile.

"I'm sorry Mr. Callahan, but where I was raised, the one who does the inviting does the cooking. So perhaps I'll just leave all the food to your doing." Meg was not about to let this guy think that he could kiss his way into home-cooked meals.

"You know what, you're absolutely right Meg. I did do the inviting, so I will take care of the picnic. All you have to do is show up and enjoy. There, done. Now I have to get home. I'll talk to you tomorrow about a time and place. Bye Goldie girl." And with a wink, Brady jumped in his truck and drove away before Meg could manage any kind of sassy retort.

The idea of Brady taking full responsibility for the picnic intrigued Meg as she and Goldie strolled from the barn to the house. It felt odd, but also satisfying. Meg had never been around a man who wanted to cook and care for her. "I could get used to this Goldie. This might be all right."

The sound of her ringing telephone prompted Meg to make a quick dash into the kitchen and answer the unknown caller.

"Hello."

"May I speak to Meg Flynn, please?"

"This is she."

"Hello Meg. It's Clara Johnson. I've been waiting for your call."

Mary began Meg's dream again within the same setting, in the living room by the fireplace. She made sure that Meg was comfortably settled, surrounded by a loving sense of those in life who had cared for her. Then gently, from among those gathered, Mary approached.

"Meg, it is wonderful that you have come. Crown Hill and I have waited to welcome you for such a long time. Now that you are here, know that your life will be surrounded by beauty and love each day, as Crown Hill wraps its protective embrace around you."

As I witnessed Mary approach Meg in her dreams, I wondered of this woman's character and strength. Dealing with the spiritual essence of a home was challenging for any soul. Only those with the unique willingness to believe in a world beyond their own could engage. Of those, only individuals of the greatest heart could withstand and ultimately connect. As I observed Mary reach out to as Meg, I wondered if she was one of the brave-hearted?

"Meg, it is my deepest hope that we can become one in spirit, as we have much in common. I too once lived in this wondrous home and experienced the joy of creating a safe haven within each room and every space. However, my time here was under the control of a man possessed with an angry and violent nature. It was the only true sadness to intrude into my life at Crown Hill. It was also the cause of my death and the reason why I am here in this place, with you now. A violent end to my life wounded my spirit so deeply that I have been trapped here on earth ever since, where I do not belong, nor wish to remain. Meg, I know that you can understand the circumstance of my life that led me to this place, as you have lived the same. It is that common connection, along with your inner strength and true heart, that I believe provide you the power and ability to help release my spirit."

Meg responded with a restlessness in the downy comfort of her bed. Moving to soothe her, I encouraged the gentle night breeze to follow the moonlight streaming into her room. The embrace of the warming air restored a peaceful comfort to Meg's sleep. Wanting to ensure her continued tranquility, I reached out to Mary.

"Proceed with gentle care, dear friend. Meg has only been with us for a short time. Yes, she possesses the strength you seek, but she also has her own wounds to heal. You cannot ask greatly of her before she is able or ready."

"Indeed, Crown Hill, I know your words to be true. I know that a soul's strength can be diminished in the healing process. Yet I can also feel the power of Meg's nature and I trust that the universe has brought us together at this time for a true purpose. In support of both of our spirits, please stay close and comfort Meg as I continue."

Honoring her request, I gathered my comforting powers around Meg as Mary once again approached in her dream.

"Meg, have no fear of me, or of those who appear around me. None mean you any harm. As for me, I humbly ask of your powerful strength and energy to heal my soul. I know that you understand my being and I have strong faith that as you come to realize our shared life in Crown Hill, you will help our spirits touch and eternally connect."

Mary's passionate thoughts reached Meg as she slept. In the depth of her dream, it was clear that Meg connected with Mary's pain, as well as in her devotion to my being. She showed no fear, no hesitation, only a strong desire to become a part of Mary and allow the same in return. Finally, Mary released the sleeping woman from the dream and into a restful state.

"Crown Hill, it is enough. I have done all that I can do. I have given Meg a true understanding of our shared spirits and she has responded with an open heart. I am hopeful that she will remain connected and stay strong, no matter how unsettled our spiritual journey may become."

"That is my hope as well Dearest, and I am grateful that Meg appears willing. Now, let us leave her, allow for the needed sleep to foster within her spirit the strength and resolve she will need. As for you and I, let us settle into the soft glow of the moonlight and await the new day with hopeful hearts."

As Mary and I joined together, I left Meg with the soft sounds of cicadas making love in the velvet summer night…and the sweet scent of her favored roses enveloping her.

CHAPTER FIFTEEN

In the blaze of the morning sun, Meg felt more exhausted than when she had climbed into bed the night before. Once again, she hadn't slept well and a groggy feeling laid claim to her mind and body. Checking Big Ben, the clock showed morning was well underway at 8:48 am.

What is up with me? I haven't slept this late since I was in high school. Yet the hour in no way inspired the sleepy woman to action. Instead, Meg rolled over into a comforting snuggle and closed her eyes. Half-heartedly she tried to imagine a reason to "rise and shine," as her mother used to say.

As her eyelids met, Meg experienced a vague memory of dreams from her restless night. Within the recall she realized a familiarity. She was once again seated in a chair in her living room with various people around her. Yet this time, something was different. This time, someone unknown but indefinably familiar approached her and spoke

Who was this person? No one from her family, no one she remembered from growing up or from her married life. Someone from Eden? So far, she hadn't met that many people. There was Brady, Jake, Kathryn, Jethro Tull, Frankie-B the egg guy, the sweet little lady at the diner--what was her name--oh yeah, Clara Johnson.

Clara Johnson!

The thought of the woman propelled Meg directly out of bed. Shedding her pj's and ducking under the shower she tried not to feel panicked. Her phone conversation with Clara the previous evening had been interesting, a bit on the creepy side, but interesting. In the end, the two women agreed to lunch at Crown Hill, Sunday at noon.

Although Meg was still a bit foggy, she was fully aware that the day was Sunday and it was but a few hours from noon. Clara Johnson would soon be standing on her doorstep.

Throwing on a sleeveless pink blouse, thankfully clean and ironed, Meg added a pair of white linen slacks and some comfy pink flats. Grabbing a cotton eyelet sweater, she called out to Goldie to head to the kitchen.

Swirling through the house, Meg created a menu using items from the freezer, the refrigerator and the pantry. She found ingredients to whip together her favored pecan apple chicken salad using spinach greens for a base. Next she blended a batch of her homemade orange poppy seed dressing. She decided to complement the main course with muffins from Kathryn Winston's gift basket. Meg knew there was a reason she put those baked goods in the freezer instead of eating them right away.

Finally, she brewed a pitcher of blueberry lemon iced tea and layered together fresh strawberries and ice cream for a perfect summer dessert. Twenty minutes later, Meg's luncheon menu was ready and waiting.

Next she moved to preparing the table. The attentive hostess began setting places in the dining room, but a soft summer breeze from the adjoining porch persuaded her otherwise. Grabbing a card table from the pantry Meg placed it on the porch, rearranging two white wicker chairs for seating. The addition of a sheer white tablecloth accented with delicately embroidered flowers furthered her garden luncheon theme. To enhance the setting, Meg partnered a cobalt blue canning jar with wild orange tiger lilies and queen ann's lace for a centerpiece accent.

At each place, Meg carefully fanned two of her great grandmother's white linen napkins atop blue chintz, ruffled placements. Next, she layered place settings of her mother's delicate rose china and rose silverware complimented by gracefully tall azure goblets. Stepping back, she deemed her alfresco setting, *Home and Garden* gorgeous.

Meg felt the need to pinch herself, to understand that the vision before her was not some kind of dream. It was almost beyond her strongest imaginings that Crown Hill and all of its beauty was a reality, truly her home. She also was realizing a sense of welcome within her heart, a joy over the prospect of a visitor coming to Crown Hill. Clearly the delightful lunch with Kathryn Winston had lightened Meg's concerns over allowing people into her home and her life.

Returning to the kitchen, Meg checked the clock. Just short of 11 am; an hour to spare. With everything in good order, Meg poured herself a glass of iced tea and was about to head out for a swing on the porch when the telephone intervened.

How life had changed in just a few short weeks, Meg mused. A ringing phone was becoming a normal part of her world again. She had to admit that it felt good.

"Good morning."

"Good morning to you Ms. Flynn. How are you and Goldie this beautiful June day?"

The sound of Brady's voice delivered a pleasurable shiver through Meg's body. *Good thing he's on the other end of this phone and not standing beside me*, Meg thought in embarrassed delight. Catching her breath and trying to control her excitement, she responded. "I'm good, thank you Mr. Callahan. Have you been to church and finished your chores already?"

"I have in fact, although my father caught me on the way out of church. He's got a bad gasket on one of the tractors and needs a hand fixing it. I'm actually headed over there in a few minutes. Figure if I play my cards right, my mother will feed me Sunday dinner as well."

Mindful that playfulness was part of their burgeoning friendship, Meg offered a quick retort. "Oh really, your mother cooking for you? After all your bragging last night about making the food for our picnic, I just assumed you took care of all the meals, Mr. Master Chef!"

"Sharp-witted even on a Sunday morning, eh, Margaret Rose? Well, if you must know, I find no shame in admitting that I encourage my mother to feed me whenever she pleases. She's a great cook and as a bonus, she always sends me home with leftovers. As for our picnic, I'm no master chef, as you suggest, but I have a few dishes that I've kind of perfected. Actually, I enjoy being in the kitchen. I like taking foods that I've grown and blending them into meals that taste good." With an easy laugh, Brady added, "Besides, being on my own, it's pretty much cook or starve."

The reference to his solitary lifestyle caught Meg off guard. The words she next spoke were delivered straight from her heart. "Brady, I am truly glad that we have met. You are a very special person and I'm looking forward to spending the 4th of July together."

It was more than she really wanted to reveal to this man, still a stranger in so many ways. Yet Meg was relying on her gut instinct in concert with her heart, and both were leading her straight to Brady Callahan.

"Well, I am honored. An actual compliment from the usually sassy Ms. Flynn. I'll be walking around with a smile on my face all day."

"Alright Brady Callahan, if you're going to make fun of me when I try to be sincere, then I'm not going to say nice things to you ever again."

"Come on Meg, you know I'm just teasing. Honestly, I am glad that you told me, as I feel the same. Thinking about spending the 4th of July together makes me happy and, as I shared with you on your porch last week, I've not been happy in a very long time."

The raw emotion accompanying Brady's words touched Meg in a way that she had rarely experienced. Again she found herself wondering when this good-hearted person was going to morph into the callous type of men she had known most of her life. At the same time, like a child waiting for Christmas, Meg wanted with all of her heart to believe.

"I'm going to say goodbye now Miss Meg, before you decide to take back all of your sweet words. I'll give you a call later, if that's ok, after dinner. Then we can talk about our plans for tomorrow."

Meg wanted to tell Brady that he couldn't hang up, unless it meant that he was coming directly to Crown Hill to be with her. But she knew that she needed to keep her feelings in check. Too fast and too soon was not the way for true hearts to connect. Plus, Clara Johnson would be at her door in a matter of minutes

"Actually it would be nice to chat later. And I have to go as well. Clara Johnson is coming for lunch today. Do you know Clara?"

Brady's answer to her question was immediate. "Everyone in town knows Clara. She's older than the hills and been a part of all that's gone on in Eden for as long as I can remember."

"Well, I met her on my first day in town at The Four Corners Cafe," Meg recalled. "I don't really know her, but I decided to invite her for lunch after talking to my neighbor, Leigh Wilson. Leigh suggested that Clara would know details about the history of my home. I'm not sure how or what this lady knows, but I'm interested in finding out."

Brady responded with a bit more information. "Like I said, Clara's been around forever and basically knows everything about everybody. Plus she does this thing. She tells people about their lives. I don't know exactly what it's all about or how it works. I do know a lot of people swear on the Bible that she's told them something from their past that they never knew, or things that are going to happen that eventually come to be."

Brady's words struck a chord, reminding Meg of her first meeting with Clara and the sweet woman's suggestion to call when she was, *"ready."* Meg remembered thinking the woman's words were odd at the time and felt more so now, after listening to Brady.

"To be honest Brady, when I talked to her on the phone last night she creeped me out a bit. When I explained why I was calling, she said that she already knew why and had been waiting for me. I really didn't know what to say to that."

Before Brady could respond, there was a knock on Meg's door, accompanied by an engaging voice calling her name. "Hello, Meg dear. It's Clara Johnson."

"Oh Brady, I've got to go. Clara is here already. Talk to you later, ok?"

Following quick goodbyes, Meg hung up the phone and headed to the back door. There, already in place stood Goldie, welcoming Clara with tail-wagging barks

"Hello Clara. It's so good of you to come." Gently taking ahold of Goldie's collar, Meg opened the door with her free hand, making room for the petite, older woman to enter.

"Please come in. This is Goldie. She's a love and won't hurt you. She just believes that she is the official greeter here at Crown Hill and is obviously devoted to her job!"

"My, my. Well as the official greeter, I must say hello to you first, Goldie. You are a beautiful girl and a very welcoming hostess." Bestowing a few soft pats on Goldie's head, Clara turned her attention to Meg.

"It's so nice to see you Meg. Thank you for inviting me to lunch today. I hope you don't mind that I'm a bit early. It's been many years since I have been to Crown Hill and I was most eager to return."

Meg immediately became aware of a purple aura materializing around Clara. *Spirituality, how interesting,* Meg thought, especially in light of all that had Brady told her. She also found herself wondering how the afternoon with this intriguing woman would evolve.

"Let's go out to the porch, Clara. I have our lunch all ready."

Meg set plates of chicken salad and a basket of muffins on her garden table, along with the tall clear pitcher of iced tea. Within minutes, the two women were comfortably settled into their wicker seats, engaged in delicious conversation about food and recipes, flowers and gardens, pets they had owned and loved and random stories about life. As midafternoon approached and the women finished their strawberry sundaes, Clara placed her napkin on the table with a request.

"Meg, would it be too much to ask for a tour? I have many special memories of Crown Hill and would love to relive some of them with you."

"Clara I'd be pleased to take you through my home. As I explained last night, one of the reasons I invited you is because of your knowledge of Crown Hill. I look forward to hearing your stories." Meg had decided not to mention Mary and Owen , the Randalls or Sir Arthur Conan Doyle. Somehow she sensed it was important to let Clara share her Crown Hill memories on her own terms.

Moving from the porch, the women stepped inside to the adjoining dining room. Without pause, Clara began her remembrances. "Oh the wonderful moments I've known in this house. My best friend growing up was Flordie George. She and I were like sisters. We spent most every day and many nights together at her house, just down the road, across from where Leigh Wilson and her husband now live. Flordie was an only child, glad for the company, and I was the youngest of five brothers, glad for the chance to escape. Flordie's mother, Dorothy, was a close acquaintance of the Randall Family who owned Crown Hill, in the 1920's. Actually, the Randalls lived in Buffalo, but spent their summers here in Eden. Flordie and I got to know their two teenaged daughters quite well, as they occasionally served as our babysitters. I have to say, we pretty much worshipped the Randall girls as they were beautiful and stylish, much more sophisticated than any of the Eden teens we knew. They were also sweet and kind, often inviting us to spend time with them, here at Crown Hill."

As Clara continued, Meg guided her into the living room where the sharp-minded woman shared remembrances of times she and Flordie played with the Randall sisters in what she called, "the parlor." Her blue eyes sparkled with delight in describing the richly upholstered mohair furniture where they sat and read books, and the piano in the triple bay window where they sang away rainy summer afternoons.

Following the house's circular design, Meg and Clara strolled from the living room, back into the dining room and through the swinging door to the kitchen. There Clara visually swept through the room, becoming momentarily transfixed by the picture window framing Crown Hill's yard and outbuildings.

"Could we go up the back stairs to the bedrooms dear? I think I'd like to save the kitchen for last."

Meg had no reason to deny the request. This was Clara's trip down memory lane. Whatever allowed her to best recall the house's history was fine.

While Goldie excitedly bound ahead, the women steadily climbed the enclosed back stairs to the second floor. Moving through the upper rooms, Clara shared engaging stories of hide and seek games, teddy bear tea parties, cross-your-heart secrets and girlish giggles. Meg felt as if Clara's words were actually reviving the childhood joys that had once echoed throughout Crown Hill's walls.

Upon exiting the last of the bedrooms, Meg cautiously led her guest down the front staircase, pausing on the landing for a brief rest. Clara was clearly tiring, which concerned Meg. Yet within a few moments, the sprightly 83-year-old was re-energized and ready to continue down the stairs into the kitchen.

"If you don't mind Meg, I'd like to sit down now."

In direct response, Meg pulled out one of the pressback chairs set around the claw-foot kitchen table.

"Can I get you a cup of tea, Clara?" Meg thought caffeine might energize the unsteady woman.

"Thank you dear, but I'm fine really. I just need for you to come and sit by me. I have something that I need to share, a gift I brought for you. But first, would you bring me my purse? I believe I set it on the shelf by the back door when I came in the house."

Respectfully Meg retrieved the quilted patchwork bag and set it before Clara, gently slipping onto the seat next to her. The kitchen immediately became filled with the sounds of Clara searching through her purse, pulling out an assortment of notepads and tissues, keys and change purses, even a roll of pennies. Finally the determined woman extracted a small leather bound notebook, appearing much like the journal Meg's mother once kept. Setting it on the table, Clara turned directly toward Meg.

"When we spoke last evening I told you that I'd been waiting for you to call. Truthfully, it's much more than that. I have been waiting for you to come to Eden and to Crown Hill for many years."

Meg could feel the tingle of the red spread beginning in her feet. Yet, concern over its heated advance was the furthest thing from her mind. At the moment Meg was completely immersed in trying to comprehend Clara's words.

"I am sure that my words sounds quite ominous to you and I don't mean them that way. But I have knowledge of you and your connection to this house that goes back more than a century. I know why you are here, now."

Meg's body burst into a full-out flush, perspiration forming on her forehead and collecting along her back and armpits. What was this odd little woman talking about? It sounded like madness to Meg, yet somehow felt like the truth. That's what scared her the most. Somewhere in her gut, Meg knew Clara Johnson was speaking honestly about her fated arrival at Crown Hill.

"Meg I know that you have heard the story of Mary Southwick and the terrible end to her life that occurred here. It is a part of this home's past that has remained an enduring part of its presence. But what you don't know is the continuation of Mary's story, specifically as it relates to the Randall Family."

Meg closed her eyes, determined to focus solely on Clara's words. As the purposeful woman continued, her story began to weave together within Meg's imaginings.

"For many years, there have been rumors about Crown Hill being haunted by Mary Southwick's ghost. For many years, my intuitive powers have allowed me to know the truth, that Mary's spirit was indeed part of Crown Hill, that the tragic circumstance of her death trapped her here in an earthly purgatory. Like any spirit so imprisoned, Mary's sole chance of redemption required a connection to a living soul who could provide her the needed strength to pass."

Within Meg's mind a vision began to form, misshapen at first, as if warped in a distorted mirror. As Clara continued to speak, the image came into focus. Meg discerned a woman distant and unfamiliar. Who was she? The question burned in Meg's mind until Clara's descriptive words helped to reveal the same woman who had come to Meg in her dreams over the last several nights. The woman who told Meg that she had been waiting for her. The woman who Meg now understood to be Mary Southwick.

"I did not experience Mary Southwick's spirit in any of the times that Flordie and I visited Crown Hill," Clara continued. "However, a young girl who moved to Sandrock Road in the 1920's did have such experiences. She was actually the daughter of a nanny for the Spaulding Family, who once lived in Leigh Wilson's house."

Through the power of Clara's words a young girl entered Meg's vision. Meg recognized the delicate child as part of her recent dreams. She recalled the girl off to one side in the living room quietly settled on a footstool.

Clara continued. "One spring day when Flordie and I were outside, this young girl came across the road to play with us. As soon as we met, I could see that she was filled with goodness and light and I felt a sense of the girl's special powers come over me. A short time later, I heard that she was working with Edward Randall and his houseguest, the famed author, Sir Arthur Conan Doyle. I was never a direct witness to anything that transpired among them here at Crown Hill, but I can tell you that after several days of working together, their collaboration abruptly ended. Further, within weeks of that abrupt end, the young girl and her mother moved away from Eden, severing all connections with the town. Equally as mystifying, within a short period Edward Randall himself departed and sold Crown Hill, never to return."

Meg envisioned the deed to Crown Hill that she had received upon purchasing the farm. There was a title section that included the hand written signature of every owner in the property's history, including hers. The precise signature of Edward Randall stood out in her vision. It empowered Meg to see the man, actually feel his presence. In her imagining, he stood next to Mary Southwick, as if protecting her. His position clearly revealed the importance of that responsibility to Randall's spirit.

"No one ever knew why this girl and her mother, or the Randalls, left Eden so hurriedly. It was really quite peculiar. I was ten years old at the time and I still remember people in town gossiping about it. There were rumors of spiritual affairs and inappropriate behavior by Edward Randall. And of course there were stories about the house being haunted by Mary Southwick. But truth be told, nothing was ever proven and no one ever really knew what happened here."

Meg's vision continued, connecting Mary and Edward with the young girl. She could see the kindness and protective feelings shared among them. They appeared much like a family to Meg and she found comfort in that image as Clara spoke again.

"One day following all of the puzzling departures, I was walking past the Spaulding's house on my way to Flordie's. It was trash day and some of the neighborhood dogs had pilfered through the Spaulding's garbage containers, leaving rubbish strewn across their property. As I passed by the debris, I noticed the edge of what appeared to be a book. Being a curious child, I stepped closer and verified that it was indeed a book, leather bound and gold edged. Looking around to ensure no one was watching, I snatched the soft covered journal and stuffed it into my coat pocket. There I left if for the rest of the day until I returned home, never telling anyone about my pocketed treasure, not even Flordie."

Meg felt suddenly uncomfortable within the boundaries of her imaginings. Forcing her eyes wide open, she decided to focus intently on Clara as the sage woman continued her tale.

"Once in the security of my own bedroom, I locked the door and set about reviewing the discarded journal. Upon closer inspection I found an inscription on the inside cover that I can still recall to this day. It read, 'Herein is written the story of Crown Hill and the spirit who claims it, as I came to know them.' Below that inscription there was a date-- June, 1922. Below the date appeared the signature of the writer, Margaret Rose Jennings.

The same Margaret Rose Jennings, Meg, who was your grandmother."

When Clara Johnson crossed my threshold that day I never imagined she would resurrect a century and a half of life within me and immerse Meg in the most startling parts.

As the intuitive woman proceeded through my being, room to room, I drew close to Meg, to ensure her comfort. When the two settled in the kitchen, I remained vigilant as Clara guided Meg through the shared journey of Mary, Edward, and Rose. Watching the innocent woman experience the complex tale was heart-wrenching. I knew the twists and turns that Clara was about to reveal before she revealed them and still I found the experience overwhelming. I could only imagine how it felt to Meg who was unaware and yet so deeply connected.

Upon Clara's revelation of Rose's journal, I moved to encircle both women in my protective care. It was obvious that the news of her grandmother's history within my walls bewildered Meg, as her complexion paled and her breathing became shallow. Next witnessing Rose's handwritten Crown Hill experiences in the journal seemed to advance Meg to a state of frightened disorientation. My own fear at that moment was that the sum of these shocks could cause the usually resilient woman to give out, both in body and mind.

Mercifully, it appeared that Clara held the same concerns as she clasped her hands around Meg's and forced the strength of her spirit to flow between them. Slowly Meg revived. Delicately, Clara began again, this time detailing Rose's life after departing Crown Hill.

Clara began with her memory of a summer day playing with Flordie at her home. She recalled how, just after lunch, Elizabeth Jennings appeared at the George's front door. Clara described the woman as clearly distraught, begging for Dorothy George's help. Through emotional sobs the overwrought woman blurted out that she needed to take Rose and leave Eden immediately, but refused to say why.

Dorothy offered to contact her cousin, who lived in the prosperous community of Ridgewood, New Jersey. It was but a few days later when Flordie made Clara cross her heart and promise not to tell that her mother had made all the arrangements for Elizabeth's employment and suitable housing In New Jersey for both mother and child. As Clara recalled, in a matter of weeks, Elizabeth and Rose disappeared from

Eden as if they never existed, leaving behind all of their worldly possessions, short of the clothes on their backs.

Clara's voice softened as she next spoke of a day, six years later, a day when Flordie's mother received a letter with a New Jersey postmark. The correspondence was from Rose. It told of Elizabeth's untimely passing, which had forced the young girl to withdraw from high school and seek employment as a housekeeper.

Clara recalled the news as devastating to Dorothy, who wrote many return letters to the young woman in sorrowful support. However, all correspondences were returned to sender. Rose was never heard from again.

Ultimately, Clara disclosed, it was only with Meg's arrival in Eden, in learning her full name and noticing her remarkable resemblance to Clara's memories of young Rose, that the intuitive woman became intrigued and started making the connection between grandparent and grandchild.

As Clara finished her story, I wondered what would come next? The woman had exploded an informational time bomb within me, affecting all who were integral to the passing of Mary's spirit at this moment in time.

Meg was now aware of Mary and more fully realizing her purpose in coming to Crown Hill.

Mary was becoming strongly connected to Meg and her goodness.

Clara was serving as the bond between the spirits of both women, helping to advance them along their shared path.

And I was in place to support and protect them all as they began this long-awaited journey…a journey clearly well underway.

CHAPTER SIXTEEN

The porch was quickly becoming Meg's treasured refuge. The gentle rhythm of the wicker swing in concert with the peaceful view of the lake, provided a haven that seemed to answer Meg's every need.

At the moment the weary woman's need was intense. Her plans for a lovely Sunday luncheon flavored with Clara Johnson's Crown Hill memories had turned into somewhat of an unsavory experience. At least that's the way it felt, as Meg tried to sort through the afternoon's turn of events.

Once she sat down at the kitchen table with Clara, Meg's entire being became immersed in the story of Mary Southwick. Even in recalling the experience hours later, Meg still had the strong feeling that she and Mary were of the same soul. Envisioning images from her recent dreams of Edward Randall and the unknown young girl served to further the force of her feelings. So it was, in the moment that Clara revealed the person of the young girl as her grandmother, Meg's mind went blank in overwhelmed reaction.

This entire day has been confusing and disturbing, Meg thought as she snuggled deeply into the wicker swing, comforted by her soft cotton blanket. Connecting her foot to the porch floor Meg gave the swing a gentle push. She found the steady rhythm soothing.

Slowly, remembrances of Clara's departure from Crown Hill played through Meg's mind. The kind-hearted older woman determinedly refused Meg's offer to drive her home. Instead, after finishing a cup of tea, Clara set off independently, but not before offering apologies, hugs and promises to return and help Meg work through all that she had just revealed.

Yet, even after Clara was gone there remained the continued presence of the leather bound book that Meg now held in her hands. She had not gathered the courage to go beyond the faded gold print on the soft worn leather cover.

"My Journal."

No doubt, she needed to fold back the cover and experience the book's contents. However, the possibilities within those gilt-edged pages kept Meg fixed in place, struggling for control or at least some sense of balance.

I moved to Eden, to this house, purely on instinct, Meg pondered. *I didn't know anyone here. I had never been near this area. I just needed to move away from my life with Cal in New Jersey, and somehow, after finding the for sale ad and seeing this house, upstate New York felt like a good place. Yet, according to Clara, I was destined to come here, destined to live at Crown Hill.*

The interlocking thoughts again overwhelmed Meg's mind and twisted her stomach. Turning her view to the freshwater horizon, Meg silently prayed for strength and guidance. She knew that she would never be able to piece together her life and move forward--never mend her heart--unless she fully understood the past that had seemingly brought her to this time and place.

Trusting in all that was good, Meg extracted the journal from beneath the blanket and commanded her hands to open the cover.

One page. Start by reading just one page. Then you can stop if need be.

The "one page" proposal gave Meg the courage to enter into the written world of Margaret Rose Jennings, her namesake, her grandmother.

As Clara had described, the opening page held her grandmothers' name and the time frame in which she wrote in the journal. Immediately, Meg was impacted by the graceful style of the faded black script. It was the first qualifier by which Meg could define this woman to whom she was connected.

The sweetness of the moment was quickly checked by the inscription above, "Herein is written the story of Crown Hill and the spirit who claims it, as I came to know them."

A compounded feeling came over Meg. The person of her grandmother was newly forming in her heart, while an overlapping awareness of Mary's spirit was invading her soul. The tag team of emotions created a relentless unease within the conflicted woman.

There is nothing in this journal that can hurt me or jeopardize the life I have found here at Crown Hill, Meg scolded herself with a greater courage than she felt. *All of my life I have wanted to know more about my family, to know my grandparents and where they came from. Now I have that chance. Am I going to pass up this opportunity because of an irrational fear of some words on a page?*

Like a pendulum, Meg's cautious nature entered her consciousness.

No doubt, there is value in reading my grandmother's words. Yet by her inscription, the story she tells could have far-reaching implications in my life. How is it that my grandmother lived near to Crown Hill? How is it that I came to this area and purchased this house? How is it that a spirit could be the connection between us both?

Meg pushed away the leather journal and the voices in her head. She needed to sit and sense. Sense the tranquility of nature surrounding her. Sense the wisdom of her instincts. Sense the being of Crown Hill that had already become a valued part of her world.

Looking out on the broad lake's horizon, Meg became absorbed in inspired thoughts. Within the confines of her grandmother's journal existed information that would help to define her as a person, as well as provide a greater knowledge of her home. That was exactly what Meg wanted in this start to her new life.

She reached for the journal and began again. The cover, the inscription, the first page.

For the next hour Meg poured through Rose's writings, reading and re-reading vignettes of the two weeks during which the young girl journaled her Crown Hill experiences. She was touched by the innocent goodness of her grandmother, as evidenced by the detailed entries describing her work for Edward Randall and Sir Conan Doyle. She was intrigued by her grandmother's passion for Crown Hill, as it so strongly mirrored her own. Moreover, in reading her grandmother's mystifying details about the unknown spirit, Meg felt a discomfort partnered with a budding awareness of something she could not quite identify.

Concluding her grandmother's journal, Meg set the book aside. The events of the day, both real and written, had exhausted her. She could neither keep her head up, nor her eyes open. Within seconds, the weary woman fell into a dreamless sleep where her mind went unchallenged while her body renewed.

It was hours later when Meg experienced a darkened awakening, as she responded to the call of her name.

"Meg. Meg. Are you okay?"

Her brain reacted ahead of her eyelids. "Um hm."

"Hey Meg, come on. Wake up. It's Brady."

Hearing Brady's name in his own voice encouraged the half-conscious woman into full awareness. Opening her eyes, Meg struggled to adjust to the passage of time from afternoon to night. Yet even in the darkness, she could discern Brady Callahan's strong profile.

"Brady. It *is* you. What are you doing here?"

Struggling to sit up, Meg found herself immobilized in her blanket. Reacting, Brady loosened the cotton wrap and in one smooth motion swept Meg into his arms and placed them together on the swing. Without reflection, Meg took full comfort in Brady's protective embrace.

"Now young lady, would you like to tell me what's going on here? I've been calling you for hours with every call going unanswered. I was concerned enough that I drove over here and knocked relentlessly at your door. Finally in total frustration, I walked in and found the house wide open, Goldie desperately looking for her dinner and you unconscious on the porch."

Meg was a bit groggy and unsure of her thoughts. Still she understood that the tone of Brady's question belied his care. As such, he deserved a valid response. The problem was that Meg wasn't sure how he would handle the truth of the matter.

After all, how many people would actually believe in family members and unknown spirits mysteriously showing up in the pages of a long lost journal, she asked herself? Meg was part of the story and even she was having trouble fully accepting it.

"Thank you for caring Brady. I'm not sure what time it is. I fell asleep at some point in the late afternoon and as you noted, it was a very deep sleep. Undoubtedly, Goldie has gone way past her usual dinner time."

"It's about 9:30 and don't worry about Goldie. I fed her and she is sitting contentedly right here with us." At the sound of her name, the affectionate dog rose and tried to draw close to Meg on the swing. Finding it impossible, she instead settled for a place near Brady's dangling feet.

"Again, thank you. I feel terrible that I neglected Goldie. But, to be truthful, the way I'm feeling at the moment, and apparently the way I've been sleeping for the last few hours, the world could have ended around me and I would not have known."

"Well, I would have to agree, based on how long it took me to wake you. What exactly went on here this afternoon? When we talked this morning everything was fine. You were just about to have lunch with Clara Johnson. Did something happen after she left?"

Meg righted herself, sitting up and away from Brady. She needed to see him, to watch his reactions as she spoke. "Clara Johnson is what happened here today. It was my hope that she would be able to shed some light on the history of Crown Hill over a pleasant lunch. As it turned out, she shared much more than I ever imagined." To illustrate her words, Meg produced her grandmother's journal.

"What's this?"

"It's a journal that Clara gave to me today after lunch. It seems that it belonged to a young girl who once spent time at Crown Hill in the early 1920's. She worked here for a short time and Clara knew her. "

"Did the girl write about Crown Hill in her diary? Is that why Clara thought it would be important to you?"

"Yes, sort of. Actually, the girl did write about Crown Hill exclusively in this journal. She experienced some unusual occurrences here and it seems that she and her mother left Eden because of those experiences. But that's not the whole story."

The encroaching darkness made it impossible for Meg to discern more than the outline of Brady's face. Before continuing the conversation, she needed to be sure of his reaction to all that she was about to reveal. "Brady, would you mind if we went inside? It's getting chilly and I'd like a cup of tea."

Moments later, the two were in the kitchen with Meg steeping an herbal brew. While she pulled out mugs and spoons, the couple chatted about Brady's afternoon with his parents and the leftovers he took home from his mother's Sunday dinner feast. Once settled alongside Brady at the table, the fragrant tea before them, their shared conversation ceased as Meg returned to her story.

"So, back to Clara Johnson. Remember our conversation about her this morning, when you told me how she knows things and I explained that she'd said she had been "waiting for me"? Well apparently, her special ability and this journal are directly related to all of that. Clara knew I was coming to Eden because she had been waiting to give me this journal."

"Well that's pretty weird. How did you describe it this morning? Creepy? Yeah, it sounds creepy," Brady responded. "I get it, that the journal is about Crown Hill, but who is this girl who wrote it? How did Clara get ahold of the book? And how does any of Clara's bizarre story confirm that you were going to move to Eden? You're not really buying into this, are you Meg?"

She wasn't really surprised by Brady's reaction. In fact, she probably would have thought the same, had their roles been reversed. Yet over the course of the afternoon Meg had decided that she absolutely believed in the wise woman's vision. Now she hoped to convert Brady to that same belief.

"Actually Brady, I had similar thoughts after Clara left, but in reading the journal entries I believe that she is right. I am connected to this house and to the girl who owned this journal, and all that is written about both. You see according to Clara, the young girl who wrote in this journal and I share the same name, Margaret Rose. That's because I am her namesake. She was my grandmother."

Brady's face mirrored the shock of his reaction. "Your grandmother? Really? And you said that this girl worked here? Did you have any idea? Did you even know that she lived in Eden? And again, are you sure that this information is correct?"

Meg knew that continuing this conversation would fully test Brady's sensibilities. Yet her choices were few. She had decided to share everything, and her hope was that Brady would be able to accept and believe.

"I have never known much about my mother's family. She would never talk about them, no matter how I tried. She didn't share much about her life growing up either. It was weird, but that was my mother's way."

"So learning about your grandmother today, if this girl was in fact your grandmother, that had to feel pretty disorienting. No wonder you're worn out. But how did Clara know your grandmother? And if she lived in Eden, what was her name? She has to be familiar to other people in town around Clara's age."

Brady's response felt slightly more supportive, but Meg knew that the toughest part was yet to come.

"Well, it seems that Clara did know my grandmother. From what she told me today, apparently my great grandmother was born and raised here in Eden. I can't recall her name at the moment, there was just so much information Clara shared with me today. Anyway, my great grandmother worked as a nanny for the Spaulding Family, who lived right here on Sandrock, in the house that is now owned by the Wilson's. As part of her salary, the Spauldings provided a small cottage on their property where my great grandmother lived with her daughter, Margaret Rose, whose name I do remember for obvious reasons."

"And you never knew any of this? Really? That's almost unbelievable." Brady's comment fueled Meg's concern about sharing further details with him. Regardless, there was no turning back now.

"Ok, just be patient and let me finish. You're going to have to pay close attention because the story gets a little confusing from here on."

"Like it isn't already?"

Brady's words hit her like a hard slap. Meg turned fully toward the doubting man and unleashed her unbridled Irish passion.

"Listen Brady, I didn't invite you here tonight, nor did I ask you to become involved in whatever it is that's going on with me and with Clara Johnson. You were the one to make those choices. And if you want to change your mind about being involved with me, or with the dysfunction that seems to be my life at the moment, now's your chance. You can just haul yourself right out of here."

As Brady flinched against her terse words, Meg realized that she had gone too far. Her new-found life at Crown Hill was affording her the courage to speak her mind, at times to a fault. Meg suspected that this was one of those times.

"I'm sorry Brady. I didn't mean to snap at you like that. It's just been a very long day and to be honest, I'm still trying to sort out a lot of what Clara told me. You have every right to wonder about any or all of it, because actually it is pretty unbelievable."

"Yeah. I don't know Meg. I'm somebody who's pretty grounded in reality. All this stuff about your great grandmother and your grandmother living here and you never knowing. Then somehow you magically move here, without any idea that this house was connected to your family; it's all pretty far-fetched."

Meg could feel her heart constricting as she listened to Brady's words. Describing her situation the way he did, it made perfect sense that he could not accept what Clara Johnson had told her. Yet she wanted so desperately to share the day's events with this man who was quickly becoming part of her life. *But, at what cost?* She wondered.

"I understand Brady. And again, I'm sorry for my rude outburst." Observing that her words had little effect, Meg was not surprised as Brady pushed his chair back from the kitchen table.

"I think it's best if I go, Meg. I came to make sure that you and Goldie were safe and clearly you are. It's late and we're both tired. I'll give you a call in the morning and see if we still want to picnic."

Meg felt like a kid whose favorite toy was being taken away in punishment for bad behavior. Not only was their picnic date in jeopardy, she was pretty sure that she was losing the chance for a relationship with Brady. The worst part was there was absolutely nothing Meg could do to change it.

She walked Brady to the back door in muted sadness, sensing the same feelings from him. As he opened the screen door to leave, Goldie bounded past Brady into the cool summer's night. Playfully she turned and blocked his path as if to entice him to stay. Yet for the first time since meeting, Brady did not respond.

"Good night Meg. I hope you sleep well." With that, Brady Callahan disappeared into the black night, passing Goldie without regard.

The disappointed pet slowly returned to Meg, tail drooped and dragging on the ground. Emitting a gentle whine, she settled beside her owner and rested her head against Meg's leg. Taking a moment to stroke her pet's softly furred body, Meg realized that even Goldie was suffering from the day's turn of events.

Retreating from the porch, Goldie shadowed Meg as she moved through the house, locking doors and turning out lights. Heading to bed, the pair was so deeply immersed in their sadness that they never noticed the soft scent of roses as they climbed the stairs. Neither did they see the pale vision of Mary in the bedroom door mirror as they passed.

The emotions swirling through me were intense and varied. Meg's reactions to Clara's revelations and Brady's critiques infused me with her own conflicted feelings. The vestiges of Clara and Brady's strong emotions lingered long after their departures, furthering my turbulent mood. Then there was Goldie's sadness, absorbed from all around her, which flooded unhappiness directly into me.

Still the emotions that impacted me most strongly were Mary's. The day's events had at once challenged and enlightened her, raised her hopes for the future within the details of the past. It was a kaleidoscope of feelings and emotions that I ultimately experienced as my own.

I was truly relieved when Clara finally departed. While the information she shared with Meg was important, it was the gift of her grandmother's journal that mattered most. I knew that as Meg read through Rose's memories, she would begin to understand Mary's significance to my being. She would also become aware of her grandmother's special sensitivities through which she experienced Mary's spirit within me.

"Dearest Crown Hill, can we be a while together?"

"Of course, sweet Mary. I was just sorting through the many moods and emotions that have defined me today. It has been a time of intense feelings for all."

"I agree my kind friend. This day has also brought with it much of the change that we have needed. I know that Meg is overwhelmed right now, but I do believe that Clara has helped her more fully realize my past. Now, I must complete our connection in the here and now. Once that occurs, I am sure that she will help me pass. We are that close, dear one."

I knew Mary was right. I also knew that she was determined to make everything happen as she saw fit. No matter Meg's circumstance or needs, Mary was going to engage Crown Hill's new mistress and take from her whatever she needed.

"Mary, the only thing I would ask is that you proceed with care. Meg received a great deal of life information today--yours and her grandmother's, as well as her own. She will need some time to process all of those truths in order to provide the strength you need. Just remember that, no matter how you decide to move forward."

"I will remind myself of such, Crown Hill. And I will hope that with all that came to Meg today, she will more clearly understand what

has been and what is possible. Her grandmother had that strength of character and I have no doubt Meg possesses the same."

In considering all, I offered a silent prayer that Meg's devotion to Mary's spirit would become as powerful as Rose's once was...and stronger than it ever had the chance to become.

CHAPTER SEVENTEEN

Meg awoke with a start that bolted her body upright in bed. Looking around the softly moonlit room she felt fully alert, aware of something disturbing, yet unknown.

Her middle of the night motion awakened Goldie as well. Immediately the protective pet jumped onto the bed next to her owner and began sniffing the air. It was as if she was tracking something unfamiliar in the room.

"What's up girl? Did I wake you?" Meg's voice encouraged a distracted tail wag but nothing more. The dedicated retriever was focused on her mission of sensory investigation. As Goldie remained vigilant, her hackles rose up along the ridge of her golden, furred back.

Oh heavenly day, Meg thought to herself. *I don't know what this dog thinks she smells, but I am in no mood to have her get all riled up in the middle of the night.* Wrapping her arms around her loyal companion, Meg attempted to pull Goldie into a full body hug. However the sizable dog was having none of it. Uncharacteristically, Goldie pulled away from Meg, emitting a soft half growl as she moved.

"Goldie! Shame on you. You've never growled at me before. What's the matter with you?"

Meg's scolding caused the dog to react in admonished shame. Gently, she sidled up to her mistress and offered an apologetic kiss

"That's better. Thank you Miss Goldie." Hugging the loving animal, Meg felt the tension of whatever had awakened her begin to ebb. Her only problem was that now she was fully awake. After a week of restless nights, Meg needed to sleep.

The exhausted woman got up and walked across the bedroom to a vintage black and white television sitting securely on a bracketed wall shelf. In the year it had taken Meg to work through her divorce, she had endured a major case of insomnia. Out of desperation, the emotionally overwrought woman turned to late night television as her sleeping drug of choice. Now that she was happily settled into Crown Hill, Meg rarely needed the electronic sleep inducer. Tonight however, she had a need for the TV's soothing drone.

Pushing the power button, images of Meg's mother flickered across her mind. The old-fashioned TV had been a second-hand gift from her mom shortly before she passed. In the waning years of her life, the aging widow kept the black and white broadcaster running continually, explaining it as a way to ward off the emptiness of living alone. The day she insisted her daughter take the antiquated television home, Meg knew the end of her loving parent's life was drawing near.

Turning back towards her bed, Meg's memories of her mother were suddenly cut short as unexplained fear bolted through her body and blinded her mind. Instinctively the frightened woman jumped forward, screaming as she felt something behind her, scraping along the full length of her body.

All reason eluded Meg as Goldie came flying off the bed toward her, in full-barking alarm. Immediately Meg was divided between her instinctive need for self-protection and her humane desire to safeguard her dog. Honoring both, she stepped forward and derailed Goldie's progress by grabbing her collar, at the same time spinning around to face whatever danger she had felt.

In the moonlit shadows, Meg was astonished to witness the television, face down on the bedroom carpet. The heavy black cord linking the television's inner workings to the electrical outlet still connected. In fact Meg could hear the voice of a familiar, talk show host broadcasting through the speaker, now muffled in the carpeted floor. The sight of the wall shelf, lying undamaged near the television compounded her confusion.

Deciding to improve her view of the calamity Meg stepped forward to turn on the overhead light. A sharp pain in the back of her right calf immediately halted her progress. Reaching down, Meg discovered a golf ball sized-welt where the television must have bruised her leg as it scraped along her body. The tender bump stimulated Meg's frightened realization of what could have happened, had she not jumped forward so quickly.

Gingerly moving to the wall, Meg flipped on the light switch. Straightaway she inspected the shelf and then the wall brackets. All were perfect, without mark or defect. Nothing Meg could imagine would rationalize the television tumbling off the shelf and the shelf separating from the wall, both without damage in any form.

Methodically, Meg placed the shelf onto the secure brackets again and positioned the television in its rightful place. At that point, the bewildered woman decided that she had two choices. She could give extended thought to all that had just happened and undoubtedly become anxious about all that was going on at Crown Hill, or she could simply dismiss the entire incident as odd happenstance and go back to bed. Turning off the light, Meg chose the latter.

Goldie joined her mistress on the bed, intent on staying protectively close. Meg took comfort in the security of her pet as she tried to dispel the array of nagging fears assaulting her mind. Turning to the reassuring pattern of her nightly bedtime routine, Meg fluffed her down pillows and snuggled into a curled ball under her cotton sheet and light-weight quilt. Forcing herself to close her eyes, the tense woman took a deep breath, hoping to release the stress that was wracking her body.

As it turned out, the only thing Meg released was another scream, as within her mind she was confronted by what had earlier awakened her so dramatically. It was a man, or more accurately the vision of a man. He was a stranger, but his threatening words were familiar.

"I will make your world a tortured hell forever and end your life at Crown Hill."

Meg again bolted upright in her bed. Goldie became fully engaged beside her, growling with hackles raised. This time Meg did not chastise her defensive dog.

Reaching out to her nightstand, Meg turned on the table lamp. In the security of the illuminating light she scanned the room, searching for the threatening man. Meg knew it was crazy, but she couldn't help herself. Whoever this person was, he came through her dreams and into her mind in a very real way. She could feel his presence in the room, as apparently did Goldie. Both woman and dog were frozen in fear.

Glancing toward Big Ben, Meg could see that it was 3 am. She was never going to go back to sleep now, especially when closing her eyes might allow a return of the fearsome man. No, she would stay awake and hope that in the light of dawn, the threatening spirit would disappear.

Meg sat motionless in bed, monitoring every sound and creak in her aged farmhouse. Within her heightened awareness, she searched her mind for traces of the dream that seemed to have activated the night's unsettling events.

Slowly she recalled that the man first materialized at the end of her bed, silently standing and waiting. It had taken Meg some time to realize his presence, as her subconscious had been fully engaged in a review of the day's happenings with Clara. However, gradually this unknown man became the center of her dream, as Meg struggled to identify exactly who it was at the foot of her bed.

Her growing awareness of the man strengthened his spirit until he became a menacing force within the room. Meg struggled to speak, but found her voice disabled. As she lay mute, the man declared his thoughts with an intensity that paralyzed her body as well.

"Your presence here in my home is not welcome. You do not belong here and you have no business interfering with my wife. Stay away from her, or I will see to it that you suffer."

Allowing for the full force of his words to penetrate the room, the spirit moved steadily closer to Meg until he loomed directly over her. Exhibiting a barely contained rage, he issued yet another warning.

"Do not discount what I have told you. Sever yourself from my wife or I will make your world a tortured hell and end your life at Crown Hill."

In recalling his threatening words, Meg became more fully aware and alarmed over the reason why. She had spent a great part of the previous day listening to Clara's story of Crown Hill, including details of Mary Southwick's tragic death and her husband's rumored part in her dreadful passing. In re-imagining the sights and sounds of this threatening man of her dreams, Meg found herself making a connection to Owen Southwick. *Could that be the truth?* She wondered. *Has Owen Southwick invaded my home, intruded into my room, and threatened my life?*

Trying to stay calm, Meg inhaled deeply and exhaled fully, but she could not slow her racing mind. *How could such a thing happen? How has my home transformed from protected tranquility to disruptive turmoil, all in the matter of hours? And how is it that spirits, séances, and a murder, or suicide, have come to define the world that I thought was so safe and protected?*

Meg could feel her heart pounding wildly, as it often would following a disagreeable shouting match with Cal. She well knew the feeling of being threatened by an abusive man. She had just never experienced such cruelty from a male spirit. Meg found that thought oddly humorous, which made her laugh out loud.

"Seems as if I am meant to be forever challenged in both mind and body by idiotic men, Goldie."

The understanding canine snuggled more closely to her owner, bestowing a gentle kiss on her hand. It was in at that moment that Meg became fully aware of the strength of her mind. Suddenly she realized she did not have to be threatened or intimidated by Owen Southwick. While she might not know exactly how to deal with spirits, she had become strong enough to rage against mistreatment by any person or being.

Meg further understood that, in some way, the spirit of Mary Southwick needed her help, her strength. And by aiding Mary she would be going against the dangerous anger of Owen. That combined realization led Meg to a clear decision. As soon as the sun rose, she would call Clara Johnson and tell her of the dream. She might even mention the television almost crashing on top of her. The spiritually-connected woman would know what to do, Meg was sure of it. After all, Clara was the one who told her she was meant to come to Crown Hill.

And the reasons for her presence in the house on the hill were becoming increasingly clear to Meg, with each passing moment.

We had underestimated Owen's ability to become aware of Meg and her growing connection to Mary. Our miscalculation extended further to Owen's foreboding ill will.

Before appearing to Meg he constrained Mary and I with his overpowering evil. We were literally immobilized and isolated, unable to protect Meg as he invaded her being.

Of equal concern was the physical harm that Owen tried to inflict upon Meg. While the brooding man lashed out cruelly against Mary during their marriage, he had never reacted with physical fury against others. His effort to injure Meg, by hurling the television upon her, provided frightening notice of his increasingly volatile strength and spirit.

In the light of the advancing day, Owen finally withdrew from me. Freed from his power, I immediately encircled Meg and Goldie, calling upon the goodness of all who had ever dwelt within me for added strength and protection. I aggregated a powerful force of the same to stand against Owen and diminish all chances of his immediate return.

Reflecting on the night's events, the only goodness to evolve out of the terror was Meg's stalwart reaction. Many would have been intimidated by Owen's menacing threats. Instead, Meg's devotion to her new home and her belief in Clara's stories of her grandmother motivated the determined woman to choose action over fear.

As Meg focused on contacting Clara, I reached out to Mary. In connecting, I sensed that she was in some way changed.

"Beloved Crown Hill, I am so grateful for your positive spirit around Meg. She needs to be protected against Owen, which I know you can do. However, I am troubled about the manner in which I should now move forward. My hope was to complete my bond with Meg before Owen became aware. But after the occurrences of last night, it is obvious that such hope is futile and we now all face the constant threat of his wrathful retribution."

The positive force that had been advancing through Mary's spirit since Meg's arrival was depleted. I understood it as Owen invading her being, a pattern through which he had controlled her in life and was now doing in the afterlife.

"Do not go without hope, my sweet Mary. While Owen's awareness makes your connection with Meg more challenging, it does not mean an end. Meg is already planning to reach out to Clara. That

makes it clear that Owen has not intimidated her. We have but to draw together the positive life-forces within me and encircle them around you and Meg, and I believe she will be able to use the power of her goodness to guide you."

I could feel Mary's spirit continue to retreat. I understood that Owen's return and his threatening actions against Meg had deeply impacted her. No matter how encouraging I tried to be, Mary was holding true to that which she had perpetually known…Owen's cruelty always won out. Feeling the battered woman drowning in despair, I reached out to her again.

"Mary, soon you will have the combined strengths of Meg and Clara within me. Together they are a force capable of all that you need. Know that if you can just come forward this one last time, put your trust in me and allow some sense of faith in Meg and Clara, all will be as it should be."

I gathered the strength of my love for Mary and centered it in the depths of my being. With every energy that I possessed, I infused my ardor into her spirit, hoping to overcome Owen's cruelty that had so deeply scarred her soul. My dearest friend had to respond, had to believe, or she would be forever trapped in the darkness of Owen's world.

Finally, from my innermost core, came her reply.

"Crown Hill, you know all that I am and all that I was…in the light of your love, I pledge all that I can be to you."

CHAPTER EIGHTEEN

Considering that she had hardly slept, Meg expected to feel exhausted. Yet every fibre of her being was energized, as if a continuous electric current was charging through her body.

As the sun filtered into her room, Meg turned off the bedside lamp and made her way to the bathroom. Doing her best to act as if the morning was a normal beginning to a normal day, she showered, dressed and made her bed.

Truth be told, the whole time she engaged in her morning ritual, Meg kept waiting; waiting for the television to magically power on, for the shelf to weaken and fall, for the threatening man of her dreams to invade and haunt again.

Immersed in eeriness, Meg knew she needed to get out of the bedroom. She also knew she needed to call Clara Johnson.

"Ok, Goldie. Let's go downstairs and make some breakfast." Hopping down from the bed, the happy dog came immediately to Meg's side and hugged her. "Aw, good morning to you too, sweet girl. How about some pancakes with raspberries and blueberries? After all, it is the 4th of July!"

Within minutes Meg was flipping patriotically colored flapjacks into butter-layered, maple-syruped stacks. Meg loved pancakes except for one small detail--living alone made them a less than ideal breakfast choice. Meg had long ago discovered that a good pancake batter required a blend of ingredients for at least 6 servings. The super-sized result meant that Meg either ate way too much, or was forced to confront the melancholy reality that she was cooking for only one.

Contemplating the lack of romance in her life, Meg's attention turned to Brady. Through all of the night's disturbances, she had not given the handsome farmer a single thought. Looking at the clock, Meg wondered if he would actually call to talk about their picnic plans? Based on his departure from Crown Hill the previous evening, Meg doubted she and Brady would speak again about anything, no less about spending the 4th of July together.

More importantly at the moment, Meg needed to talk to Clara Johnson--the sooner, the better.

As Meg recalled, Clara was an early riser. A first-thing-in-the-morning call shouldn't disturb the sprightly woman. After the nightmarish adventure that Meg had endured, she needed someone to share in her mysterious experience. Heading to the phone, Meg felt quite sure Clara Johnson was that someone.

Dialing Clara's number, Meg wondered how best to explain all that had transpired. In truth, if it weren't for the purple lump on the back of her leg, Meg would have a hard time believing any account of last night's turbulence

"Good Morning! Happy Independence Day!"

The cheery phone greeting caught Meg off guard.

"Hello? Is anyone there?"

"Yes, yes, I'm here Clara and Happy 4th of July to you as well. It's Meg Flynn. I hope I'm not calling too early."

"Oh not at all dear. I was just enjoying a second cup of tea while my biscuits bake. I always serve a dessert of fresh baked buttermilk biscuits topped with strawberries, blueberries and vanilla whipped cream at our family's 4th of July picnic. Already have my biscuits in the oven, before the day gets too hot. But enough about me, how are you Meg? I've been thinking about you since I woke up this morning. How did you survive the night?"

"Well, actually, my night was about as unsettled as our day yesterday Clara. That's why I'm calling. I know it's a holiday and I heard you say that you have family plans, but I wondered if you might have a bit of time to come by Crown Hill today? I would like to try and explain to you all that happened here last night, and I need to do it in person."

I completely understand dear. I was quite sure when I awoke this morning that something unusual had occurred. In fact, I was expecting your call. So, I'm glad to stop by. What time did you have in mind?"

The woman's uncanny ability to know things about Meg's life was unsettling. At the same time, her innate sensibilities were exactly the reason Meg was reaching out to the clairvoyant woman.

"Actually, I don't think I'm going to be busy today Clara, so whatever suits your schedule."

"Well, once my biscuits turn golden, I am free for the morning. So I'll see you in a bit."

Hanging up the phone, Meg was soothed by the thought of Clara's imminent arrival. Beginning with her first day in Eden, the intuitive woman had made a point of connecting with her. Now with all that Meg was enduring in her dreams and in waking, she was beginning to understand that their meeting was not by chance. Meg needed Clara Johnson in her life and she was becoming most grateful for her presence.

To pass the time until Clara arrived, Meg moved through the house collecting remnants from the previous day's luncheon. She had been too wrung out by Clara's revelations to tackle any cleanup before going to bed. Stacking dishes on the cast iron sink sideboard, Meg created soapy dishwater in one of the double basins and clear rinse water in the other. With deliberate care she began washing the heirloom china plates, as she had watched her mother do countless times.

The memory of her mother comforted Meg and allowed her to mindlessly move through her remaining clean-up chores. When a knock came at her back door, she was ready to welcome Clara to Crown Hill.

"Be right there. Clara." Meg called out as she took one last look around the kitchen. Yet as she stepped onto the back porch, Meg discovered it was not Clara standing at her door.

"Brady? What are you doing here?" Meg realized her reaction was not the most gracious, but on this particular morning she was far from concerned about manners.

"Um, good morning Meg." The self-conscious man's tone was clearly one of unease, but nonetheless he forged ahead. "I wanted to be the first to wish you a happy 4th of July and, actually, I brought you this red rose from my garden as a patriotic peace offering, sort of...kind of...I guess."

The sight of the practical-minded farmer, struggling like a young man courting his true love, touched Meg. She was also amused. Trying not to giggle, she accepted the gorgeous rose and invited Brady into the kitchen.

"Would you like a cup of coffee?" Meg hadn't brewed a pot, but she felt as if the offer should be made.

"Actually, no, thank you. I've had my fill today already. I'd just like to sit and talk, if that's ok with you?."

The earnest tone in his voice and the tenderness in his penetrating blue eyes left Meg no choice. She responded by leading the way into the kitchen and sitting down at the table, offering Brady the adjoining chair.

Nervously clearing his throat, Brady began. "I'm not really sure where to start. Guess maybe where we left off. I'm sorry for the way I walked out of here last night. I'm sure it must have seemed pretty selfish and that's not who I am; it's not my way."

Brady paused. Meg allowed silence to fill the space between them. This was his time to speak and she was not going to interfere with whatever the man had to say.

"Anyway, when I was driving away last night, it was all I could do not to turn around, to come back and take you in my arms, hold you through the night. I knew it had been a tough day for you and I wanted to help, wanted to make it better. But truthfully, all the talk about your grandmother and the journal and the stuff about Clara Johnson knowing you were going to move to Eden, it was all confusing and kind of disturbing to me. Like I told you, I'm a pretty basic guy."

Meg wanted to reach out and touch Brady, be supportive of his heartfelt explanation, but her conscience told her otherwise.

You don't always have to make it better for everyone else. Just sit there and let him talk.

Doing her best, Meg compromised by giving Brady an encouraging smile as he continued.

"I tried to sleep, but truthfully, thoughts of you kept me awake. You are the first woman since Julieann that I have cared about. Being with you, talking with you, hell, just thinking about you makes me happy. The more I thought about all of that, the more I realized that I had to figure out my reactions from last night."

Pausing for breath…and courage…Brady reconsidered Meg's earlier offer. "Could I take you up on that coffee now?"

Feeling as if his request left her hanging on the edge of a cliff, Meg managed to scrape herself off the chair and get to the coffee pot. Sensing Brady's eyes on her the whole time, she brewed and poured some deep roasted java and set it before him in a steaming mug. The only language that passed between them was the magnetic attraction of their bodies as Meg again took her place at the table, next to Brady. After a few inhales of the liquid caffeine, the determined farmer began again.

"Thanks, Meg. This is my fifth cup this morning. Anyway, like I said, I couldn't sleep after leaving here last night. Finally, about 4 am, I got up and made a pot of coffee and went to the barn, over at the homestead. Actually going to the barn is something I've done ever since the accident. After Julieann and Colin died, sleepless nights were all I knew. The only way I got through was by driving over to the barn and tinkering on equipment or cleaning out grain bins or haymows, anything to keep from facing the reality that that they were gone."

Tears pooled in Brady's eyes, spilling over onto his face. Meg wanted to kiss away the outward sign of this engaging man's pain. Yet she was afraid that connecting their bodies would overpower Brady's mind and interrupt his thoughts. Instead, she sat and continued to listen.

"Over the years, my mom would come down to the barn in the early mornings as well. She started in those first months after the accident. She'd show up with some coffee and cinnamon rolls or muffins and just sit there and let me spit out every thought I had, good or bad, crazy or sane. Honestly, I think that those times were what got me through. She didn't try to tell me how I should feel or what I should do. She just let me get it all out."

The description of his mother made Meg want to meet the wise woman. It also provided insight into the character of Brady, a man who obviously respected and cared for the women in his life. His appeal to Meg was intensifying with every word.

"This morning mom stopped down to the barn. She knew that we were going to picnic today and the early morning lights kind of made her wonder if I was ok. Anyway, it didn't take long before I was telling her what a jerk I'd been in leaving you last night and how I was unhappy with my reaction to everything--Clara, the house, your grandmother. As usual, mom listened, but this time she talked as well."

Brady paused for another bolster of caffeine. As he did, Meg left her chair and grabbed the still warming coffee pot. She refilled his cup and returned to the table, hoping her actions would not interfere with his train of thought.

"Thanks. Anyway, my mom laughed at me at first, saying that I was definitely my father's son. Then she said I also carried her ways within me as well, and because of that she wanted to tell me a story; a story about her and Clara Johnson."

The woman's name caused Meg to emit her first sounds since Brady began. "Clara? Are she and your mother friends?"

"Well, Clara is sort of everyone's friend. Like I told you yesterday, she's been around Eden forever, knows everyone in town and most everything about them as well. However, I never knew anything about the story that my mother shared with me this morning. It seems that mom learned about Clara's special ability to know things when she was first pregnant with my oldest sister, Karen. One day at a church meeting, Clara came up and hugged my mother. She whispered that she was sure the baby would be a perfect image of her, when she gave birth in June. My mother said she stared at the odd woman in wonder because at that point, no one, not even my father, knew she was pregnant. Apparently Clara did the same thing in each of my mother's four pregnancies, always telling my mother whether the baby was a boy or a girl, and the month each of us would be born."

In listening to Brady, Meg felt a strong sense of satisfaction. His mother's story was validating much of Meg's experience with Clara. She wondered how complete the validation would become.

"My mother then told me that just weeks before the accident, Clara invited her for Christmas lunch at The Four Corners. They often got together around holidays and my mother agreed without thinking anything of it. As they finished lunch and were about to leave, Clara took hold of my mother's hands and said that when the heartbreak struck, she would be there for her and for our family. Mom decided against asking Clara for an explanation, thinking that the woman was just growing old and odd-minded."

Meg smiled in acknowledgment. She recalled having the same thoughts as Clara had explained Meg's connection to Crown Hill and her family's history. It had definitely been disorienting to hear the all-knowing woman's words. Meg could only imagine the impact if Clara had been suggesting something of a tragic nature. Brady's next statements reinforced her thoughts.

"Obviously when Juilieann and Colin were killed on Christmas, our family was devastated. After we finished with the police and the hospital and all the paperwork, my parents took me home with them. They gave me a sleeping pill from the ER doc and put me to bed in my old room. However, my mother wasn't able to sleep and somewhere in the middle of the night she was struck with a remembrance of Clara's words from their Christmas lunch. Well, she called Clara on the phone right then and there."

Having suffered her own nighttime terror, Meg understood the need to reach out to someone who could allay the night's darkest fears. As Brady continued, Meg's heart ached for his mother.

"Despite the late hour, Clara answered on the first ring. She greeted my mother by name before mom even spoke. My mother said that she was so overcome with emotion that she could only sob while Clara offered words of comfort and understanding. To this day, my mother says that she has never understood how Clara seemed to know about the accident beforehand, or how she knew it was my mother calling in the middle of the night. But ever since, mom has come to fully believe in Clara's abilities and her wisdom, especially now--since you moved to Eden--since Clara told my mother that you were meant to come to Crown Hill, and meant to become part of my life."

The stunning end to Brady's story froze Meg in place and time. She wanted to ask him to repeat the part about coming into his life, but didn't dare for fear that she had misheard. Instead Meg reached her arms to Brady and allowed the powerful man to lift her into his embrace. Amid gentle tears, the two sat silently within the moment, aware only of each other.

"Oh I am so pleased to see that you two have finally found each other." Looking up, Meg and Brady realized that Clara Johnson was standing in the entryway of the kitchen. Bestowing her kindest smile upon them, the wise woman added, "I have been waiting for you two."

What had been a frightening night was advancing into a morning of hope. I was heartened by the uniting of Meg and Clara. The older woman possessed special gifts and abilities that I was sure could connect Meg's life force with Mary's spirit.

Then there was the surprise of the dawning day, with Brady's appearance and the sharing of his mother's story. While there was no way to be sure of this man's part in Mary's passing, he brought a spirit of goodness into my being and I knew that alone would help discourage Owen's return.

My only true concern now was Mary. While she had pledged her willingness to be present and believe, I knew that she still struggled. In fairness, I could not fault her, but in reality her time was now. Of all the chances her spirit ever had to pass, I was sure this was the moment.

"Sweet friend, after so many years, your time is almost at hand and our time is almost complete. Draw near and let us speak of those things that will forever remain a part of us. Let us one last time remember the wonders of our shared life, so that when we are separate, we will not be sad for what is lost, but rather cherish all that has been."

I was unsure if Mary would respond, as she had been quiet since the dawn. There was such little time left. I could only reveal my heart and hope. At last, I heard her.

"Dearest Crown Hill, amid the fears and excitement now within my spirit, there is quieted sadness knowing we may soon part. Just as you say, it has been many years and much shared. I often am unsure of how we are different, as for so long we have been the same. But of all that I hold in my heart I want, no need, I need to tell you that your love has been the guiding force of my life. You have given me strength, confidence, kindness, joy and an endless sharing of your heart. In both body and spirit, my life within you has been defined and fulfilled. No matter what awaits my spirit in passing, I know that nothing will ever truly separate us. "

"My dearest Mary, so many thoughts fill me at this moment. There is so much that I want to say. But, in truth, we have shared our thoughts and hopes and dreams since you first came to me so many years ago. And within that sharing we have come to be one, as you say. So in these moments, which may be our last, I will simply tell you that of all who ever dwelled within me, you are the most loving and kind. I

am sorry for the pain in your life that seared your soul and splintered your heart. You did not deserve such sorrow and I hope that in some way my love helped, for you received all that I possessed, forever and always."

Time passed with only the echoes of our words between us. I began to fear that the intensity of the moment and the many fears connected to passing had driven Mary away. Then I heard her soft voice.

"Kind friend, your words touch my heart and provide my soul with peaceful courage. Please stay close one last time, as together we face whatever is about to come."

"Your wish is mine, Mary. With all that I am, I will be with you."

"Beloved Crown Hill...one last thing"

"Yes, My Mary?"

"Promise. Promise that you won't forget me."

"Mary, I promise that I will forget everything about myself...before the slightest memory of you ever fades."

CHAPTER NINETEEN

Clara's quiet presence felt unnerving to Meg and Brady. It wasn't just that her arrival had uncoupled their lover's embrace. It was that the elderly woman's silent appearance bordered on mysterious.

Meg immediately tried to restore normalcy to the situation. "Good Morning Clara. I'm so glad to see you. You know Brady Callahan, don't you?"

"Good morning, Meg. And yes, of course, Brady and I have known each other since before he was born, haven't we young man?"

As Brady struggled to regain his composure, Meg deemed the expression on his face priceless. At some point she was going to engage this man in a high stakes poker game, as he had absolutely no ability to hide his feelings. Finally, the usually engaging farmer recovered his composure enough to speak.

"Yes m'am, we have known each a long time."

One sentence. That was all Brady could manage. Taking pity on him, Meg moved toward Clara and escorted her to a chair at the kitchen table, setting her oversized patchwork purse nearby.

"Can I get you some tea, Clara?"

"No, thank you my dear. I've had my two cups for the day. I would like some ice water though, if you don't mind."

While Meg filled a tall glass, Clara engaged the reticent farmer. "How are your parents, Brady? I heard that your father had a bit of a spell a while ago."

"They are both fine, thank you for asking, m'am. Dad did have a blood pressure issue back in May, but you know my mom. She got him to the doctor and found out everything there was to know about his problems. Now she's got Dad eating healthier and taking vitamins and he's doing great."

Meg listened with interest to the exchange about the Callahans. Brady hadn't really shared much about his parents. The quick vignette created a charming image of the couple within Meg's mind. Yet in returning to the table, Meg refocused her thoughts on the reason for Clara's presence, and how Brady might to react to that reason.

"So my dear, how are you managing?" Clara inquired as Meg joined them. "I'm sure it was a very long night for you."

Feeling Brady's eyes upon her, Meg took a deep breath and forged ahead. "Yes, it was very long and scary, actually. That's why I'm grateful you could come by this morning, Clara. I truly believe that what happened last night is connected to all we discussed here yesterday."

Placing a reassuring hand on Meg's arm, Clara spoke with gentle authority. "I have no doubt that you are correct Meg. But I would like to hear exactly what happened last night. Then I can better understand what we need to do. Crown Hill is your home. You belong here and I intend to ensure that you are protected in your happiness here. It is a purpose I accepted long ago when I laid claim to your grandmother's journal."

Clara's words caused a powerful sense of relief to flood through Meg's being. The strong-willed woman hadn't realized just how much Owen's threatening actions had frightened her. The idea that there was someone who not only wanted to help her, but was able to do so, caused Meg to release a cascade of tears over the comforting response.

"Meg, sweetheart, what's wrong? Why are you crying?" Brady tenderly reached out and raised her face to his. Meg could see the care of Brady's heart reflected in his passionate blue eyes. His kindness caused Meg to cry more freely, a reaction that softened the usually strong man.

"Meg, I don't know what's going on or why you're so upset, but if I can help I will. That's why I'm here. It's why I came back after last night. Please, stop crying. Please tell me what it is you need, what I can do."

"Brady, you are such a fine young man and I am so pleased that you and Meg have found each other." Clara's words carried a compassion that encouraged Brady's trust.

"Possibly I can help explain what is happening here, and what is going on with Meg as well. The question is, where to start? Perhaps, with a story about Crown Hill. You see Brady, over the years, Crown Hill has been home to many people including a couple named Mary and Owen Southwick. I speak of the Southwicks specifically, because of a tragic event that occurred here involving them both. There's really no delicate way to say this, so I'll just tell you directly. Mary was found hanged in a woodshed out behind this house. In fact it's the woodshed that still stands by the barn."

Brady's mind zeroed in on the first day that he came to Crown Hill. It was in response to Meg's emergency call about a danger in that woodshed. He remembered thinking that her panic was a bit extreme, but eventually dismissed it as Meg's inexperience with rural life. As Clara told the Southwick's story, Brady began to wonder about Meg's true fear that day.

"Of course, as news of Mary Southwick's death spread through Eden people started to talk. The town sheriff at the time immediately ruled her death a suicide, ending any investigation of the case. However, neighbors of the Southwick's and friends of Mary believed that Owen had murdered his wife and made it appear like suicide. Soon people were telling stories of Mary's spirit appearing as a terrifying ghost, haunting her own home."

Clara paused to allow Brady to process the details of Mary Southwick's demise. The wise woman could see that his mind was evaluating the story and its likelihood. She now needed to unravel the rest of the tale in a manner that would keep Brady moving towards belief.

"Over the years Crown Hill declined from a home of life and light to a place of despair and darkness, primarily due to accounts of Mary's hauntings. People in Eden truly feared being anywhere in or around the property. In fact, according to one of the most enduring Crown Hill stories..."

Clara's revelation was cut short by the shock of a sudden and deep chill spreading through the kitchen. Not a cooling breeze coming through a window, but more like a chilling winter's day invading the house. The cold virtually froze Clara, Meg, and Brady in place, arresting their words as well. As the three sat suspended in time, a pale blue light steadily appeared and remained near them. From within the light, a voice spoke.

"I am weary of these constant stories portraying me as a cruel and haunting spirit. I am neither. I am a woman who lived a tortured life and died a painful death. It is because of those circumstances that my spirit is trapped on this earth and I have become a misunderstood and desperate soul."

Clara immediately identified the voice and understood the moment. It was Mary Southwick reaching out and trying to connect to all that had drawn Clara to Meg and that which had brought Meg to Crown Hill. Clara's clear understanding of the moment freed her mind and allowed her to speak.

"Dear Mary, we understand that the manner in which your husband, Owen, ended your life has kept you painfully bound to this world. And while your resultant actions have often been deemed evil and cruel, we know they are only reflections of the evil and cruelty inflicted upon you through your husband's menacing nature. Mary, know that we feel your goodness and we are here to help you. Your time is now. It is in this moment that you are free to leave all of your pain and sorrow and move to the light."

Meg and Brady sat tangled in a web of confusion. The voice invading the kitchen was unknown and frightening, unlike anything the couple had ever experienced. It was only when they heard Clara speak the name, "Mary" that they realized the mysterious voice belonged to Mary Southwick. Instinctively, the two turned to Clara in watchful wait, wordlessly listening as Mary spoke again.

"I understand that your gathered strength has the power to help me pass from this world. But it is not only about your power. It is about the truth. The truth of my passing and why I have been so long trapped between body and being. So many times I have heard people say that my haunted spirit was caused by my death at the murderous hands of my husband. Within the core of such accusations is the truth. It was Owen's evil nature, his cruelty, which caused me to die. Yet understand, my life did not end within the force of Owen's hands."

With each word spoken Mary's voice became stronger and more compelling, particularly to Meg. In reading through her grandmother's journal, the turn of every page had caused Meg to feel a growing connection to Mary. Now, hearing the haunted woman's voice and listening to the passion of her words, Meg was moving beyond a connection of written imaginings. She felt a bond of spiritual intensity forming with Mary, centered within Crown Hill.

The kitchen remained immersed in a deeply chilled state as Mary confessed the final moments of her life and death. "After years of enduring a marriage of angry words and hurtful actions, I realized that life as I knew it would never change. Owen would always seek to control me through his fury and my fear. There would never be a time or a place where I would be safe, protected and able to live in soulful peace. Within that understanding came an enormously hopeless need to end my painful despair. I simply could not go on one more day."

As Mary continued her words became images and actions within Meg's mind. It was as if the two were connected as one.

"After preparing Owen's dinner and making his fresh bread, I went to the back hall and pulled out a wooden crate that I often used as a make-shift step stool. With crate in hand, I went out to the yard, and stood on the wooden box to reach and untie my clothes line. I placed the length of rope into the crate and set off for the woodshed. Once there, I threw the clothesline over a beam and made a tight knot against the wood's rough-hewn edges. I then gathered the free end of the rope and tied a noose, as I had watched Owen do so many times in slaughtering livestock on the farm. Stepping onto the crate, I placed the noose around my neck."

Meg could feel the clothesline around her own throat and wondered if she would actually experience the tightening of the noose as well. She silently offered a quick prayer for her well-being, as Mary continued with her end-of-life story.

"Then it was the moment. My moment. My own moment when I could actually choose life or death. Savoring one fond, final view of my beloved Crown Hill through the woodshed doorway, I closed my eyes and made my decision. With all of my will, I kicked the crate away and launched my body into a violent swinging motion from the beam. There I dangled until I drew my final breath, hanging until the neighbors found me hours later. And that is the truth of my death, as it needed to be told, before my spirit could be free to pass."

Mary's words caused an intensity within Meg's being. It was as if a lifetime of words had been stored within her, all of them saved expressly for Mary Southwick. Fully inspired, she spoke.

"Mary I can feel all of you within me. Your love of nature and beauty, your kind and giving heart and, most of all, your devotion to Crown Hill, our home. I know leaving this place that you love so dearly will be heartbreaking. But it is something that you need to do now, now before Owen returns and again robs you of your choice to move to the light. But before you go, know I will ensure that Crown Hill continues to reflect the love you shared in the gardens, on the porch, in every room where I have sensed your lingering rose fragrance. Mary, you will always be the heart of this home."

As Meg's words tumbled out, the stack of dishes she had washed earlier came flying off the drain board, crashing to the floor. Without hesitation, Clara raised her hand as if to deflect a blow as she loudly commanded. "You are not welcome in this house. Do not stay here. Leave now and do not come again."

Upon Clara's challenge the spirit of Owen Southwick materialized before her as a menacing black force. As Brady moved to try and combat the disturbing vision Meg cried out. "Mary, you have to go now. Please. You are free to leave and know that all will be well once you are gone."

Meg was silenced as Brady was forcibly knocked back against her by Owen's enraged power. As the two struggled to rise, they again heard Clara's voice calling out.

"You will not win this fight Owen Southwick. I possess a power stronger than yours and will use it against you ever more."

As she issued her threat, Clara reached beneath the collar of her dress, extracting a silver chain from around her neck. At the end of the chain hung an amulet, formed in the shape of a Celtic knot. Centered in the knot was a gem of black tourmaline that had long protected Clara against possessions and intrusions by evil spirits.

Pushing herself away from the table. Clara stood and raised the amulet in sacred ritual. "Within this house exist spirits of love, kindness and caring. In both day and night may the goodness of these spirits embrace all who enter and bless all who remain. And to the spirits of hatred, cruelty, and malintent, know that you have no place in this house. In both day and night, you are banished and forbidden from ever entering or remaining. I pray this in the name of all that is good in this world and beyond."

A tumultuous fury descended upon the room as Owen unleashed his malevolent spirit. "This is my home. Mary is my wife and your power is meaningless here, old woman."

At that moment, Mary began to weep with an enduring sadness that beleaguered Meg. She could feel the lifetime of suffering that Owen had inflicted upon his wife, as fully as she had experienced it in her own life with Cal. She understood Owen's control was the only thing now preventing Mary's spirit from passing. That impact fueled a resentment within Meg that flamed into an overpowering passion. Mary did not deserve to suffer any longer. If she could not choose to pass, then Meg would choose for her.

Standing and stepping into the middle of the kitchen, Meg closed her eyes and took a calming, deep breath. Within her mind, she envisioned Mary as the woman she had seen in her dreams. Petite, dark haired with deeply brown eyes, a gentle smile, a kind spirit. Within that vision she placed herself next to Mary, gathering the woman's hands in her own. As she looked into the core of the woman's brown eyes, Meg began to transfer the power of her spirit to Mary, willing her the strength to pass.

It was not enough. Meg's force was not enough against the might of Owen.

"Help. I need help." Meg's plea brought Clara and Brady immediately to her. Without pause, Clara linked her hand to Meg's while Brady moved to do the same on the opposite side. Flanked by their spirits and joined in their strength, Meg shared her reinforced power with Mary. In painful frustration, Meg heard Owen's mocking laughter as Mary's spirit began to fade from her vision.

"No. No. Mary, you cannot give up. You can't let Owen overcome your spirit again. Not when you have me here with you. Please, please try. Believe in your goodness and know that your spirit deserves to pass to the welcoming peace of the hereafter."

The heartfelt intensity of Meg's words echoed through the house, enchanting spirits and beings alike. Meg could feel a change swirling around her. What was the source? From where was this energy coming?

Then within her vision Meg saw someone approach Mary, a being that drew near and connected. All at once a surge of energy poured through Mary's spirit. It was stunning to both women as Mary became visibly brighter and stronger, her energy force increasing and increasing, until her spirit literally surged into a crystalline cascade. Mary was passing, Meg knew it to be true. And amid Meg's overwhelming emotions, amid the brilliance of Mary's crossing over to the light, Meg saw a clear vision of the power that had finally helped Mary pass and immediately she understood the reason she had come to Crown Hill.

The vision was of a woman that she clearly understood to be her grandmother, Margaret Rose.

It was done. She was gone.

For the first time in more than a century, I was without my Mary. I understood that it was her time. She had suffered for so long, desperately wishing to pass from this world. Yet as I watched her spirit dissolve, I remained focused on the bright light of Mary's eternal being...as if doing so might somehow keep us, forever.

The joy amidst my sadness was that Owen's spirit was gone from my being as well, banished, never to return. The protective spell cast by Clara's blessing ensured that it would be so, and I was grateful for her transcendent powers.

As a warming air again permeated my being, I encouraged a scent of roses from the arbor to drift through my windows and doors. It was a needed and soothing action, as the past days had been exhausting for all.

I watched as Brady and Meg gently guided Clara back to her chair at the kitchen table. I listened as the three reflected upon all that had happened. From Meg's traumatic experience with Owen, to Mary's passing, all of it reinforced the stark reality that my world, the world I had known for so long, was now gone.

Yet as that life within me was ending, so a new one was beginning.

In dealing with the spirits that had so long defined me, Meg had claimed her own place within my being. As it was meant to be, Margaret Rose Flynn was now the spirit of Crown Hill, joining with Mary and Edward and the many who had played a part in my 150-year existence.

For that is the life of a house...a patchwork of the people and the experiences that filter through its being, leaving traces to forever be.

And so, to those with whom I may someday share a future, know that whatever path you take to reach me, no matter where your journey begins. Whether you have the heart to give or if the obstacles you have overcome have taken too much. In that moment when you walk beneath Mary's gracious rose-covered arbor, when you rest on Meg's treasured wraparound porch, know you will have found a place of peace and caring, a place where you will be forever safe, a place where together we will make and meet life, a place that you will always be able to call...Home.

AUTHOR'S AFTERWARD

The year was 1979. My husband and I were immersed in the process of purchasing our first home.

We had been married for almost nine years and in that time our family had expanded with the birth of two wonderful children. We had also traveled around New York State and across Canada like a gypsy family, moving 12 times in 10 years. It was a tough experience, finally made better by the fact that we were going to have a place to call our own.

Home. It was my dream.

After much married-couple debate, my husband and I agreed to locate our family in the country, specifically on a farm where we could raise our family and some horses as well. Between budget and locale, there were a small pool of choices. Yet in our home search we came to a farm that sat on top of a hill with a distant view of Lake Erie. A farm which, from the moment I walked through its entry, was more than roof and timbers, more than barn and pastures. It was home.

Despite weeks of negotiations, my husband and I were never able to complete the sale to buy that property. Ultimately discouraged, but accepting, we moved on and eventually bought a nearby farm that served our purpose. Yet the spirit of that farmhouse never left my heart and soul. For years, I would take the long route to events and meetings just to drive by that house that felt so much like home. In looking back, I now wonder if my side trips were a way of staying connected, or more some fanciful method of self-torture!

Fast forward through 17 years of life, and I was newly-divorced, my children onto their own lives and my horses in need of more space than the three-room apartment where I had temporarily relocated. I had an immediate need for land with a barn and a house and, as any good story would have it, the house on the hill was once again for sale.

This time, I would not be denied.

On June 3, 1995, I began my life's journey within the caring shelter of Crown Hill. This was not a name that I chose, but rather one that was given to me in the form of an old concrete sign, dug up by a friend helping me to clear some of my farmland. It is one of many secrets of this home that I have been given, one in particular that served as the inspiration for this book.

One warm and sunny spring day. I took a leisurely stroll out to the mailbox and therein found a plain white, business-sized envelope bearing my name and address. The envelope was stamped, but missing a postmark or return address. Looking much like an unwanted solicitation, I earmarked the envelope as trash. Yet something stopped me from discarding the correspondence...curiosity perhaps, or an unknown sense of destiny.

I opened the envelope and discovered a paper imprinted with a page photocopied from a book. The book was identified simply as, "The History of Eden," the town in which I live. As the title promised, the copy was a story based on the history of the town.

Within the middle of the black and white print, a paragraph was highlighted by red pen, obviously meant to capture my attention.

In scanning through the printed lines, I realized that the words detailed information not just about Eden, but about my home.

287

Deciding that it might be wise to read, rather than scan, I sat down at the kitchen table and carefully considered all that was written.

At the end of my review, I was slightly shaken, as much by the delivery style of the letter as the story it told. For within the unmarked envelope, upon the plain white paper, lacking note or signature, there was the story of a husband and wife who had lived in my home in the late 1800's. A husband and wife whose marriage ended on the day that she died and was found hanging in a shed behind my house.

The story detailed that the cause of this woman's death was never truly determined. Her husband claimed suicide, while the neighbors strongly felt the woman was murdered...at the hands of her husband.

I never found out who sent that letter, although I admit, I never really tried. One day I did mention the rather cryptic correspondence to a friend of mine. This friend was also connected to my home in that her son had been the owner of the property in the years between my two purchase bids. Upon hearing the odd circumstance and the even odder lore of the letter, my friend smiled with a twinkle in her eye and said, "My, wouldn't that make a good story?"

And, as it turned out, she was right.

After much research, many shared memories with Eden friends and neighbors and seven years of writing efforts, Crown Hill has, for me, become a good story and a wonderful book; one that I hope you will enjoy reading as much as I enjoyed writing.

Yet, before completing your Crown Hill journey, here are a few things you might like to know. The characters of Mary and Owen Southwick, Edward Randall and his family, Emily French and Sir

Arthur Conan Doyle are all based on their real lives and experiences at Crown Hill.

The characters around them and the dialogue they share are primarily based on my writer's imagination. Most significantly, most all of the spiritual happenings in the book are based on my own Crown Hill real-life experiences.

Finally, Crown Hill would not be a book without the love and support of my family and friends. As any good Irishwoman is wont to do, I'm going to take the time and space to acknowledge them all!

To James, thank you for inspiring your mother to reach higher and try harder---and always telling me the truth, even when I really didn't want to hear it!

To Lisa, thank you for believing, not only in me, but in Crown Hill and its story. And thank you for making your edits with pink ink, instead of red. They were just so lovely that way.

To Glenn, thank you for being the first to believe in my writing and to convince others that they absolutely had to believe as well.

To Suzy, thank you for believing Glenn and for continuing to support and admire my writing these many years.

To Vicki, Laurie, Karen, Sherry, Robyn, Marion, Jill, Bob, Peter, "Z", Patti and John, thank you from the bottom of my heart for loving me, my house and our story.

To Candi, thank you for connecting me with Mary, and for helping me to truly hear the voices of both Mary and Crown Hill.

To Jocelyn, thank you for never confirming my worst fears in your email reviews of the chapters that you read as I wrote. Each positive word you sent allowed me to continue to imagine and to write.

To John, there are neither words nor payment that can properly communicate my gratitude for Crown Hill's cover. It is perfect and beautiful. Thank you.

To Marc, as always, you took my Crown Hill words and my thoughts and brought them to life. I never fail to be touched by your video translations. Thank you.

To my editors, Holly Lorincz and Brian, thank you for making sure Crown Hill was readable and properly formatted while allowing it to remain true to the story in my heart. Your patience, kindness and belief in me and this book changed my life. I hope that someday I can support other writers in the same wonderful way that you have supported me.

To the men in my life who, in one way or another brought me to this place in time, thank you. You have helped me fulfill my lifelong dream of having my own safe haven; my home.

To Mary Southwick, thank you for sharing your story and for helping me to tell that story in moments when I had no thoughts or words of my own.

To Crown Hill, for all that you have been in the lives of so many before me, for all that you are in my life and in the lives of those that I love, thank you for sharing your story with me and for your willingness to tell your story for others to read. Most of all, thank you for being my home.

When it is my time, I will pass peacefully having experienced the wonders of life within your caring shelter...leaving behind a trace of my spirit to forever be.

Love always,
Christina